After the host's collapse, the party came to a sudden halt

Robert turned quickly, intending to catch up with Diann, only to find himself literally running into her. Instinctively, he caught her bare shoulders to steady them both and saw her look of startled uneasiness.

He was suddenly acutely aware of the hot, silky feel of her firm shoulders beneath his hands, the light glow of her maple-syrup hair, the lovely warm liquid of her caramel eyes.

She was having trouble breathing. He sensed it with every one of his own uneven breaths.

And right at that moment—despite everything he knew about her—he wanted nothing more than to hold her in his arms.

ABOUT THE AUTHOR

M.J. Rodgers is the recipient of *Romantic Times* magazine's Career Achievement Award for Romantic Mysteries. She lives with her family at the base of the Olympic Mountains in Washington State.

Books by M.J. Rodgers

On the Scent
M.J. Rodgers

Harlequin Books

TORONTO • NEW YORK • LONDON
AMSTERDAM • PARIS • SYDNEY • HAMBURG
STOCKHOLM • ATHENS • TOKYO • MILAN
MADRID • WARSAW • BUDAPEST • AUCKLAND

For Theresa Scott—a writer, a friend—whose inspirational call on January 26, 1993, came just at the right moment to save me from being committed to the local loony bin

ISBN 0-373-22271-8

ON THE SCENT

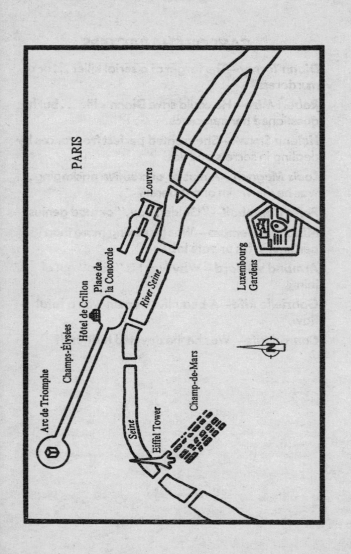

CAST OF CHARACTERS

Diann Torrey—The target of a serial killer . . . or a murderess?

Robert Mize—He could save Diann's life . . . but he questioned her innocence.

Helena Strunk—She created perfect fragrances by dealing in secrets and lies.

Louis Magnen—A master of creative packaging . . . was he the victim or murderer?

Peter Campbell—"Golden boy," or mad genius?

Miskka Kanemoto—Was he mixing more than perfume in his private lab?

Armand Vuillard—Why was his "nose" out of joint?

Gabrielle Rife—A beautiful woman with a fatal flaw.

Conrad Rife—Was he the devoted husband?

Prologue

"Get out of my way!" master perfumer Armand Vuillard yelled at his startled Paris staff as he steamrolled into his lab, making a beeline for the new box of natural fragrance oils next to his worktable.

His head assistant, Paul Rimbaud, swung around, to see the crimson cast to his boss's round face and bald head, and wondered what had set him off this time. Rimbaud stood ready for the worst, his thin shoulders straightening into a stiff T beneath his elongated neck, his face wearing the long-suffering look that had become so much a part of him since being promoted to his "exalted" position.

Vuillard screeched to a stop, his short, plump body tensing, his dark eyes widening in horror at the telltale splits in the packaging of his expensive scents. He whirled around, his arms flying in threatening arcs as he shouted at his staff, "Imbeciles! Idiots! You've opened the box! You dare to presume!"

"No, Monsieur Vuillard, it was that way when it arrived. We—" Rimbaud began, but never got to finish.

Vuillard's dark eyes blazed at his assistant's, their angry light slashing as sharp as silver sabers. "Cease your petty excuses, you...you...assassin! Get out! You're fired! All of you are fired!"

Rimbaud's shoulders slumped.

Another firing. Another week of strained silence. Followed by the muffled telephone call where *he* would be forgiven.

Such was his suffering. But there would be the raise in salary. And the return to normal routine. Until the next time.

Rimbaud shrugged in abused resignation, motioned to the staff to leave, wrapping a bony, sustaining arm around a cowering new recruit to the famous Parfumerie Vuillard. Gently he ushered her outside.

She would learn in time. They all learned in time that Armand Vuillard must be forgiven his displays of temper—just as true artists had been forgiven them throughout the centuries.

ARMAND VUILLARD FUMED as he slammed the door behind his staff's retreat. He locked it with shaking hands and threw the key against the counter. Betrayed! Everywhere he was betrayed! He stomped back to the open box. Betrayed and insulted!

He tore at the already open packaging, flinging the special aluminum containers onto his pristine worktable as though they were tins of cheap cologne instead of the fortune they represented in natural fragrance oils and absolutes from southern France's Grasse, the acknowledged perfume capital of the world.

For more than two hundred years France had been synonymous with the best in perfume, its crops of night-blooming jasmine and rose the sweetest in all the world, its perfumeries the unqualified best.

How dare Gabrielle Rife select that…that *chemist* Diann Torrey to receive half the coveted NOSE Award! Why, Torrey wasn't even fit to be called a "nose," much less considered on a par with the great Armand Vuillard! Weren't there even rumors she used synthetics in her perfumes? Yes, he was sure he had heard as much. How could Gabrielle Rife, a Frenchwoman, no less, have made such an error in judgment?

Hands still shaking with the rage burning through him, Vuillard grabbed the aluminum container of precious rose absolute and emptied exactly sixteen parts into the waiting beaker. He'd show Gabrielle. He knew the special formula that would fix Madame Rife's betraying little heart. Had he not used it before?

Armand savagely snatched a container of oakmoss from the carefully distilled absolutes sitting on a lazy Susan at the back of his worktable. Measuring only with his eye, he dipped precisely the right amount into the waiting crystal beaker. Next followed an exact sequence of several exotic oils.

His hands blurred with the speed of his work. Gradually the classical floral chypre perfume that was his trademark began to burst into its symphony of perfection.

Gabrielle Rife would sink to her knees before him after smelling the aphrodisiac quality of this perfume. After her insult, nothing less than having her on her lily-white knees before him would do. She would be begging him to let her retract that Torrey woman's name from the PERFUME awards. Literally begging.

Vuillard's eyes gleamed as he visualized the beautiful Gabrielle Rife pleading, with tears in her eyes. He splashed in the just-arrived, exquisite Grasse jasmine absolute, once again using his practiced eye and uncanny expertise to measure out precisely another sixteen parts. He ignored the motorized blender waiting on the counter. With the bold caress of an impatient lover, he swept the crystal stirrer through his ingredients before bringing the beaker to the most educated nose in all of France.

A bounty of fragrance soared into his skull, its top note singing in dizzy magnificence. Still, beneath the lovely symphony of scent, he unerringly detected the strident chord.

But only for an instant.

Because in the next instant, Armand Vuillard could smell nothing at all.

Chapter One

Diann Torrey might have been able to resist the colossal Arc de Triomphe welcoming the surging traffic through its twelve radiating avenues, or the thirty-two shoelace bridges deftly tying together the Right and Left banks of the blue-gray Seine. She might even have been able to resist the Eiffel Tower, seventy tons of delicately braided iron soaring into the skyline, visible from nearly everywhere in the city.

But Diann could not resist Paris's smells.

Since she'd dropped her suitcases at the Hôtel de Crillon that morning after an eight-hour plane ride, she'd been out walking in the glorious April day, poking her head into the bakeries to catch the heavenly fresh-bread aromas, pausing to sniff at the paints of the artists lining the banks of the Seine, getting quick snatches of the deep, rich delicacies of the chocolate shops and the cafés.

Now it had started to rain, and she inhaled the sweetest of all Paris's scents—her damp chestnut trees. If only Diann could reproduce that fragrance in a bottle, she would call it Paris Spring and have the perfume world at her feet.

But some scents eluded poor human imitation—as perhaps they should. Diann leaned against a mosaic of delicate gray-and-green stone lining the broad, tree-graced Champs-Élysées, the busiest and most famous of all Paris's boulevards, and lifted her face to let the shower patter gently upon her cheeks and chin.

After hours of walking she was hungry. She was weary. She was wet. But, ah, she was in Paris!

She closed her eyes against its liquid baptism, drank in its scents, inhaling every sweet note with infinite pleasure. And like Ernest Hemingway, Gertrude Stein, James Joyce and all her other predecessors, she did not struggle within the bewitching bonds of this fantasy city.

Suddenly Diann felt a rough shove of reality as her purse was yanked from her shoulder. Her eyes popped open in surprise, and her hands shot out to break her fall. Her palms slipping against wet stone, she tumbled onto the unyielding pavement, landing sharply on her right knee and hip. The impact shot through her bones and rattled her teeth.

She rolled to her bottom and blinked in disbelief. *I've been mugged!*

She raised her head and searched for her assailant, but got only a flash of a blurred figure darting through the busy crowd of the broad Champs-Élysées.

Anger flicked over her nerves as the pain registered in her knee and hip. The pain quickly retreated. The anger, on the other hand, advanced. This thief had not just stolen her purse. He had robbed her of Paris's wonderful spell.

And for that he should be guillotined.

Diann started as a deep masculine voice asked from beside her in perfect English, "Are you all right?"

She twisted in its direction. Her eyes followed a long, lean line of well-fitting black slacks to a white shirt with a dark sweater tied over impressive shoulders. She stared into a preposterously handsome face, haloed by bold, dark-brown curls and eyes as blue as a warm spring sky.

The rain was soaking him by the second. But his expression was full of unhurried concern as he bent to offer her his hand. "Allow me to help you."

Diann took a deep breath and let it out slowly. Now, this was the kind of man to take a woman's mind off an insignificant mugging. She slipped her hand into his and let its warm strength bring her to her feet. At five-eight she found herself barely coming up to his shoulders. His very broad shoulders.

"How do you feel? That was a nasty fall."

Diann raised her eyebrows in surprise. "A nasty fall? Are you saying you saw the man who stole my purse?"

"Only his back. He took off at a run."

He captured both her hands in a warm, firm grasp. As he leaned over to examine her palms, an exotic, rich, almond scent wafted up her nose. Damn, he even smelled terrific.

His deep voice again vibrated in her ears.

"You've scraped your palms."

She glanced at the slight abrasions, hardly feeling their light sting, so much was she enjoying the way his warm palms cocooned the backs of her hands.

She smiled. "A little soap and water, and they'll be fine."

He raised his head, returning her smile with a bright dazzling flash that highlighted every one of his chiseled features. Diann knew she'd never met this handsome stranger before, and yet contrarily, maddeningly, he seemed so familiar. Why was that? Perhaps she'd seen him in her dreams?

No, she would have remembered such dreams. This man went beyond attractive—*way* beyond.

He still held her hands in his. She made no effort to remove them. His deep voice caressed her ears.

"Would you like me to take you to the police station?"

Her emotions had her thoughts pursuing a far more interesting destination. With ever-increasing difficulty, she kick-started her brain into a semblance of rationality. "No. Thank you. I didn't really see the man, so it would be a waste of time. Besides, my purse contained only a Paris tour book and a few francs."

The smile flashed at her again.

"Good. I'll buy you some refreshment before I walk you back to your hotel. Luckily Fouquet's, the premier café on the Champs-Élysées, is just over there."

He had her arm curled in his and was strolling over to the aforementioned café before Diann could catch her next breath.

She sighed to herself as the strength and sensuality of this man invaded every receptor in her skin. She knew she was acting very uncharacteristically, letting this marvelous-looking and -smelling Frenchman take control, but at the moment she had absolutely no inclination to resist. Paris had obviously sent this handsome magician to reweave its spell. What an absolutely enchanting city.

Fouquet's sat behind a barricade of struggling potted spring flowers at the edge of the sidewalk. Its outside tables and chairs had been vacated with the start of the light rain.

He led them into the glassed-in, street-level grill room and selected seats for them on the leather banquettes.

The delicious smells of coffee and food surrounded Diann in the warm, elegant café. She sat back and listened to the rich liquid sounds of murmured French drifting into her ears. A waiter in a snow-white jacket approached, a pristine towel draped neatly over his left arm. Her companion ordered several things in French. Diann caught just one familiar word.

When the waiter left, she leaned forward. "I appreciate all the trouble you're going to and I don't mean to appear ungrateful, but I hope the cognac was for you."

One dark eyebrow arched in inquiry. "You speak French?"

"No. That was the only word I understood."

Diann felt guilty with the admission and hastily added, "I know I should have found time to learn some French. I don't like being ignorant of the language of a country I visit. Or insensitive to its customs. But it would take a far bigger shock to get me to drink something alcoholic when it's barely past noon."

He leaned closer and rested a large, warm hand on one of hers. "As you wish. But a sip or two will warm you."

He had no idea how warm he was making her just by his look and the touch of his hand. She couldn't remember ever responding to a man this quickly or unqualifiedly. The thought was both exciting and sobering.

She decided a temporary retreat was definitely in order. "Will you excuse me while I go wash my hands?"

He rose as she did and smiled. "Of course. Would you like me to show you the way?"

Such nice manners. So wonderfully suave and urbane. Now, why couldn't American men be like this? "I see where it is, thank you. I'll only be a moment."

HE ROLLED her small purse with the long strap back into the concealing folds of his sweater and replaced the sweater around his shoulders. The waiter deposited the café au lait, cognac and sandwiches made with fresh-smelling crusty baguettes at the table. He saw her emerge from the door on the other side of the room.

She had slipped out of her wet, hooded windbreaker. With growing approval he took in her soft pink sweater, swelling with gentle curves. A cascade of thick, light-brown hair flowed past her shoulders.

The planes of her face took on new, alluring shapes within the frame of that luxuriant hair, a tumble of wavy strands that glistened like spun maple syrup in the subdued light of the café. She moved in long, graceful sways toward him.

He rose as she approached. She smiled at him. No coy flirtation. A straight study from lively, intelligent eyes the color of light melted caramel. Her expressions, walk, smile, even the way she held herself, exuded an abundant energy for and curiosity about life.

Not a beautiful woman. But lovely. Very lovely.

He'd never thought of a woman as lovely before. He doubted he'd ever think of a woman precisely that way again.

He never should have approached to see if she was all right. But every time he saw the way she looked at him, he had a hell of a time being sorry.

Of course he knew the assumptions she was making about him. He had a momentary stab of regret that he was going to be bursting her bubble. He shoved it aside. He had time to regret nothing. Not even what he might eventually have to do to her.

She ate ravenously, and her enthusiasm for the fresh sandwiches became infectious. The food quickly disappeared from both their plates. He sat back and sipped his cognac and watched her until she finally leaned back and reached for her rich café au lait.

She sighed from some contented inner cavern. "The last meal I had was on the plane several hours ago. I didn't realize how hungry I was. How did you know to speak English to me?"

"The same way that the thief knew you were an American tourist and thought you'd be carrying a lot of money."

Her smooth brow crinkled. "I look like an American tourist?"

He motioned toward her clothes. "The Gloria Vanderbilt designer jeans, the Saucony walking shoes, the bright-pink windbreaker with 'New Jersey— Next To New York Anything Looks Like A Garden State,' embossed on the back."

She considered his observations, and her full lips twisted into a smile of self-acknowledged chagrin. "And I thought when I left my camera back at the hotel I'd be blending right in."

She took her mistake well. Sign of a lady with a strong sense of herself. He liked that.

"Even if you had dressed to fade into the crowd, I don't see how you ever could."

She smiled at his compliment, and he felt a curious tightening in his gut. Damn. He couldn't afford to like her too much. Deliberately he dropped his eyes to his cognac. "Of course, the way you stopped to stare at everything was also a dead giveaway to a watching thief."

"You were watching me?"

Whoops. Small mistake there. Still, no major problem. He looked up. "I didn't have to watch you to know what you were probably doing to attract a thief's attention."

She nodded, accepting his explanation. "I suppose I was gawking a bit."

"And you won't find too many Parisians who stop to let a spring rain bathe their faces."

That smile again. There was danger there and he had the sudden sinking feeling he'd already stepped right into it with both feet.

"You speak English so beautifully. I can't even detect an accent. Have you spent time in the States?"

He sipped his cognac, prolonging the explanation for that fraction of a moment more. "I was born in Philadelphia. I'm American."

He saw the information drop with a disappointing splash into those liquid caramel eyes.

She stared at him a moment before a soft, private laugh escaped her lips, rumbling from deep in her throat. "I feel rather foolish. I just assumed when you spoke such fluid French to the waiter—"

"I'm glad you think it sounded fluid. I had only two years of French in high school, and that was quite a while ago. Sorry to disappoint you."

The denial on her lips tried to fill her eyes, but came up half-empty. "Why should I be disappointed?"

This lady obviously never played poker. "To learn that it isn't a real Frenchman extending the hospitality of Paris to you? Of course you're disappointed. An American woman doesn't travel all the way to Paris to meet an American man.''

Her chin raised as her shoulders straightened into a formidable block. "I haven't come to Paris with the thought of meeting any man. I'm here to attend a symposium for the International Fragrance Fraternity.''

In an instant the inexperienced tourist had been replaced by the competent professional. He watched the transformation with growing interest. Maybe the lady did play poker.

"My name is Diann Torrey. I'm the head chemist for an American pefume company called Man to Woman. Perhaps you've heard of it?''

His cue had come. He donned a well-practiced look of surprise. "Yes, you could say I've heard of it." He put down his cognac and held out his hand to her. "I'm Robert Mize. I've just signed a year's contract with the advertising department of Man to Woman perfumes.''

Her features seemed to freeze for a moment. A very long moment. And then he watched the information fully erupt on her face. She didn't take his extended hand. She reached for her previously untouched cognac with unsteady fingers, nearly spilling it, took a hasty gulp and then promptly choked.

He dropped his hand and let her get her breath back and compose herself. He didn't offer to assist. Her look told him just how unwelcome any assistance from him would be.

He had expected surprise. Maybe a hint of suspicion for the coincidence. But not this look that approached repugnance. For the first time since he'd seen her that morning, he was not happy to be studying her very expressive face.

Finally she took a couple of deep, steadying breaths and seemed to regain a semblance of control over her breathing and speech. She shot a direct glance at him, her eyes no longer warm and liquid, but dry and hard.

"I knew there was something familiar about you. I guess I just didn't recognize you with your clothes on."

As soon as the words were out of her mouth, Diann regretted their literal truth and realized that the shock of learning who this man was had made her even more outspoken than usual. She jumped to her feet, eager to be placing her full weight on them before she ended up sticking both of them into her mouth.

"Mr. Mize, thank you for your kind attention. If you'll let me know where you're staying, I'll be happy to reimburse you for this excellent lunch."

He rose slowly. She caught some unreadable emotion tugging at the corners of his lips as he dumped what seemed to be an enormous number of francs on the table. "My treat, Ms. Torrey. I'm sure you won't insult me by trying to reimburse an act of kindness with money. And as for where I'm staying, my room is at the Hôtel de Crillon. Where you're staying and where the symposium is taking place."

Another second of shocked silence passed before she found herself able to form the question. "The company sent you here?"

"A last-minute decision. They felt my presence would help in the current campaign to promote your newest perfume, HEAT."

Her brow crinkled. "I'd have thought the advertising manager would have been a better selection. She could have used the opportunity to negotiate the European contracts."

"Contract negotiation will come later. Right now generating interest in HEAT is considered tantamount. That's my job. Come on, the rain has stopped. I'll walk you back to the hotel."

"There's no need—"

He treated her to a composed blue stare. "You've had a nasty experience, despite how well you've taken it. I will see you safely to your door."

Diann hadn't expected that kind of quiet, cool command in his voice. Not from a man who did what he did for a living. Naturally she would have preferred to be rid of him here and now. Her memories of her previous reactions to him embarrassed her beyond belief. But considering his earlier assistance, to refuse his escort would be rude.

She led the way out of the café and back onto the famous Champs-Élysées.

They walked quietly side by side for the next couple of blocks. Paris's lure was all around, but Diann no longer noticed. Her entire focus was on the man next to her. Although this was the first time she had met him face-to-face, she'd been hearing about Robert Mize for months.

Only too vividly she remembered the preview of his televised spot three weeks before, that still had nearly the entire female staff at Man to Woman swooning.

And after the spot aired on national TV a couple of weeks later, the rest of the American female population had succumbed. Even her sister, Connie—the world's best barometer when it came to locating a loser—called her in the middle of the night, begging Diann to get her an introduction to the incredibly sexy Robert Mize.

Diann cast a glance at his smooth, powerful stride. She knew his statistics: thirty-three, six-two, two-hundred twenty-five pounds of pure muscle. And sitting on top of all that muscle, a far-too-handsome face surrounded by that bold, incredibly sensual hair. Did it naturally grow in those loose, sexy curls or did he have it permed?

"Ms. Torrey, why do I have the impression that you're just bursting with unasked questions?"

Her eyes flashed forward. Perceptive devil. Well, he asked. "Okay. What makes a man pose nude in a commercial to air on all the national networks and for a magazine ad sold on all the major newsstands?"

He turned toward her slightly and studied her a moment in silence as they walked. She felt the pressure of his scrutiny but kept her eyes straight ahead. His voice sounded mildly amused.

"Do I detect an air of disapproval in your tone?"

"I'd be a fool to disapprove of the phenomenal increase in sales we've experienced since the HEAT campaign began. Everyone in both the television and perfume industries has said it's launched a new era in advertising—the adult commercial, aired only after ten at night. Your spot has gotten a higher Nielsen rating in its first week of running than any of the network shows. The magazines featuring the ad have sold out."

"People are always attracted by something new."

His nonchalant tone as well as his words broadcasted his familiarity with success. Diann again studied his face.

He oozed sensuality in a way she'd never experienced—or even imagined a man could. His was not an abstract sensuality. It had a corporeal quality that played across her skin and excited every cell in her body, not only forcibly reminding her she was female but making her exceptionally happy of the fact.

Diann quickly reminded herself that he was not a dashing and debonair Frenchman after all, but just a plain American male model. The kind of man who traded on his good looks to get him through life. The kind of man she had happily crossed streets all her life to avoid.

But they were walking on the same side for the moment, and she had to admit her rampant curiosity was getting the better of her. "Have you always been a model?"

A knowing, slight smile lifted the left side of his full lips. A challenging, mysterious light glowed in his impossibly blue eyes.

"No. Not always. Why?"

Damn. He might just be a face and body, but it was one hell of a face and body. She looked away from those eyes—eyes that threatened to drown a woman's rational thought in one warm sweep if she wasn't careful.

As always, Diann intended to be very careful. "There's been a lot of talk about you around MW. I just thought I'd take the opportunity to get the straight story."

"What's MW?"

"It's short for Man to Woman. All the insiders call it MW. I'm surprised nobody's told you."

"I've only been on contract to the company for a little over a month. I really don't know anything about the perfume business. Most of the time I've spent in front of studio cameras."

Yeah. Stark naked. The reminder puckered Diann's forehead. She had never understood how a woman could pose nude to satisfy the prurient interest of a nameless, faceless, salivating male public. She was no less understanding of how a man could.

"So what do the rumors say?" he asked.

"There are several. They range from a former Chippendale to an unsuccessful actor."

He laughed in a deep, robust way that surprised her for its unrestrained force and honesty.

"Looks like I'd better set the record straight. I've worked at several different jobs before signing on with MW's advertising arm. But never a Chippendale. And never an actor."

"What, then?"

"Last year I played baseball."

Diann stole a glance at his profile. "Major league baseball?"

"Maybe you heard of me. I was a pitcher."

She shook an internal, judgmental head. An ex-jock turned model. Could it get any worse? "No, I don't follow sports. What made you quit?"

"I injured my shoulder."

"Don't ex-players try to become sports announcers when they can no longer play the game?"

"If they've had time to make a big name for themselves. And if there's a position open. And if they can announce as well as play."

"Wasn't your name big enough?"

"Not after only one season in play."

"Still, aren't there other things—like being a manager or coach?"

"There are."

"Didn't you want to become one of those?"

"No."

"But you wanted to become a model?"

"I'm doing it, aren't I?"

"But why?"

"For the same reason I became a baseball player. Money."

"There must have been other jobs."

"Not at the salary I'm commanding."

"You need money? Are you supporting a family or something?"

He smiled at her, the light of humor still in his eyes. "You mean it would be all right if I was modeling to pay for my little gray-haired mother's dialysis machine or my autistic child's expensive counseling care. But being single without dependents and modeling because I enjoy being well paid means I should apologize."

"I didn't ask you to."

It was a lie. She knew it the moment the words tumbled from her lips. That was exactly what her pointed questions had been doing.

"You disappoint me, Diann. I thought you were more honest than that."

Diann stopped at the edge of the place de la Concorde, one of the most beautiful urban squares in the world, with its yards of cascading fountains and imposing statues.

She ignored it all as she turned on Robert, her growing anger focused as much on herself for getting caught in a lie as on him. "So you want honesty? All right, I'll give you honesty. Maybe you should be apologizing. What kind of a man *wants* to pose for airbrushed photographs on the slick pages of a magazine, or to stand nude in front of a TV screen with nothing between him and the camera but a strategically placed shadow?"

He surveyed her silently for a second, that challenging, mysterious glow within the blue depths of his eyes. "You said it yourself. Women are tuning in by the millions. The magazines carrying the ad are selling out. I must be giving the public something they want."

His voice had remained calm, controlled, that slight lift to his sexy lips still in evidence. He didn't even begin to see what she was getting at. Well, what did she expect? It didn't take any brains to pump iron and pose in the altogether.

She turned away. "Oh, just forget it."

"You've judged me solely by the job I do, haven't you?"

"I'm sorry if that bothers you. But I happen to think that what a person does is far more important than what he looks like."

"Do you, now?"

She eyed him, surprised at the suppressed laughter in his tone.

"Would you have been more impressed if I were still a baseball player?"

"No," she admitted.

"Oh? Why not?"

"Well, it hardly takes much mental matter to throw a ball at a bat all day. Institutionalized adult sports are a complete waste of human and other resources. Just think what society could accomplish if all that time, effort, energy and money devoted to sports were concentrated instead on building roads and schools. Or on health care. Or on teaching kids how to use their brains and treat the Earth and one another with respect."

"Athletic prowess develops important mental as well as physical skills."

Behind Diann in the middle of the magnificent place de la Concorde sat the incredible thirty-three-centuries-old obelisk from Egypt, covered with hieroglyphics. But it was the thirty-three-year-old man standing before her whom she found far more incomprehensible. "What mental and physical skills are being developed by the millions of beer-guzzling couch potatoes who spend their lives in front of a TV, watching all that athletic prowess? The truth, Mr. Mize—"

"Call me 'Robert.'"

"The truth, *Mr. Mize,* is that it's the scientists, not the game players, who have brought humans out of their cold, dark caves to live in warm, bright homes."

"And you're making your contribution to these warm, bright homes by developing perfumes?"

Diann turned and headed for the front of the Hôtel de Crillon, Robert right beside her. The staid exterior of the eighteenth-century building made it look like just another one of the government offices lining the square, instead of the luxury hotel it was.

"Being able to discover new olfactory pleasure for people is a way of brightening their lives," Diann called over her shoulder. "But I don't expect you to see the connection."

"So it would appear. You were graduated from Cornell with honors, I believe. Wasn't Paul Goldman, the guy who's up for a Nobel Prize for his work on combating mutant viruses, in your graduating class?"

The subtle shift of inflection in Robert's voice caught Diann's attention. Her head swiveled in his direction. "He was. So what's your point?"

"I was just wondering how you felt about devoting your life to catering to rich women's whims for yet another unnecessary perfume on their dressing tables, while your classmate—who probably doesn't pull in a fourth of your salary—is successfully fighting diseases plaguing human-kind?''

Diann stopped in her tracks, feeling the sharp blow of the words he'd just pitched at her so deftly.

Her eyes flew to his and met a candid, cool-blue stare. She'd found fault with his chosen profession and he'd just repaid the compliment. Damn. For an ex-jock and a male model, this guy could throw an intellectual punch and then some.

She laughed in surprise at the thought that her opponent in the cerebral cat-and-mouse game she'd been playing had just metamorphosed from mouse into full-grown grizzly.

He didn't laugh back. His eyes held that same challenging mysterious glow that had seduced her when she thought him a Frenchman and now warned her that, like the Hôtel de Crillon, this man's exterior could be deceiving.

"*Mademoiselle!* Mademoiselle Diann Torrey!''

Diann knew only one Frenchwoman who could sound that excited and collected at the same time. Diann whirled around to see Gabrielle Rife sweeping toward them, as always a picture of French sophistication and fashion in a Lanvin haute-couture burgundy dress and gold Hermès silk scarf. Her shoulder-length dark hair was as elegant as every other detail of her grooming.

Gabrielle engulfed Diann in a warm embrace and nearly squeezed the breath out of her. She smelled of the sweet red wine she'd had for lunch and a dab of Armand Vuillard's classic floral chypre perfume.

Diann looked over Gabrielle's shoulder to see her shiny-domed, pointed-eared, round-faced husband, Conrad, getting out of a taxi. His facial features and the natural upward slant to the ends of his lips made him look like a perpetually happy, well-dressed elf.

Gabrielle was scolding. "Finally, you are here! Yesterday you were supposed to have arrived. You will not be ready for the dinner this evening? You will be too tired, no?"

Diann extricated herself from Gabrielle's enthusiastic welcome, wondering how a woman ten years older, two inches shorter and ten pounds lighter could possibly be strong enough to nearly crack a rib with every embrace. "I'll be fine. I slept some on the plane. And as for late, well, perhaps you'll forgive me when you see what I was finishing."

Gabrielle's bright hazel eyes sparked instantly with curiosity as her expressive hands flew into the air. "What you were finishing? You have brought a new fragrance for me?"

"You'll be the first woman outside my lab assistants to smell it. But it's not just a new fragrance, Gabrielle. It's more."

"More? What is this more?"

"No. I'm wise to your browbeating tactics, and I promise you you won't get it out of me prematurely. You'll find out with everyone else at the Man to Woman presentation."

Conrad finished paying the taxi and walked up to them. Diann gave him a big smile. "Good to see you, Conrad. I'd like to introduce Robert Mize, Man to Woman's new model for our just released perfume, HEAT."

Diann paused as she turned back to Robert. "Mr. Mize, this is Gabrielle Rife, the co-director of the International Fragrance Fraternity and the editor in chief of the organization's magazine, *Redolence*, the absolute last word in perfume. And this is her husband, Conrad Rife, the other co-director and an American businessman who owns and operates the latest in recycling plants."

Conrad Rife stepped forward and took Robert's hand, his typical hearty smile in evidence. His expertly cut suit nearly succeeded in covering his generous girth. "Gabrielle and I are pleased you could attend our little symposium."

Gabrielle swept forward then to claim Robert's hand with hers, an appreciative gleam in her eyes as she looked up into his face. "Mr. Mize needs no introduction, Diann. Videos of his sensational TV spot have been making the rounds everywhere in Europe. You are marvelous in it."

"That is kind of you to say, Madame Rife."

"No. You must call me 'Gabrielle.' And I will call you 'Robert.' You will be on hand to make a personal appearance after we run the spot in the packaging presentation, no?"

"Wait a minute," Diann interjected. "You're going to be showing *that* TV spot here at the symposium?"

"But of course! This is big news to the whole industry!"

"But—"

"Man to Woman has executed an industry coup d'état, Diann. You must take your opportunity to show off your Robert. He is a man who should be enjoyed by all women."

Robert smiled at Gabrielle as a small chuckle rumbled in his throat. "Thank you, a very nice compliment. But being enjoyed by all women might be a feat beyond my abilities."

Diann watched Gabrielle listen to the words, translate them and then tardily understand. She laughed, waving her hands. "No, no! I mean, your TV appearance is what should be enjoyed by all women. Ah, but you know that is what I mean. Come. Both of you. We will go in now."

Despite the fact that Gabrielle professed to be going inside to get Diann settled, it was Robert's arm she held as they started toward the doorman. Conrad let them pass and then stepped up to Diann, offering his arm. He smelled of an unfortunate mixture of the red wine he'd consumed at lunch and the chemicals that had been used to clean his expensive suit.

"Forgive Gabrielle for being a bit proprietary and pushy about things. She got a bootlegged copy of your commercial precisely because she knew it would be a hot point of conversation. She's worked long and hard on this symposium, seen to every detail personally. She's so eager to make it a success."

Diann let out a little sigh. "I know, Conrad. Besides, when I'm reasonable about it, I realize I should be welcoming showings of the ad."

"But you don't wish to be reasonable about it?"

"Silly, huh? It's making the female population clamor for my perfume."

"So what's wrong?"

"I'd rather my perfume be sold on its merits, not because some sexy naked man is associated with it."

"Ah, but my dear Diann, that is the primary force of a perfume—its ability to deflect a woman's mood away from the mundane elements of her existence and focus it on her sexuality. Robert Mize's spot reminds women of this."

Diann looked into the round elf face. "You think sexuality is at the core? I don't know, Conrad. When I'm searching for the right scents, I'm not thinking of sex. I'm trying to detect odors that will make me feel good."

"Something feels better than sex?"

Diann grinned into the mischievous light resting in Conrad's bland eyes. "You got me there. By the way, I've always meant to ask. What's your favorite fragrance on Gabrielle?"

"I have none."

"Come on. You must."

Conrad headed them toward the hotel entrance. "No, that's the truth."

"You have to have a preference. Don't worry. If it's not one of mine, I'll just drown myself in the Seine."

His lips extended into an ear-to-ear grin. "Okay, Diann. To put your mind at ease. I have no favorite perfume because I'm a victim of anosmia. I cannot smell a thing."

Diann's head shook in sympathy. "Conrad, no. I never guessed. How awful for you!"

He shrugged his round shoulders as they negotiated the revolving glass door that marked the entrance to the Hôtel de Crillon.

"I realize for someone like you, such an affliction would be a tragedy. But it's been so long since I could smell anything that I've almost forgotten things have odors."

"How did it happen?"

"Oh, I was hit in the nose with a wrench by my father when I was in high school. Not intentional, you understand. Just an unfortunate accident when I was giving him a hand in his workshop. I was knocked unconscious. When I awoke I had a broken nose and no sense of smell. It's never come back."

Diann nodded. "Trauma is one of the most frequent causes of anosmia. I'm happy you seem to take it so well. I can't imagine a life without fragrance."

"If it wasn't for Gabrielle, I'd probably not miss it much. But you know how perfume-crazy she is. Here she has the world's most luscious scents to wear, and I can't share them with her."

Diann watched as the perpetually happy tilt to Conrad's lips quivered.

"Strange how nature decrees whom we will fall madly in love with and when, despite how inconvenient either proves."

Diann hadn't heard many men who could show love simply by the tone of their voice. But Conrad Rife's feelings for his wife came through loud and clear and left a lump forming in her throat. She swallowed it quickly. Mushy had never been her style and she wasn't about to adopt it.

"And what about you, Diann? Haven't you found this to be true?"

"What I've found is that a woman is happiest when she falls in love with her work, not a man."

Conrad chuckled and patted her arm, circled within his. "Your time will come. Despite all your brave protestations,

I predict you will be hopelessly smitten. Now, promise me something."

"What?"

"That you will keep my little confession about my anosmia to yourself. It would not do to let it be known that this codirector's sole contribution to the international Fragrance Fraternity is to provide the money to keep it running."

Diann flashed him a smile. "Your secret is safe with me."

They walked through the Hôtel de Crillon's lobby, a study in graceful elegance from its black velvet upholstered Louis XV-style chairs to its gleaming crystal chandeliers reflecting off golden Siena and Portor marble. And everywhere the wonderful fragrance of great sprays of fresh flowers.

Conrad stopped and released her arm, blowing a quick kiss across her knuckles before turning toward his wife, who was waiting for him, still on Robert Mize's arm, at the entrance to the grand staircase.

Robert Mize was looking at Diann across the lobby, a very intent look that made Diann's skin quiver. The subtle invitation and challenge in that look was unmistakable and almost irresistible.

Almost. Jet lag and Paris's enchantment had combined to make her act a bit foolishly earlier, but the foolishness was now over. She wasn't the kind of woman to get involved with a male model, even one who proved he had a brain dwelling beneath that sensational packaging.

Actually, the fact that he had a brain made his chosen profession even harder for her to accept. How could a man with intelligence waste it on such an empty, inconsequential pursuit?

"The welcoming dinner begins at nine here in the hotel's les Ambassadeurs restaurant," Conrad called over his shoulder as he moved to join his wife. "See you then."

Diann waved goodbye to Conrad, turned resolutely away from Mize's look and stepped up to the long marble reception desk. Instantly a desk clerk in an impeccable dove-gray uniform appeared before her, a polite inquiry in his voice.

"Mademoiselle Torrey, I hope you enjoyed your walk?"

The Hôtel de Crillon thoroughly impressed Diann. Even with two hundred registered guests, this desk clerk had made it a point to learn her name and face.

"Yes, thank you. It's all true. Paris is quite special in the spring."

He allowed his mouth to melt into a small smile. "Your room is ready now. I will have your luggage taken right up."

With the mere flick of his hand, the desk clerk summoned a bellboy attired in a bright-red jacket and flat red hat. He was such an old and wonderful visual cliché, Diann found herself smiling as he proceeded to carefully stack her luggage from behind the marble reception desk onto his luggage cart.

But as she glanced at her neatly stacked luggage, her smile quickly faded. She turned back to the desk clerk. "Excuse me, *monsieur*. I had three pieces of luggage, not two."

The desk clerk's eyes fastened on the cart. His slim body bent, barely creasing his uniform as he looked carefully beneath the marble reception desk. His forehead puckered into a slight frown.

"*Mademoiselle* is correct, of course. I remember her two pieces of matching luggage and her third piece, nonmatching."

Diann bit her lip and clutched the marble counter, trying to keep calm. "*Monsieur*, that third piece of luggage is...very important. Please, I cannot lose it."

The desk clerk nodded at her stiffly. "If *mademoiselle* will excuse me a moment?"

At her affirmative nod, he walked the entire expanse of the long reception desk, searching for the missing piece. By the time he had returned to her, Diann could see his frown had deepened.

He straightened and stiffened resolutely. "*Mademoiselle,* your third piece of luggage will be found. And quickly. This I promise you." He leaned over to the bellboy and snatched the room key out of his hand, replacing it with another from the back wall.

"You will have one of our finest suites overlooking the place de la Concorde, at no additional charge. Perhaps the beauty of the view will in some small way make up for this unforgivable delay."

Minutes later Diann stepped inside the palatial suite and halted in awe. Bronze busts, chintz, silk and velvet wall coverings and upholstery caught her every glance. In the ceiling a multitiered chandelier acted like an eloquent prism, sending sunlit rainbows to dance in every corner. Faced with such elegance, she forgot all about looking out the windows at the view.

But even the spectacular suite could not make her forget about her missing luggage.

It had to be found. It just had to.

She tipped the bellboy and saw him to the door. She checked her watch. Reached for the phone. Dialed the number she had carefully memorized. And waited while the electronic whine echoed in her ear. When it stopped and a man's voice answered, she took a deep breath.

"It's Diann. I'm here."

"Where are you calling from?"

"My room at the hotel."

"Say nothing more. Meet me tomorrow at five o'clock, Luxembourg Garden, at the pond. Make sure you are not followed."

The phone went dead in her ear.

Chapter Two

Robert Mize picked up the telephone the moment he entered his room. He punched in a number. When his ring was answered, he wasted no words. "Did you search them, Cassel?"

"Yes," the man on the other end of the line answered. "But there was a problem."

Robert sat on the soft, lemon-yellow bedcover and leaned back against the similarly colored upholstered headboard. "What problem?"

"The small case had a combination lock. I had to take it with me."

"You *did* open it?"

"And hit pay dirt. It contained two vials of liquid—one white, one grayish. I took samples of them both and sent them off to the lab."

"You followed the precautions? The gloves? The mask?"

"I'm not a novice at this, Mize. The lab will have them tomorrow. If the guys hop to it, we should know in forty-eight hours."

Robert's body sagged against the headboard as both anticipation and a curious disappointment vied for expression. He made an effort to coat his voice with some enthusiasm. "Good. If that's it, we've got her and we're finally getting to the end of this thing."

"There was a further complication."

Robert's spine immediately straightened to attention. "What kind of complication?"

"I didn't get the case back in place before the desk clerk returned from his break."

Robert rose from the bed uneasily. "Don't tell me you still have it?"

"No, no. I left it on an empty luggage cart in the back room. They'll find it if they do a thorough search."

Robert rubbed at the back of his neck as though it was developing a pain. "Yes, but they will wonder how it got there. This is a hotel that doesn't make those kinds of mistakes. There will be questions. Unanswerable ones. I don't like it."

"I know. Sorry. But it couldn't be avoided. You learn anything from following her?"

Robert looked out his window to his view of the inner courtyard, a study in hushed elegance. The afternoon sun splashed over the rain-washed flowers and plants.

"No. She played tourist all the way. Even got herself mugged."

"Mugged? Mize, what's wrong with you? That's the classic setup of how to pass merchandise to a contact. The mugger could have been a partner."

"Relax, Cassel. I lifted the purse he stole from her before he'd even turned around and then booted him into the crowd. I hid the purse in my sweater until I could check it later. She said there was just a guidebook and some francs in it and that's all there was."

"She said? You talked to her?"

"I played the rescuer to see what I could learn while she was vulnerable. No harm done."

"But she'll suspect—"

"She'll suspect nothing, Cassel. She thinks I'm a glorified male model."

"Good."

"Yeah. Terrific."

"That's what you wanted, isn't it? What's wrong?"

Robert laughed mirthlessly. "Wrong? What could be wrong? I've got money rolling in, women writing me torrid love letters, threatening to leave their husbands, and even a few energetic ones determined to form a fan club. I might dump you guys and make this my new career."

"You're kidding. Aren't you?"

Robert snickered. "What do you think, Cassel?"

"Yeah, you're kidding. It's just that . . ."

"It's just what?"

"Well, you've got to know the way you've insisted on handling this one is making everyone very nervous. It's not like I don't understand. You know I do. But you must also know your butt is on the line with the guys back in Philly."

"Not to mention on the TV."

"What?"

"Nothing."

"Yeah, well, it won't be nothing if this turns sour. Or if the local gendarmes find out who we are."

"You backing out of volunteering for this job, Cassel?"

"Naw. You know me, boss. I'm just complaining. Hell, what fun would there be if I couldn't complain? Besides, you need me on this one to keep you from screwing up again."

Robert smiled. He knew the special history Cassel and he had together made Cassel loyal to him, not to the guys in Philly. "Well, see that you do keep me from screwing up, Cassel."

"Don't make it too hard on me, Mize. Play things straight this time."

Robert dropped the receiver onto the telephone base, Cassel's last words echoing in his ears.

"Play things straight this time."

He leaned against the polished-wood window casement and stared out at the garden again. But he no longer saw the lush plants or shining sun. What he saw was cascading maple hair. And liquid caramel eyes.

And the idea of playing it straight dripped a steady stream of acid into his stomach.

DIANN COUNTED six kinds of marble surrounding the head table in the exquisite les Ambassadeurs restaurant, once the Grand Salon of the Hôtel de Crillon. And grand was the adjective for it, all right. The crystal in the chandeliers, as well as the dinnerware, glowed with the polish of quiet aged elegance.

But the room was far from quiet. Every table buzzed with the formally clad attendees to the International Fragrance Fraternity Symposium's welcoming dinner—perfume buyers and aficionados, nearly sixty strong.

And at her table, gathered around Conrad and Gabrielle Rife—the king and queen of the event—sat the chosen few who had received the coveted PERFUME awards.

Japan's Kohei Kanemoto of Oriental Blossom, far and above the best diversifier of fragrance in the world, sat to Diann's right. Next to him was Germany's Helena Strunk of Mit Luv, the industry's undisputed best blender. Next to Helena was France's Louis Magnen of La Belle, a packager without peers. Beside Louis sat Gabrielle Rife. To her right was England's Peter Campbell of Regal Bouquet, an absolute genius at fragrance distribution. Next to Peter was Conrad Rife. Between Conrad and Diann lay a conspicuously empty chair.

Diann had exchanged polite table conversation for a full five minutes before she could no longer stand the tension of that empty chair.

She turned to Conrad. "Where is Armand Vuillard?"

An uncomfortable look descended into Conrad's eyes. He leaned toward her and lowered his voice, obviously in an effort to be discreet. He only succeeded in immediately drawing attention to himself and hushing all other table conversation.

"Gabrielle phoned him a few hours ago when she found out his room had not been claimed. She tried at his home and lab. He wasn't there."

"Or if he was, he didn't answer," Gabrielle called from across the table in a voice filled with pique.

"Vuillard did not talk to you on purpose?" Helena Strunk sniffed disdainfully through her perpetually runny sinuses.

Gabrielle shrugged. "It is possible."

Helena's short, straight, ginger hair vibrated with a disapproving shake of her head, the white expanse of her voluptuous breast following suit above the confines of a black strapless dress.

"I for one would not be surprised," Louis Magnen said after taking a quick sip of wine. He was an amiable, painfully thin, angular Frenchman with a full head of slick black hair and a pencil-thin black mustache that had been groomed to perfection.

He traced it with a reflective finger. "There is no bigger ego in all of Paris than Armand Vuillard. I expected something like this when Gabrielle announced the winners of the PERFUME awards from the finalists last week."

"I don't understand," Diann said, turning to Louis Magnen. "You expected Armand Vuillard not to show?"

"Diann, Armand is not the man to share the limelight. He's been mad at Gabrielle since last year, when others made the finals along with him."

"And now he's angry because I've won an award along with him?"

Louis Magnen looked away and shrugged in that inestimable way that only a true Frenchman seemed capable of pulling off. Diann had learned it was a wonderfully ambiguous movement that could communicate the messages of "Life dictates the terms," "What did you expect?" "That's just the way things are'' and ''Maybe, maybe not'' all at the same time.

''Vuillard is an excitable man, Diann,'' Peter Campbell said from across the table, his refined blond good looks in perfect harmony with his straight British carriage and precise diction. ''Nearly everyone in the Fragrance Fraternity knew he expected to be the sole recipient of the NOSE Award. Perhaps—''

''Perhaps when he found out he was to share it with Ms. Torrey, he got his nose out of joint,'' a deep voice said from both above and behind Diann.

She twisted to see Robert Mize standing behind Armand Vuillard's empty chair, breathtakingly handsome in a flawless indigo blue tuxedo that had to have been custom-made for those broad shoulders and narrow waist. In that tanned sculptured face under the subdued light, his eyes glowed a midnight blue.

A polite chuckle made its way around the table at his small witticism. When it reached Gabrielle, she cried out, her expressive hands waving in the air. ''*Oui!* Robert. You are too clever. Come. Sit down. You will have Vuillard's place at this symposium. Let his nose be out of joint.''

''Thank you, Gabrielle. I would be delighted.''

Robert's eyes swept from Diann's face to her flowing hair to her off-the-shoulder, golden gown, leaving warm licks of heat in their wake as he pulled out the chair to her left.

As soon as he sat down next to her, Diann immediately smelled the rich almond fragrance that seemed a part of him. She thought she knew all the men's colognes and after-shaves, but this was new. She was curious to know what it was, but asking him outright might give him the impression that she was interested in him and not just the cologne.

She was honest enough to admit to herself that she was interested in him.

No, she quickly amended. Curious. A scientific curiosity. He'd proved he was no dummy in that afternoon's verbal exchange. Why wasn't he using his brains for more than conversational jabs?

Gabrielle played hostess and introduced Robert to the other diners at the head table. She seemed delighted to learn that although everyone had heard of Robert Mize's TV spot, none of them had seen it.

"It will precede Louis's packaging presentation two days from now," she said, an excited twinkle in her eyes. "You see the connection, yes?"

Helena brought her ever-present tissue to her runny nose and shook her square head of ginger hair. "*Nicht.* I do not see."

Gabrielle gestured impatiently with her expressive hands. "My dear, Helena. Robert is a form of packaging, no?"

Helena squeezed her profuse ginger eyebrows together in contemplation before shaking her head. "Gabrielle, you must be precise. He is an advertisement, a display, not a package."

A small frown found its way between Gabrielle's fashionable brows. "Perhaps you are right. But we do not have a PERFUME Award for advertisement. But wait. I know. Next year *Redolence* will include a category for advertisement and honor that perfume company's whose advertisement is the best. A wonderful idea, yes?"

The general murmur around the table seemed to agree.

Gabrielle chatted on happily as the dinner courses began to arrive, informing them that she'd already held private screenings of Robert's taped TV spot for many of her friends.

When the discussion switched from him to more elemental aspects of the perfume business, Diann felt Robert lean closer to her. His scent came first, then his warmth and palatable sensuality made themselves felt on every nerve ending in her body.

"So, Diann, what does being the best 'nose' in the perfume industry mean?"

Diann focused her eyes on the elegant dinner setting. "It means you have the olfactory capability that enables you to find the ingredients that produce the best-smelling perfumes."

"In other words, a super sense of smell?"

"Maybe not super, but certainly a sensitive sense of smell. And an educated one."

"How do you educate your sense of smell?"

"Much the way you educate any sense—by using it with focus and intent. It's the subject of my presentation at the symposium. If you're still interested in a few days, maybe you'd like to sit in."

"I'll be interested."

She glanced at him, hearing the subtle, intimate inflection in his tone. She came eye-to-eye with a seductive midnight blue. She glanced quickly away again.

She could feel him lean slightly closer as he asked his next question.

"You've moved from the room originally assigned to you. Anything wrong?"

"How do you know what room was assigned to me?"

"Gabrielle told me what room was yours."

"Did she also tell you I moved?"

"No, I found that out for myself when I knocked on the door I thought was yours and announced I had come to escort you to dinner. A short surprised man from Brussels declined my offer. I think this will be his last trip to Paris."

Diann couldn't quite stifle her laugh. When she had composed herself again, she braved another look at his face. "Why should you come by to escort me to dinner?"

His eyes deepened with a quiet intensity. "Because I've been trying to meet you for a long time, and now that I have, I plan to spend as much time with you as I can."

Diann tried to ignore his very matter-of-fact declaration of intent and the flutter it was causing in her stomach. She looked quickly away, suddenly not wanting to read what she might find in his eyes and not wanting him to read what he might find in hers. He gave her but a second to regroup.

"So why the room change? Lumpy bed?"

"No, of course not. A clerk misplaced a piece of my luggage. In an effort to make it up to me, they gave me a suite overlooking the place de la Concorde."

Robert brought a glass of wine to his lips and took a leisurely sip. "That's one of the most impressive sights in Paris. Too bad they didn't lose a piece of my luggage. You get it back?"

"Yes, fortunately. About an hour later, nothing less than the manager himself appeared at my door with it and more apologies. They made me feel as though that was the first piece of luggage that had ever been misplaced in the entire history of the hotel, and who knows how long it's been in operation."

"Since 1909. Prior to that it was the home of the duke of Crillon."

She looked into that handsome face with more surprise. "How did you know that?"

His eyes rested on the wineglass as he reset it beside his plate. "Must have read it in a guidebook somewhere."

That could explain it. However, Diann could think of a few other explanations. "Where were you educated?"

"I've always found life to be the best educator."

"But you've been to college?"

"Several."

"Several?"

"I didn't stay long."

A euphemism for the fact that he didn't apply himself? Or was it because he didn't have a clue as to what he wanted to do? "What did you study?"

"Nothing useful."

Great. Another illuminating confidence. Why was it so hard to get a straight answer out of this man? "Did you get a degree?"

He looked away. Examined his wineglass for a moment. "And if I did, would my stock go up or down with you, I wonder?"

He glanced back at her face, his blue eyes sparking with speculation. "Down, I bet, since you'd find that further evidence that I was wasting my brain."

He smiled as he watched the telling response in her face. She looked away, irritated he could read her so well.

"Degrees often have nothing to do with the work a person ends up doing, Diann. Take you, for example. You're the only 'nose' in the perfume business who has a graduate degree in chemistry. Most of the industry is made up of people who signed on with a perfume company and learned their trade by doing."

"And how did you become such an expert on the perfume industry all of a sudden?"

"I read *Redolence* magazine on the plane trip over here. The last issue had a background profile on all the PERFUME Award winners."

"So now you know all about me."

"Not yet. But I will. How did you get into the perfume business? The article didn't say."

"Not yet? I will?" Such confidence. Both irritation and excitement leafed through Diann's emotions. "I got a job at MW while I was attending graduate school. I found I enjoyed the work, so I stuck with it after getting my degree. Simple enough."

"You could have gotten a proper job in chemistry after you'd completed your schooling. One that might have enabled you to make all those discoveries you talked about being so vital to humankind. Why didn't you?"

Diann scanned his face to confirm that curiosity and not condemnation had prompted the question. A small smile curved her lips. "Maybe I will one day."

She concentrated on her food then, hoping that would convey her wish to end the subject. The *blanquette,* a stewed meat with white sauce enriched with cream and eggs, melted deliciously in her mouth. She savored every bite, steadfastly refusing to think about the calories she was consuming.

He leaned perceptively closer. "Did I tell you my room's view is of an inner courtyard reminiscent of the eighteenth century? The grounds are quite impressive. Come up with me later and I'll show you."

He smiled and gave her a knowing look of pure suggestion.

Diann put as much cool displeasure in her voice as she could muster. To her chagrin, she found she couldn't muster a whole lot. "Thank you, but I'm not interested, Mr. Mize."

He leaned a bit closer. " 'Robert,' remember? Don't decide too hastily, Diann. There are several things I'd enjoy showing you. You might even surprise yourself and enjoy them, too."

His thick, rich almond scent combined with the suggestive warmth of his whisper to whip her heartbeat into double time. Diann took a quick breath and then another, angry at her body's interested response and angry at herself for being so tardy in getting it under control.

This was not like her. This was not like her at all.

"Mr. Mize?" Conrad called from his other side. "Can you tell us about how MW selected you as their model?"

Diann felt Robert turn and move slightly toward his left to answer Conrad's question, and she sighed in relief. Conrad might be dumpy and bald, but at that moment he was wearing a suit of shining armor as far as she was concerned.

She reached for her water glass and took a quick gulp.

Kohei Kanemoto's head inched toward her. "You all right?"

She put the glass down slowly and then turned to her right. "Yes, thank you. Why did you ask?"

"You look... warm."

"I am. A bit. So what's new in the wonderful world of perfume diversification?"

Kohei leaned closer. He moved a little like a penguin in his tuxedo, stiff and cold. His straight black hair sported a full-fledged, flying-buttress cowlick. Kohei had always struck her as a comfortable, baggy-pants, bare feet, rolled-up sleeves kind of guy, ill at lease in formal wear and at formal functions.

She recognized the excitement in his voice as he whispered in her ear. "Something I want to show you."

Diann had met Kohei several years before at a conference and had ended up talking with him for hours. His love of combining both perfume and gadgetry were wholesomely infectious, and she always looked forward to what new manner of wonder he had devised.

Now, like a little boy who could not wait to share a secret, he carefully drew a small block-shaped tissue out of his pocket and set it on the table, looking around furtively to see if anyone else had noticed.

Sensing his need for secrecy, Diann found herself looking around, too, like a coconspirator. The others at their table appeared appropriately absorbed in their own conversations. Only their attentive waiter and a sharp-featured, copper-haired man from an adjoining table glanced even momentarily in their direction.

Obviously feeling safe, Kohei slowly unwrapped the small square of tissue to reveal a pair of earrings, soft shimmering jade dangling at the end of a single, glistening golden thread. As exquisite as they were, Diann waited, knowing there was more.

"Pick them up," Kohei whispered in her ear. "Put them on."

Diann didn't wear jewelry as a rule, but she knew these would be something special. As inconspicuously as possible, she clipped each earring on her ear. She had no sooner gotten them into place than a lovely fragrance seemed to explode all around her. She recognized it immediately. It was called Blossom, the heavy, intensely exotic, most exclusive and expensive fragrance of the Oriental Blossom line.

She turned to Kohei. "How is the perfume being released?"

His dark eyes danced with the surprise in her voice. "Ear warmth excites gold thread. Gold thread special heat-sensitive coil, traveling to scent solids encased in jade, releasing scent molecules into air."

Diann nodded. "Similar principle that Annette Prince of Prince Perfumes employed in her perfumed bracelets, which she introduced last December at a conference in Las Vegas."

"Annette Prince? Yes, I know name. I remember bracelets."

"But her fragrance solids encased in the grove of her bracelets had to come in contact with a woman's skin in order to be released. These are superior. Now a woman won't have to worry about the fragrance of a perfume changing when it mixes with her skin. Too bad Annette will never see these."

"She will not? But why not?"

"Oh, I thought you knew. She died, Kohei. Only thirty-five, and she suffered a heart attack right after the conference. The perfume industry lost a true star when it lost her. She was one of the finalists for the PERFUME Award you will receive in diversification."

"Yes. I read in *Redolence* about all finalists. Perhaps she would win if she not die."

"No. Annette was an inventive genius and a formidable talent, but as far as I'm concerned, this century has not seen your peer."

Kohei did not smile, but his eyes glowed in appreciation. He fingered his cup of tea. "Many women also allergic because ingredients in perfumes interact on sensitive skin. Now they can buy earrings of favorite scents and wear them. Ingredients never contact skin."

Diann knew his natural modesty had made him change the subject. She was happy to cooperate, since it would help her to find out more about his newest invention. "How long does the scent in a pair of earrings last?"

"Three months if wear every day."

Diann gently slipped the earrings from her ears and laid them back in the protective tissue. "Even women who don't have allergic reactions to perfume ingredients would want to buy and wear their perfume this way. Think of how easy it would be to change their scent. Instead of having to wash it out of their skin, all they'd have to do is put on a different pair of earrings."

"Yes. And no chance perfume stain garment or be transferred when embracing."

"Kohei, as always, you are a marvel. Are these what you plan to present at the Oriental Blossom presentation tomorrow morning?"

"I introduce at end of presentation. After you smell earrings tonight."

Diann understood immediately. "You were testing them out on me because the bottom note isn't quite stable yet in this new process."

His shoulders dropped perceptively and he let out a sigh that resembled a low hiss. "Computer told me this. I could not smell difference. I hoped your nose could not smell difference."

Kohei rewrapped the earrings in the tissue paper and slowly returned them to his pocket. "So. Unveiling another time. Another place."

Disappointment filled his voice. Diann rested her hand on his arm. "Armand Vuillard is the only other person who would instantly have noticed the flattening of the fragrance. And he isn't here. Why not present your innovation? With a short exposure, no one else will detect the problem. Just say the earrings won't be on the market immediately. I know you. You'll find the answer soon. You're the best."

Kohei shook his head. "Thank you, Diann, but no. Earrings must be right before presentation. I wait."

Diann should have known that would be his response. Kohei, like the rest of them at this table, was a perfectionist. If they shared nothing else, the winners of the PERFUME awards had that in common.

Diann started as her attention was drawn by a sudden, sharp cry. She looked up to see Gabrielle jumping to her feet, knocking her chair onto its side, waving her billowing sleeves like enormous signal flags of distress. Diann immediately understood why. Gabrielle had spilled champagne all over the milk-white tablecloth and her blood-red designer dress.

Diann did not have to understand the furious French escaping the woman's lips to interpret its meaning. The wail of her tone was enough.

Instantly all the men at the table seemed to be up and racing over to lend their assistance.

Diann didn't know what the horde of them thought they could accomplish by all attempting to dab at Gabrielle's wet dress at once with their dinner napkins. But she understood that it was probably the damsel-in-distress, hero-coming-to-the-rescue scenario that drew the men so irresistibly. Diann exchanged glances and shrugs with Helena Strunk, the only other one at the table who had remained seated.

It took several moments for the commotion to die down and the men to finally return to their seats. Their attentive waiter brought another glass and more champagne for Gabrielle and refilled all the other glasses at the table. Then he deftly covered the wet spot on the tablecloth with a piece of matching white linen and quietly withdrew.

Gabrielle's skin was flushed. She looked more embarrassed than irritated by the mishap now.

Diann's attention was drawn by the tinkling of silverware on the side of a glass. She looked up to see Peter Campbell rising languidly, one of the red rosebuds from Gabrielle's corsage now worn prominently in the lapel of his impeccable black tuxedo. He waited politely for the various conversations in the room to cease. They did finally as everyone looked expectantly in his direction.

"Ladies and gentlemen," he said, his diction so crisp and clean even Professor Henry Higgins would have approved.

He paused, waiting for those gathered to pick up their goblets of champagne. Diann knew she'd be hard-pressed to select her favorite between the deliciously sensual sounds of French and the beautifully enunciated English that only the well-educated British seemed to have mastered.

"I propose a toast to the elite of the International Fragrance Fraternity, the men and women at this table who are the recipients of the PERFUME awards, and to Gabrielle and Conrad Rife for making it all possible. May we all reign forever."

Not exactly a modest toast, but then, Peter Campbell was known for his excellent diction and his distribution, not his modesty.

Diann brought her goblet of champagne to her lips and took a sip. She wasn't much of a drinker, but she enjoyed the pleasant refreshing swallow as the liquid bubbled down her throat.

Then she started, nearly dropping her goblet as an even sharper cry broke into the air. Diann twisted immediately toward Gabrielle. But the cry had not come from her this time. It had come from her husband, Conrad.

Diann stared at the Fragrance Fraternity's codirector, her eyes growing large in alarm.

Conrad had turned absolutely gray. He tried to stand, his hands clutching at the tablecloth and his round body wobbling like a top. Then he collapsed into a boneless heap on the shiny, mirrorlike surface of the les Ambassadeurs parquet floor.

Chapter Three

Robert dropped to Conrad Rife's supine form. He had time only to determine that Conrad's breath was labored and his pulse thready. Then he was literally shoved away as Gabrielle swooped to her husband's side and coolly called out for someone to get an ambulance. The copper-haired man at the next table quickly volunteered and scurried off.

Conrad gasped, his words breathy and barely audible. "I just feel a little weak, dear. And a little nauseated. Something I ate, that's all."

Gabrielle held her husband's head on her lap as she sat on the carpet, her dress spread full around her like damp rose petals—and her white face and shoulders stemlike above its dewy folds. Her voice soothed as her steady hand stroked his brow. "Yes, of course, dear. But we'll let the doctor make sure. An ambulance is on its way."

Robert watched Gabrielle Rife with interest. She seemed amazingly calm and in control over her husband's collapse, in contrast to her earlier explosive outburst over the spilling of some wine on her dress.

His eyes traveled to Diann, who stood in back of Gabrielle, her face white, solemn, still.

The room had grown quiet as the other tables emptied, their previous occupants slipping into a watchful circle around the fallen man. A murmur of speculation drifted through the mass of bodies as everyone strained to get a better look.

Robert began to wave the watchers back to their tables. "Let's give Mr. and Mrs. Rife some air. Crowding around will just inhibit the rescue team from getting through."

"Mr. Mize is correct. This will not do," Peter Campbell declared, his distinct clipped tones carrying to every corner. "Please return to your seats, ladies and gentlemen."

The crowd finally began to retreat, retaking their places. Most resumed quietly eating, still periodically turning their heads in the direction of the fallen man.

Some didn't resume eating, but looked at their plates with noticeable suspicion.

Robert understood. A man collapsing in a restaurant always conjured up thoughts of food poisoning. But if there had been something wrong with the food, someone else should have been showing symptoms by now, since everyone had been served the same.

Robert did not have a good feeling about this. Not in the context of everything else that had gone before. Still, Conrad Rife was one of the last people he would have guessed would be singled out.

If he was singled out. This could be coincidence. Rife might just have a bad case of indigestion. He might be having a legitimate heart attack.

Or he might have been slipped something on purpose. Or by mistake?

Robert kept getting flashes of the commotion caused by Gabrielle's spilling of her champagne. Glasses had been deposited every which way on the table. Nearly everyone had left his on her seat. Nearly anyone could have slipped something into Conrad Rife's champagne—or into the goblet that was Conrad Rife's, thinking it was someone else's.

Robert and the rest of the dinner guests at the head table stood around the stricken man in strained silence.

Conrad's labored breath was audible. Everyone else's was silent—uncomfortably silent—as though collectively their breaths were being held.

When the ambulance attendants finally arrived, Diann turned to Gabrielle. "Do you want me to go with you?"

Gabrielle's attention focused on the attendants as they lifted Conrad's bulky frame onto their stretcher.

"No, Diann. You stay. Please. Finish your dinner. Everything will be all right."

She didn't look as if everything would be all right. Neither did her husband. She seemed to realize this and collected herself. Plastering a bright expression on her face, she raised her voice and addressed the rest of the room, which had drawn quiet and speculative again when the ambulance team had arrived.

"My husband is just suffering from a little indigestion. Please enjoy your dinner, everyone. Conrad and I will see you tomorrow morning when the presentations begin."

She waved her hands in a jaunty farewell. When the ambulance attendants had rolled her husband away and she followed, those at the head table stood looking at one another uncertainly. No one appeared to have much of an appetite left.

No one but Helena Strunk, that is. Robert was amazed to see she had already taken her seat and, in several hearty bites, had finished her meal.

She rose as though totally oblivious to his scrutiny and that of her other diners, wiped her generous mouth with her linen dinner napkin and her ever-runny nose with her tissue.

"Eating dessert would not seem right—not after Herr Rife's illness," she announced. "So I will leave now. Good night."

And with that she juggernauted, hefty arms and legs spinning, out of the dining room.

A stunned silence froze in the air for a moment until Louis Magnen broke it with a chuckle that sent his pencil-thin mustache into a little jig. "Who can match such a farewell? Please excuse me, *mademoiselle, messieurs*. I, too, will retire for the evening. Au revoir."

Kohei Kanemoto turned to Diann and gave her a small, stiff bow, then excused himself. Before Robert could say anything, Peter stepped up to Diann and offered his arm to escort her to her room. A small, irritated frown emerged on Robert's brow when Diann smiled and accepted it.

Robert waited until they were out of sight before using his napkin to carefully pick up Conrad Rife's champagne goblet and slip it into his inside pocket. Then he turned, intending to catch up with Peter and Diann, only to find himself literally running into Diann.

He caught her bare shoulders instinctively to steady them both and saw the look of startled uneasiness that immediately entered her expressive eyes.

He found himself suddenly, acutely, aware of the hot, silky feel of her firm shoulders beneath his hands, the light glow of her maple-syrup hair, the lovely warm liquid of her caramel eyes.

She was having trouble breathing. He sensed it with every one of his own uneven breaths. And right at that moment, despite everything he knew about her, he wanted nothing more than to look at her and feel her this close to him.

She took a deep breath, straightening her shoulders beneath his touch. Whatever had kept her still for that moment vanished. "I left my evening purse on the table. I came back for it," she said in a hasty, unsolicited explanation.

Robert relaxed his hold on her shoulders, let his hands slowly drop to his sides. "Where's Campbell?"

"He took the elevator up to his room. I told him I'd get the next one."

She slipped around Robert and moved to the table. He watched her pick up her evening purse, knowing she could just as easily have left it there to give herself an excuse to return.

Had she been looking for an excuse to return to the table? The thought drew an unsettling frown across his brow.

He moved to her side. "Let me buy you a nightcap."

She immediately withdrew from his hand on her arm. "No. Thank you. I've had a very long day and I'm tired."

"It's barely ten-thirty."

"Paris time. But I'm still on New Jersey time. And I had a long plane ride."

She avoided looking at him. Was she afraid her eyes would reveal guilt? He retook her arm. "I'll see you to your room."

She said nothing until they were alone in the elevator. Finally she raised her eyes to him, their look of accusation flooring him completely until he heard her words.

"Why did you take that champagne goblet?"

He was slipping. He laughed to give himself time to control his surprise at her having seen him pocket the goblet. And time to think up a logical excuse. When the practiced chuckle had ended, he let his lips curl into an ill-behaved grin. "Looks like you caught me."

"Caught you at what?"

"Some people collect ashtrays. Other people collect towels. I collect champagne goblets."

She frowned. "You mean you steal them."

The dismay and disappointment in her voice couldn't have been greater had he just admitted to pocketing the 137-carat Regent diamond out of the Galerie d'Apollon at the Louvre.

How could a face that looked that stricken and lovely at the same time possibly hide the kind of secrets he'd been imagining it must?

He moved closer to her, determined to find out several things—right here and right now.

Her eyes widened in alarm. And excitement. He could see it flashing with every quiver of light in their luscious liquid centers.

He lowered his voice, let it nestle in her right ear as he drew aside her silky curtain of hair. He leaned forward as though he meant to impart a secret. "What can I say? The impulse to take them is too strong. It's a disease, you know. I should be pitied."

The look in her eyes told him she wasn't pitying him. Her chin rose in disdain.

"You should be turned in."

He switched to her other ear, moving past her face slowly, her nearness and scent tantalizing him. "Are you going to?"

Her eyes followed his every movement. He could see the rapid beat of the pulse in her throat. No matter how hard she was trying to be cool, he knew his closeness was affecting her far more strongly than she liked. Just as hers was affecting him far more strongly than he liked.

His thoughts fogged from the warmth of her. He pushed through the distracting haze of her allure and concentrated. "Well, Diann?"

"Return it tomorrow morning. Not a moment later."

"You won't turn me in?"

"Not if you return it tomorrow morning."

The elevator opened and she bolted around him and out the door. He was right on her heels. He had no intention of letting her get away. He told himself the job he had to do meant he must learn how good a liar she was. But he knew that wasn't the only reason he followed her to her door and waited while she unlocked it.

When she turned to say good-night, he rested his arms on either side of her, in mock restraint. "Invite me in to see your view."

She said nothing for a long moment. Nor did she move. "Some other time. I'm tired."

She didn't look tired. She looked alert and flushed. He moved closer until he was just a heartbeat away. Her warm, rich vanilla-icing fragrance swarmed through his brain. He wondered if she could possibly taste as good as she smelled. "I won't keep you up long."

"It's too...late, Mr. Mize." She nervously licked her lips. Their moist, soft-pink shine drew his eyes.

"It's 'Robert,' remember?"

For a fraction of a second he let his chest brush lightly against hers to see her reaction. He could hear and feel the quick intake of her breath. And his own.

Her eyes were enormous, liquid drops of light caramel, whirlpooling before him.

His heart beat loudly in his ears. His voice erupted into a hoarse whisper. "I'm reforming my criminal career for you. Who knows what other imperfections you might be able to correct in me?"

He had to know if she would retreat from or advance into the kiss they both knew was coming. He waited what seemed to be a lifetime. Infuriatingly, she remained as still as a statue.

He moved closer. Her hair rustled against the sleeve of his tuxedo. Their breaths met, mingled. The muscles in his biceps and up and down his back tightened almost painfully as he forced himself to stay that mere whisper away.

He had to taste her. Just one taste. That would be all. He brushed her lips with his.

She exploded like hot taffy on his tongue, and he felt an insatiable greed rock through his body. He sucked in a quick breath and pulled away immediately, knowing he must while his brain still functioned marginally.

He didn't retreat a second too soon.

Her eyes swam before him—pools of surprise and barely controlled rage. "How dare you!"

Before he could think of a coherent thing to say, she ducked under one of his restraining arms and slipped inside her room, firmly locking the door behind her.

DIANN STOOD on the other side of the hotel-room door, trying to calm her heartbeat. Damn it. What in the hell was wrong with her? It was just a kiss. A quick brush that even the Disney channel could have run prime time.

But it *wasn't* just a kiss.

She had seen it coming. Her curiosity had not let her back away. She'd kissed a few men in her time. She knew a man's kiss said a lot about him. She wanted confirmation of what she expected this man would say.

She had awaited the showman's smack—forceful, intense pressure, a mere simulation of desire with maybe a back-bending dip thrown in for effect. Either that or the sportsman's kiss—all domineering lips and shooting tongue, full of the sound and fury of passion with none of its substance.

But she had not expected a sensuously tender, mind-boggling, spine-tingling brush that had ignited the peach fuzz on her forearms and singed the bandage off her scraped knee. No, she had not expected that kiss at all.

Damn it, he was a male model. And a petty thief!

How could he kiss her like that?

And how could a thirty-year-old, levelheaded, intelligent chemist with an IQ over 140 possibly be quivering now on the other side of the door, wishing he'd do it again?

THE PHONE WAS RINGING when Robert entered his hotel room. Cassel's voice popped into his ear even before he'd had a chance to say hello.

"What in the hell went on at your table tonight?"

Robert let out a heavy breath. "You tell me. Have you checked with the hospital?"

"Yeah. Rife's vital signs are now stable. They've admitted him overnight to give them a chance to run some tests to see what happened."

"And you'll get copies of those test results, right?"

"As soon as they're issued. You think this ties in?"

"I suppose if we stretch it we could say he fits the parameters of the profile. I just expressed his champagne goblet to a local lab to avoid delay."

"A local lab? Can you trust them to keep their mouths shut?"

"Don't worry. I know the right places and the right palms to grease. This is my territory, remember?"

"Yeah, well, I'm familiar with the terrain, too. By the way, Torrey was rubbing heads with that Kanemoto guy at dinner. I could have sworn they were passing something. You see that?"

"Yes. A pair of earrings. She put them on and then took them off and gave them back. She kept nothing."

"You sure?"

"I'm sure."

"You check her ears?"

Robert's smile quickly formed, then dissipated. "Closely. Are the bugs all in place and operating?"

"Everywhere but her new room. You'll have to find a way to get inside and plant it."

"I'm working on it."

"Her background check says she's cautious when it comes to men. She's dated several, but only after knowing them for months and then only men from her field of chemistry. Even so, it's only her work she ends up taking seriously. She's a real workaholic. Her colleagues call her 'driven.'"

"I've read the background report, remember?"

"Just thought I'd remind you you're up against a lady who definitely has a direction to her life."

"So?"

"So I know from experience that women with a focus are your downfall. Be careful, Mize, that while you're seducing her she doesn't end up seducing you."

Robert didn't answer. He just replaced the telephone receiver on its base.

Then he sat down on the bed and rested his head in his hands.

He could still smell her fragrance. Taste her on his lips. See the surprise and quiet rage in her eyes. Hear its edge in her voice.

He knew why she'd been surprised at a kiss she'd been fully expecting. He knew why she'd raged quietly at its execution. And he knew why the edge of that rage had nearly strangled her words.

He was feeling pretty surprised and rage-filled himself.

DIANN WATCHED Gabrielle Rife whisk her way through the throng to the presentation podium and rap repeatedly for the occupants of the Marie-Antoinette Salon to come to order. The room was spectacular with its life-size marble statues tucked into marble alcoves, sumptuous paneling with elaborate friezes, gleaming parquet floors and enormous crystal chandelier.

Tasteful polished-wood tables had been set up to accommodate the sixty attendees. Finally, the din retreated, and people took their chairs and came to a hushed attention.

Gabrielle's voice thundered enthusiastically through the microphone. "*Mesdames* and *messieurs,* as most of you know, I am Gabrielle Rife, codirector of the International Fragrance Fraternity and official sponsor of this spring symposium. I would like to take this opportunity to officially welcome you one and all."

Diann joined in with the polite applause rumbling around the room. She turned to see Robert taking the seat beside her. He looked absolutely wonderful in a French-cut casual suit with dark slacks and a light-blue jacket. He tipped his head in her direction, his warmth and scent invading her every nerve ending.

"Good morning, Diann. Sleep well?"

"Fine," she lied. Truth was she'd had a hard time getting to sleep. She knew he guessed this truth and the reason why the second she saw the sudden satisfaction of his smile. She looked quickly away.

The clapping died down and Gabrielle resumed her address. "I assume everyone knows that my husband, Conrad, was taken ill last evening."

A murmur greeted her words.

Gabrielle raised her hands to quell it. "He's doing fine, just fine. But the doctor has prescribed bed rest for a few days, so, regrettably, Conrad will not be able to join us for the remainder of the symposium."

A sympathetic rumble greeted that announcement.

"But Conrad has urged me to go ahead with our plans to make this the absolute best symposium," Gabrielle said quickly, her voice rising over the babble, quieting it again.

"We will display and pay tribute to all that is unsurpassed in our fabulous and fascinating industry. And to start that off this morning, I have the distinct pleasure of introducing you to our first presenter and the recipient of the DIVERSIFIER Award, Kohei Kanemoto from Japan. Please give Mr. Kanemoto a warm welcome."

The room exploded with enthusiastic applause. Kanemoto was no stranger to this in crowd of perfume's elite, and neither was the quality of his presentations. He walked up to the podium in stiff, straight strides, impeccably attired in a dark suit, and waited until the applause had died down. Then, with a slight wave of his hand, Kohei signaled a heavyset, bushy-haired hotel employee with thick glasses and a magnificient mustache to close and lock the doors, preventing an inadvertent interruption.

The room hushed to an anticipatory quiet. Slowly, confidently, like a magician who commanded all that he saw before him, Kanemoto waved his hand again and the dark, velvet drapes were drawn, blocking out the light from the terrace. Then the bright overhead lights were extinguished, plunging everything into immediate and absolute darkness.

A collective intake of surprise hissed about the salon.

A voice that Diann realized was a high-quality tape suddenly seemed to be coming from everywhere and nowhere. It was not Kohei's voice, but that of a smooth announcer's overlaid on the background of a soft undulating rhythm of barely discernible drums, like a distant and comforting heartbeat.

"Scent is our most mysterious of senses," the voice droned to the beat of the drums, "coming out from the invisible world, having the power to change our moods more quickly and completely than sight, taste, touch or hearing. It is an intimate, subliminal sense that we respond to instinctively and often unconsciously."

Suddenly a magnificent, enormous yellow rosebud appeared and hung suspended in the air above Diann as the sweet fragrance of rose surrounded her. The flower looked so real she was certain that if she raised her hand, she'd be able to touch it. She could tell from the exclamations of awe and delight around her that she wasn't the only one experiencing this wonderful smell or holographic image.

The drumbeat had mellowed into a violin's strings behind the announcer's voice as the flower turned, its glistening petals opening before the audience's eyes, the scent becoming more pronounced.

"Unlike sight and hearing, our sense of smell actually allows minute molecules to enter our brains when we inhale. Messages from those molecules invade several parts of our brains simultaneously. Rational thought, memory, mood, emotion and the area of the brain that controls body chemistry, hormonal release and sexuality are all instantly engaged."

The yellow rose expanded until it suddenly burst into a thousand golden lights. In the blink of an eye, the lights reformed into a splendid monarch butterfly that flew high until it was silhouetted against a full silvery moon, then swooped down to brush against the precious petals of a night-blooming jasmine.

The delicate petals fell and the heavenly scent of jasmine filled the air. The violins began a waltz and the butterfly suddenly became a beautiful pin on the long flowing dress of a twirling woman wrapped in the arms of her smiling partner.

Exclamations of delight chorused throughout the salon. Diann heard her own exclamation joining them.

"The scents of rose and jasmine evoke a relaxing mood, a romantic mood," the announcer's voice went on. "But that mood can change as quickly as the scents that surround us."

Diann detected the rose fragrance dissipating and being gradually replaced by the faint notes of a sexually stimulating ylang-ylang fragrance.

The violins faded as the sound of the drums increased. With each of the waltzing couple's turns, a piece of their clothing spun off until they ended up in scanty garb. Their dancing became a primitive and exotic tantalization of each other.

Diann could feel the entire room shifting in their seats.

Faster and faster the drums beat as the bodies of the dancing man and woman, glistening with perspiration now, edged ever closer and closer.

Diann felt her own perspiration erupting uncomfortably on her skin as her mind drifted to thoughts of the man sitting beside her.

The couple dancing in the air above her finally touched, only to have their glistening bodies explode into the fiery eruption of a volcano. Diann jumped back as images of hot lava flowed toward her.

From the startled exclamations of others around her, she knew she hadn't been the only one to respond to the realistic imagery.

Diann could swear she smelled the heat and smoke of the trails of living fire digging rivets into the air around her. She drew her eyes back to the exploding volcano, just as the glistening eruption fused and changed into a powerful, stainless-steel piston in the internal-combustion engine of a car.

The announcer's voice once again rose around her. "Scent is everywhere, an invisible world that constantly invades us."

The car was now on an assembly line, being hammered together by the robotic arms of powerful machines in a deafening percussion beat as the less-than-desirable smells of lubricating engine oils were released into the air.

"Industry seeks to keep their workers' attentions on the jobs they must do in order to maintain production and eliminate injury. And yet with all its attention to the comfort of its workers, it often ignores the all-important sense of smell."

The car drove off the assembly line and landed toy-size, on an office worker's desk. The background beat had slowed to intermittent strokes that alternated with a single, jarring piano key as the musty odor of old air and the sharp odor of chemicals from office machines combined in a swirl around Diann. Many office workers at many desks shuffled papers in slow, methodical moves.

"We in the perfume industry are familiar with how to use scents for pleasure. But we have barely touched on the importance of using scents to mentally stimulate and thereby help humankind achieve its ever-expanding potential."

The cloying chemical smells dissipated into a tangy scent of citrus. The drumbeat increased, as did the activity of the employees, who were now working together to build models of spaceships out of the paper from their desks.

The background beat lightened and sped into an energetic frenzy. The paper models were launched, becoming silver spheres that blasted into an endless black space twinkling with stars, ringed planets, purple comets and bursting orange suns.

Diann felt herself a part of that silver rocket. The images speeding by her were glorious, electrifying, mind-blowing, soul lifting.

She let them spin her along, until she suddenly had the strangest sense she was falling into that black endless space that vibrated like jazz and smelled like hot licorice. And something else. Something cloying, deadly. For a split second she fought it. But only for a split second.

Because in the next second she couldn't fight anything.

Chapter Four

Robert awoke to an irritating buzzing in his brain and an energetic shaking of his shoulder. "Mize, come out of it. Come on, Mize."

He opened his eyes to find Cassel's worried face and compact frame looming over him. "Can you get up?"

Robert looked around in surprise to find himself lying on one of the beautiful carpets laid across the parquet floors of the Salon Marie-Antoinette. He was even more surprised to see that the floor was littered with the other unconscious attendees to the International Fragrance Fraternity's symposium.

Her image and name flowed into him with his next breath. *Diann.*

He twisted to his other side and found her. She was lying very still, her long, light-brown hair streaming across her face. A slice of panic cut into his gut. His heart raced until his exploring fingers finally registered the slow, steady pulse in her neck. He let out a deep, soundless breath before turning back to Cassel.

"What in the hell happened to everybody?"

"I was hoping you could tell me. I was late getting here, because I was checking on those things we discussed. When I tried all the doors and found them locked, I banged but no one answered. Got me spooked, so I climbed in through the terrace. The lights were all off, and the place was as quiet as a tomb. When I flipped the lights back on, everyone was just lying there, including the uniformed hotel employee positioned in front of the locked doors. For a moment I thought you were all dead."

"Anybody but me come to yet?"

"No. And believe me, it took some doing to get you out of dreamland. What were you people doing?"

"We were watching a very impressive holographic display being presented by Koehi Kanemoto. Next thing I knew you were shaking me awake. What time is it?"

Cassel checked his watch. "About ten to eleven."

"Eleven? The presentation began at ten. Damn. I must have been out close to forty-five minutes. And my head is still buzzing."

Robert rolled to his feet and swayed there a moment, waiting for the dizziness to stop. "Looks like we may have been wrong. That diversifier, Kohei Kanemoto, was the one orchestrating this show. Come on. Let's go find him."

Robert got to his feet, feeling steadier by the minute. They scissored carefully through the unconscious throng on the floor to the presentation podium. At its base lay Kanemoto. Robert studied his quiet features.

"He looks to be a victim, as well."

Cassel moved closer for a better look. "He could be faking it."

Robert dropped to his knee and shook Kohei's shoulder. Once. Twice. When that drew no response, he frowned, positioning his fingers against the pulse point in Kohei's neck. Then he rested his ear against Kohei's chest. After several long moments, he sat back on his heel. "He's not faking anything, Cassel. He's dead."

"Dead?"

"Yes. Quick, let's check the others. I'll take the right side. You take the left."

They went around the room, finding pulses as fast as they could. And they did find pulses. On everyone but Kane-moto.

Cassel's thin lips tightened as they met by the diversi-fier's body. "Not a mark on him. Just like the others. Want to bet what the autopsy is going to say?"

Robert shook his head. "That's a sucker's bet."

"You know who's been present at all the other deaths. You know who I've got my money on."

Robert knew. He took a deep breath. Let it out slowly. "You'd better get out of here. I'm already involved, so I've got no choice but to call the police and report this mess. You stay loose. I'll contact you as soon as I can."

Cassel nodded, took another look at the body of Kohei Kanemoto and then headed for the terrace, carefully wip-ing the French doors of any stray fingerprints he might have left.

Robert stood and looked out at the bodies strewn over the parquet floor.

How had Kanemoto been killed? The doors had been locked from the inside. Conceivably someone could have come through one of the terrace doors as Cassel had done. But it was more likely that the person who had killed Ka-nemoto was at this moment lying on the floor in front of him, playing possum.

Robert looked over at the table where he had sat with the recipients of the PERFUME awards and the fraternity's codirector. Its occupants still lay beneath it on the elegant Oriental carpet. He studied each one in turn, trying to judge the depth of their slumber by the periodic rise and fall of their breathing.

One of them could be faking.

Gabrielle Rife. Peter Campbell. Helena Strunk. Louis Magnen. Diann Torrey.

Any one of them.

But the odds-on favorite was Diann Torrey.

DIANN COULDN'T complain about her interview with the French detective who greeted her almost the instant she regained consciousness. His name was Inspector Jean Pinchot, and he gave her a small bow when he said it. He was a trim fifty, exceedingly polite and infinitely patient with her disorientation and disbelief that not only was Kohei Kanemoto dead, but she and an entire roomful of people had been rendered unconscious.

"But it was only a demonstration of how combining the scent of smell with the other senses could help to alter perceptions and mood," she protested to no one but herself.

"You are familiar with how Monsieur Kanemoto did this?"

Kohei's face flashed before Diann's eyes, his eyes full of the sparkle of discovery. A sad little pain shot into her chest. "No, Inspector Pinchot. Kohei is...was a marvel at electronic as well as scent wizardry. And you have to understand that the perfume business is laden with secrets. Millions of dollars go into the research and development of a scent or, as in the case of Kohei, finding a novel way to use it. The results of all research are kept strictly confidential."

"Could someone have wanted to discredit Monsieur Kanemoto by sabotaging his presentation?"

Diann shook her head and then wished she hadn't as a new crescendo of buzzing followed. "I can't think why. The room was full of people from the industry, eager to see what new and exciting ways Kanemoto and his company would use perfume. Everyone was there to learn. What would have been the point of trying to discredit him?"

"Professional envy?"

"Inspector Pinchot, it's true that Kohei is...*was* a rare talent. And I suppose such genius raises jealousy in some of those less talented. But Kohei would never have explained the techniques of his presentation to a colleague, much less a rival. I'm convinced the unconscious episode we all experienced was accidental."

"And how did this accident occur?"

"Maybe by some weird aberration in the sound waves or—"

"Yes, *mademoiselle?*"

Diann didn't want to verbalize the thought she had deliberately cut off. The impression was far too dim to be relied on. "Inspector, my field is not electronics. Surely if someone were to examine the equipment used—"

"Someone is, *mademoiselle*. But it does seem strange, does it not, that if some aberration did occur it would result in so many being rendered merely unconscious while taking the life of Monsieur Kanemoto?"

Diann looked at the detective in alarm. "I just assumed Kohei died of natural causes. Are you saying he didn't?"

Inspector Pinchot's polite smile drew his lips but did not reach to his sharp, dark eyes. "We don't know yet, *mademoiselle*. But we will find out soon. Very soon."

"HE WAS BRILLIANT. It is heinous that Kohei should die, and before his marvelous presentation was even over!" Helena Strunk raged angrily and loudly. She dug into her large purse and brought out an aluminum tissue container, broke the seal and fished a tissue from it before resealing the top. Diann caught a flash of the powerful, but pleasant, Der Winter scent, one of the seasonal offerings of Mit Luv perfumes that had a distinctive menthol component.

Helena swiped at her nose with her scented tissue before resuming eating. Diann watched her polish off her wild strawberries and honeyed ice cream drizzled with raspberry sauce, smacking her lips in obvious gusto.

Diann turned to look at the rest of the perfume industry's acknowledged greats, sitting together once again, this time in the Hôtel de Crillon's l'Obélisque restaurant, a rich, dark-paneled room. A late lunch sat before them, provided by the hotel after all had been checked by the nurse and interviewed by the gendarmes, France's military police.

Unlike Helena, the other occupants of the table were quiet.

And unlike Helena, no one seemed to have much of an appetite. Diann's body and mind still felt weak and unsteady. She suspected the acceptance of Kohei's sudden, shocking death was more to blame than whatever had made her lose consciousness.

Her untouched lunch and dessert lay before her on their plates. A cold queasiness rolled in her stomach. Their attentive waiter of the night before was on hand to pour her a second cup of black coffee. She wrapped her fingers around the delicate china, thankful for its warmth.

Gabrielle sat on her right, tears spurting periodically out of her eyes. Robert sat on her left, his arm resting on the back of her chair. Diann could feel his warmth, too—a different kind of warmth. She had a sudden, insane desire to lean back against his solid flesh and feel it fold around her, encasing her in strength and security.

She took a quick sip of black coffee. What a pathetic cliché—looking for a big, strong man to lean on. She knew perfectly well that getting strength or security from someone else was an illusion. Real strength and security came from within. Besides, when a woman really needed a man was generally when he made himself most scarce. She'd learned that lesson early.

Diann took yet another sip of her coffee and wondered why the caffeine was taking so long in getting to her brain. She desperately needed to think clearly. Something at the back of her mind was trying to get through.

Across the table, Louis Magnen propped up the side of his sharp chin with the knuckles of his right hand, a pained expression on his angular face that even seemed to droop the ends of his slim mustache. Finally he broke the prolonged silence.

"I cannot grieve for our esteemed diversifier. My poor head, she still buzzes. And I keep thinking that if Monsieur

Kanemoto is responsible for this buzzing, he has met a just end."

Gabrielle sucked in a horrified breath as she rose to her feet. "Louis! You are too cruel! Kohei did not intend to hurt anyone!"

Diann raised her hand to rest on Gabrielle's arm, wishing the woman's voice had not been so loud. Gently she eased her back onto her chair.

Louis straightened, letting his knuckles drop from his chin as chagrin filled his eyes. "My apologies, Gabrielle. You are correct. A joke too cruel. Caused by a shock to the system. I am not myself."

Gabrielle sat down and set about repositioning her yards of skirts comfortably beneath her. Her hands flew about, as did her loose hair. "Ah, *oui*. None of us can be ourselves. Such a shock. Such a dreadful, dreadful shock."

It was then that Diann's brain finally registered the fragrance that had been nibbling at the edge of her consciousness for minutes. She turned toward Gabrielle, surprise raising her voice. "You're wearing Kohei's earrings."

Gabrielle turned startled eyes to her. "Diann. How can you possibly know this?"

"By their fragrance, Gabrielle. Koehi showed me the earrings last night at dinner. However did you get them?"

Gabrielle's eyes drifted toward her plate like someone caught in a questionable act. "Koehi gave them to me, of course. How else?"

"But I thought he wasn't going to tell anyone about them."

She raised her head and squinted at Diann. "Why should he not tell anyone?"

"For the same reason that I knew you weren't just wearing Blossom, the top-line perfume from Oriental Blossom. The fragrance released from the earrings is flawed. The bottom note has relinquished its life support."

"What do you mean, 'relinquished its life support'?" Robert asked from Diann's other side.

Diann twisted in his direction. "It's the language of the perfume industry. A perfume is like a symphony for the nose. Its top notes are what you perceive with the first sniff. They should sing to you like sweet strings. The middle notes are the full melody, carrying the principal aromatic theme. Then the bottom note is the tempo, the heartbeat of the fragrance, that helps to retain the character of its melody."

Gabrielle inhaled loudly to test the scent. Then her nose quivered. "How extraordinary! There is something different. Diann, you are right. I do not think I would have noticed if you had not said something. The fragrance is slightly off."

She slipped her fingers beneath the thick sweeps of her hair and brought the earrings out to set them on the table.

Louis Magnen, on the other side of her, immediately confiscated them. "Very delicate and exquisitely made. I'm sure La Belle's diversifier will enjoy taking them apart to see how Kohei managed this engineering feat."

Gabrielle snatched the earrings. "No, Louis. I promised Kohei I would return them after his presentation. I will send them to his company." Gabrielle stopped a moment as quick tears filled her eyes. "Such a brilliant man! So dearly he has paid for his mistake. If only he had let Conrad help him with the setup of his electronic equipment when Conrad offered."

Peter Campbell fixed his precise gray eyes on Gabrielle's distraught face. "His presentation dynamics are as secret as any of our specialties. Why should he have shared them?"

"Conrad is not a perfumer. He would have no reason to steal secrets. And he is so competent at these things. He would have detected any problem."

"Kanemoto set up his equipment totally by himself?" Robert asked quietly from the other side of Diann.

Gabrielle wrung her hands. "And insisted on keeping my key to the salon with him so no one would have access."

"When did he set up his presentation?"

"He worked on it most of yesterday. After he was through, he instructed the hotel personnel to lock the salon until just before ten today, when the presentation was to start. This is my fault. I should have insisted he have help."

"He shouldn't have needed any help, Gabrielle," Diann protested. "He was a master at electronics. I can't believe he could make a mistake that would incapacitate a room. Or one that could end up taking his life."

"Perhaps his heart was weak," Helena offered with an unemotional sniff. "What knocked us unconscious killed him."

Peter nodded. "Or maybe he just got a bigger blast of whatever it was because he was standing at the podium, where the controls were."

"How do you know the controls were at the podium?" Robert asked.

A manicured hand straightened Peter's already straight tie. "Since Kohei set up and directed his presentation without outside help, it would only be logical that the controls had to be close to him."

"That bushy-haired mustached hotel man helped when he locked doors and turned off lights," Helena noted.

"True," Robert confirmed. "But that's the only way he helped."

Peter turned an inquiring eyebrow in his direction. "How do you know?"

"I asked."

Diann looked at Robert. "Why would you ask?"

He smiled at her, a smile she couldn't fathom.

"Because I wanted to know."

Diann studied his face, finding something very unfamiliar in his expression. She had the fleeting impression that suspicion lay behind that controlled look in his eyes. Then she assured herself she must be wrong. What could he be suspicious about?

"How can this have happened at my symposium? I have worked so hard to make it a success. This is so distressing!" Gabrielle screeched suddenly, more tears streaking down her face.

After Gabrielle's outburst, an uneasy quiet descended on them. Helena Strunk let out a grunt of disapproval as she crossed her sturdy arms across her sturdy chest. She made it obvious that such displays of emotional weakness were beneath her.

Diann couldn't get a disturbing thought out of her mind. She finally gave it sound, hoping that would solve its question somehow. "If Koehi was the only one controlling his presentation, I don't see how anything could have gone wrong."

Helena unfolded her arms, dabbed at her runny nose. "I do not understand you, Diann. How can you make this statement after what was done to us?"

Diann put down her coffee cup and leaned forward. "You've seen Kohei's presentations before. Have they ever been anything but perfect?"

Helena shook her head, then stopped as something occurred to her. "The earrings. You have said it yourself. The earrings were not perfect."

"And that's precisely why Kohei wasn't making them part of his presentation," Diann countered. "Kohei went public only with something he was sure was right. He never would have conducted that presentation without making sure everything in it was perfect. That's simply who he was. He wouldn't have made a mistake that would render us unconscious, or take his life. And I can't accept that he did. I just can't."

Louis rested his gaunt frame against the table. "None of us is perfect, Diann. We strive to be, yes. Maybe we even convince ourselves we have achieved that perfection for an instant in time.

"But then the next instant comes along and surprises us with the evidence of an error. We tumble off our high perch. And if the fall has not seriously injured more than our pride, we get the opportunity to get back up, dust ourselves off and try the climb again."

Peter interlaced his long, well-formed fingers and set his steady gray eyes on Diann's face. "I can't say I agree totally with Louis's claim that we *all* are fallible, but he does make a point. Perhaps Kohei's pride was too great to let him recognize his error. Perhaps pride is why he cannot get up this time to resume the climb."

Helena's hair blew around her head in new energy. "*Ja*, this is so. Too much pride. Kohei's death humbles us, as it should. We will all be more careful now. We have seen the sign. Now we heed it."

Helena punctuated her words with a decisive dab at her nose with her scented tissue.

A strained silence followed Helen's words. Everyone else seemed so ready to accept Kohei's having made a mistake. Diann began to wonder if she was wrong to feel so strongly he couldn't have. It would have been easier for her if she agreed with her colleagues. But she couldn't. With every passing minute she was more certain that another explanation existed. But what?

Gabrielle finally broke the strained quiet after looking at her watch. "You must please excuse me. Conrad is to be released from the hospital soon." She rose from her chair. "Since the symposium's activities have been canceled for the rest of the day, I've decided to accompany Conrad to our home in Macon to get him started on the doctor's prescription for bed rest. I will return in time for Louis's presentation tomorrow."

"Shall I come with you to the hospital?" Diann asked as she rose. "Perhaps I can be of some help?"

"No, no, Diann. All is arranged. Go out and enjoy yourself. Louis, will you play host to our country's guests and show Peter, Helena, Diann and Robert the sights of Paris?"

Louis stood, set his heels formally, if very quietly, together and bowed his head toward his hostess. "I shall strive to do my very best, *madame.*"

"You are a dear, Louis. Au revoir, everyone."

And with that Gabrielle Rife swept out of the room, leaving only the faintest scent of Kohei's flawed Blossom in her wake.

"Well, what shall it be, *mesdames* and *messieurs,*" Louis asked as he turned to those remaining at the table. "The old Paris of Napoléon's Arc de Triomphe and Louis XIV's Versailles or the new Paris of Mitterrand's glass pyramid of the Louvre, the Opéra Bastille with its moving stages and the Grande Arche de la Défense?"

"I'd love to see it all," Diann said, taking a quick look at her watch as she stood up. "But I don't want to make it too long a day."

Peter rose briskly. "Let's see the new Paris. I for one have seen the old Paris many times. It will be a refreshing change to concentrate on its progress."

Helena's stout frame seemed to vibrate with her small exclamation of displeasure as she pounded to her feet. "Progress, he says. I suppose that means you want to see Euro Disney?"

Peter raised an aristocratic eyebrow. "Why not? Can you deny it possesses many architectural and engineering feats?"

"Humph!" Helena dabbed at her nose. "What charm is there in such architectural and engineering feats or progress defined as structures of steel and glass? Paris's heart is in her ancient stone and the brush strokes of her artists."

Diann felt Robert getting up beside her. His warmth and distinctive scent flowed up to her in rich waves.

"Perhaps a visit to the Louvre would satisfy your tastes for both the old and new," he said. "Peter can see the new glass pyramid, and Helena can feast her eyes on the old masters.''

Helena nodded. "*Ja*. And the Louvre has a small Egyptian antiquities department I have yet to see."

Peter's eyebrow raised an interest. "Interested in old Egypt, Helena? Well, at least there we have something in common."

Louis turned to Robert. "Apparently you have selected a good compromise. Come, the time slips by quickly. An all-day trip to the Louvre would not be too long, and we only have a few hours left."

LOUIS WAS RIGHT, Diann decided after two hours of literally racing through what was without a doubt the greatest museum in the world. She promised herself that she would be back someday to experience it slowly and properly.

They started at the newest addition, the seventy-one-foot-high glass pyramid in the Louvre's courtyard. They explored its architecture as well as its underground complex of shops and restaurants. Peter left his card at the perfume shops. It seemed he could never stop being a businessman.

At the very start of their gallery tour in the Greek antiquities department, Diann knew they would not be through in time.

Yet she sensed that if she excused herself from the tour on some pretext, Robert would follow. He'd remained visually and relentlessly close to her since the moment Inspector Pinchot had released them all after taking their statements. Robert had made no move to hold her hand or arm, but his proximity was consistent and had a determined feel to it.

A very determined feel. To have such a handsome, sensual man in obvious pursuit of her played excitedly on each one of her feminine chords, despite all her mental arguments.

Still, she had to get away. She decided she was going to have to trust someone. Her first thoughts went to the debonair Peter Campbell. On several occasions in the past he'd made it known—in his very correct and subtle way, of course—that he enjoyed her company and would be open to pursuing a closer relationship. And although she had never been interested, she felt reasonably sure that he'd come to her aid, upholding the tradition of the staid and steadfast Englishman.

However, when she looked and found Peter momentarily capturing both Robert's and Helena's attention, she changed her mind and pulled Louis aside, instead.

"Louis, I'm not going to stay with the group. I'm going to slip away when I get a chance."

Louis eyed her with more than curiosity. "*Slip* away?"

"Yes. I have...something I must attend to. If anyone asks where I've gone, will you tell them the ladies' room?"

"You are coming back?"

"No."

Louis's mustache twitched. "And what do I say when you do not return?"

"Tell them I told you I was ill and decided to go back to the hotel. Give me enough of a head start so it won't be possible for anyone to follow me."

Louis's angular face lengthened. "I don't understand, Diann. Why do you need to slip away? Why would someone follow you?"

"Please Louis. No questions. Will you do this for me?"

The bothered expression in Louis's dark eyes suddenly cleared and was quickly replaced with a small knowing gleam. "Ah. An affair of the heart. You have an assignation with a gentleman, no?"

Diann gave him a small smile. "You are too clever to fool, Louis."

Louis's mustache danced above his smile. "But why did you just not say so?"

"Then you'll help me?"

"For an affair of the heart? But of course. I am French, am I not? And this man you go to meet, he is French, too, no?"

"Yes."

Louis's smile broadened. "And you prefer this other man to this Robert who has become your attentive shadow?"

Diann stole a glance at Robert, uneasy to see his gaze had become fixed on her again. A frown creased his forehead as he saw her move closer to Louis. She lowered her voice. "If he has a chance, I think he might try to follow."

Louis patted her arm in mute understanding as the others caught up. Diann realized he noticed Robert's pointed study of their position and swept his hand to gesture at the serene statue of the *Venus de Milo,* a superb study in graceful sunlit marble before them.

"As I was just about to tell Diann, this lovely lady was located in a cave in 1820 on the Greek island of Melos."

Robert retook his position beside Diann and stayed there. Several times over the next hour she tried to move away, only to find him right beside her. She could tell that Louis tried to give her a chance to slip away, as he endeavored to draw Robert's attention, along with the others', at every opportunity.

Louis had wholeheartedly entered into what he imagined was the furthering of her romantic liaison with some mysterious waiting Frenchman.

She decided to let him go on believing what he would. There was no way she could tell him the truth, and the subterfuge seemed harmless enough.

At the magnificent *Winged Victory* statue, Louis kept insisting that everyone look up at her cloak and imagine it rippling in a wind that had blown two centuries before the birth of Christ. Diann knew what he was trying to do. But although Robert did look up with the rest, Diann found when she took a slow step to the side, he took one, too.

She glanced at her watch nervously. Time was running out.

Diann was beginning to think she might just have to come out with a blatant announcement that she was leaving and pointedly and publicly ask that she be allowed to leave alone. Surely social decorum would prevent him from following under such a prohibition.

Trouble was, she couldn't be sure. There was a determination about Robert Mize's interest in her that she thought might win out over a contest with social decorum. Fortunately she didn't have to test that theory, because an opportunity suddenly came to slip away and she grabbed it.

They were in front of the gently smiling portrait of the *Mona Lisa,* and Louis was explaining it was called *la Joconde* in French, when two large tour groups jostled through.

Robert had been caught between them. His good looks were thoroughly occupying several young women in one of the groups. They had apparently decided he was a far more interesting sight than the artworks the museum had offered thus far.

As he politely answered their questions, framed in imperfect English, and attempted to fend off several intimate suggestions that needed no translation, Diann slipped into the bustle of the rest of the crowd's forward momentum, hiding within their circle until they rounded the next corner.

Then she ran. Because she wanted to be out of sight as quickly as possible. And because her watch told her if she didn't, she was going to be late.

She almost lost her way several times in the labyrinth of the Louvre. She was out of breath when she finally found her way out and flagged down a taxi, telling the driver to take her to the Luxembourg Garden.

She kept her eyes glued on the back window, alert for any pursuit. She saw nothing suspicious. Still she kept watch, until the taxi driver pulled over to the curb and announced they had arrived.

What breath she had stored in the ride over she quickly lost again when she raced down the pathways of the formally laid-out and well-groomed gardens. All the splendid statues, including the one of Sainte-Geneviève, the patron saint of Paris, with pigtails to her thighs, were treated to only a fleeting glance. The flesh-and-blood inhabitants of the park held Diann's total attention.

Unfortunately her hurrying was also attracting their attention. Deliberately she slowed her forward rush. Before she proceeded to the rendezvous spot, she paused and slipped behind a tree and watched for anyone who might be following. No one was.

With a sigh of relief, she turned and proceeded more slowly, searching carefully. Finally she saw the familiar white shock of hair and bent shoulders. Her quarry was sitting on the edge of a large pond, watching a group of model ship makers testing the seaworthiness of their small crafts.

She approached him from the back as he followed a spirited boat race, its youthful captains in vigorous verbal interplay on the shore as their vessels battled for supremacy on the water. She waited until she was standing just behind him before calling softly, "Dr. Béraud?"

He turned sharply, uneasily, until he recognized her face. Then a tension in his shoulders relaxed and he smiled. "Diann. I was beginning to think you wouldn't come."

She circled to his side and sat down on the concrete, searching the aged face she remembered so well, finding the new lines etched from time and pain.

"Nothing could have kept me away. Dr. Béraud, letters are never long enough nor my writing skills good enough to tell you how empty the years have been without your wisdom."

He took her hands in his, his eyes suddenly sparking with a light she thought had gone dim.

"I'm glad when we meet again it is in these historic gardens. They have fed the starved minds and souls of many before us with the beauty of their lawns and fountains and statues and peace."

"And the starved bodies," Diann said with a smile. "I seem to remember a certain professor of mine telling the story of how a hungry Hemingway pushed an empty baby carriage through these walkways, waiting for the gendarme to go across the street for a glass of wine so he could catch a pigeon for his dinner."

The old man with the old hands and shock of white hair smiled a very young smile. "You remembered."

"Everything you ever taught me."

His eyes flared once more before other memories extinguished the light. "If Roth had listened to me merely one-tenth as well as you, I would be a different man and this would be a different world."

Diann fixed her eyes on the boat race that was now drawing to a noisy climax. She heard the excited, triumphant screech of the youthful victor as the bow of his craft collided with a makeshift finish-line ribbon. He jumped into the air, buoyant with victory. His vanquished opponent, also about twelve, sank onto the grass. His face wore the same expression she had just seen in Dr. Béraud's eyes.

"Tell me you were not followed, Diann."

"I was not followed."

His grasp on her hands tightened as she looked back at his face. His sharp, ancient eyes studied hers as though they could read any secret that might lie within her—and he *knew* that one lay within.

"You have brought it?"

"Yes."

He sighed almost in relief. Then he was up on his feet in a sudden flash of energy and impatience. "Come. We will find a taxi and go to my apartment. Over the years I have built a laboratory there. Inferior, but I have had little money and a big need to be discreet. We'll buy our supper bread and wine on the way. Hurry. Time is not to waste."

ROBERT LET OUT a frustrated breath. "I lost her, Cassel," he said into the phone.

"When? How?"

"This afternoon when we went to tour the Louvre. She gave me the slip. Deliberately. Louis Magnen covered up for her. By the time I got wise and went after her, she'd vanished."

"Magnen helped her? You think they're in on it together?"

"Who knows? Maybe she just conned him. He claimed that she wasn't feeling well and just decided to go back to the hotel without a fuss so our tour wouldn't be interrupted."

"She never came back here."

Robert let out a frustrated breath. "Yeah. What I figured."

"What are you going to do?"

"Wait until she shows up. Not much else I can do. What did you find out about Rife?"

"He had a pretty calm night in the hospital. He met with his doctors early this afternoon to go over his lab tests."

"Did you get a look at those lab tests?"

"Yeah. It was his heart, all right. But before you go leaping to any conclusions, Rife has a preexisting condition. Heart-rhythm thing. Suffered a major attack a couple of years ago. Problem's controlled by medication."

"Then why wasn't it?"

"Doctors can't answer that one. Anyway, he's expected to recover. After sufficient bed rest."

Robert's eyes strayed to his room's view of the inner courtyard, where several couples were having a civilized late-afternoon tea. "More unexplained heart problems. I don't like it."

"Yeah. Know what you mean."

"Were you there when his wife came to pick him up?"

"Yes. They left for their home in Macon almost immediately."

"Autopsy in yet on Kanemoto?"

"An Inspector Pinchot is pushing for it to be done tonight."

"Pinchot was the one who interviewed me. He was involved in that business twenty years ago. Remember?"

"Pinchot? Really? No, I don't remember. But then, I wasn't as close to it as you."

"Fortunately Pinchot didn't recognize me. Still, he's no one's fool. He's being very thorough. You can tell he knows something is very wrong with this perfume crowd."

"That jibes with what my sources say. His electronics experts went over every inch of Kanemoto's equipment and learned a few things about holographic projection, but couldn't find anything wrong. They did find a tubing that conveyed the scent beneath every table. And a computer synchronized to the presentation, which released the scents. Pinchot's pushing the labs to analyze every scrap of electronics and everything else connected with the presentation."

"I told you he's no fool. Any news yet about the stuff you got out of the two vials from Torrey's luggage?"

"Nothing's come in. Probably won't for another twenty-four hours. What about the champagne goblet?"

"The local lab found champagne. Nothing else."

"Maybe Rife's collapse was just coincidence?"

"I don't believe in coincidence. What are the bugs telling you?"

"That Louis Magnen's having a dispute with his wife. She wants to send their daughter to private school because apparently the kid's missed a lot of regular school lately. He's adamant they don't have the money. Claims they're probably going to lose their Paris apartment."

"How did the Magnens look on our financial background check?"

"Their bank accounts have gone from healthy to sick over this past year."

"Any reason?"

"Nothing we could trace by paper. Could be they're like a lot of couples these days and are just spending beyond their means. Their arguments sound like petty domestic strife to me. And speaking of petty domestic strife, Peter Campbell's girlfriend wants to join him here in France. Apparently she thinks he's refused to take her along because he's here fooling around with another woman."

"Is he?"

"No evidence from the bug in his room. Or over the phone. Not yet, anyway."

"Anything on Helena Strunk?"

"My German isn't all that good and her sinus problem sometimes adds a watery quality. She's made two calls to the same number in Frankfurt. She's talked to two different young men. From the music in the background and the few words I could pick up, I gather they're her teenage sons. If she had decided to murder anyone, I think she'd knock them off first judging by the frustrated tone of her voice."

"What about Conrad and Gabrielle Rife before the husband got carted off to the hospital?"

"Husband-wife things like 'Zip me up' and such. She doused herself in a perfume called BLOSSOM yesterday afternoon and then pounced on him. Not that he complained. They had a hell of a good roll on the bed before they washed and dressed for dinner. With an aggressive woman like that, no wonder the guy's heart is giving out. Hell, I hope that's the way I go."

Robert let out an irritated grunt. "You're supposed to tune out on some things, Cassel."

"Don't try to mess up my fun, Mize. That's the best part of the job. Oh, there was one call from the Rife room."

"What?"

"Gabrielle Rife called Kohei Kanemoto early this morning. Told him everything was all right with her husband and she'd meet Kanemoto an hour before his presentation to help him set up things."

"To help him set up things? She said that?"

"Yeah. Kanemoto thanked her but said he'd already taken care of everything and didn't need any help. Then she asked him about those earrings she'd seen him pass to Diann Torrey at dinner the night before. He sounded surprised she'd noticed. He obviously didn't want to talk about them, but she pressed him pretty hard. He finally agreed to meet her quietly before his presentation and show them to her."

"This sounds promising."

"You think so? Kanemoto told her he'd see her at nine because he'd already agreed to meet with Diann Torrey at eight."

"Kanemoto met with Diann before his presentation? Where? About what?"

"Don't know about the where and what. Just know what he said over the telephone to Gabrielle Rife. But I got a pretty good idea. What do you want to bet that Diann Torrey talked him into letting her see his equipment and then took the opportunity to sabotage something in it?"

"We don't know that, Cassel."

"Don't we? Come on, Mize. She's the one who's been at all the other deaths. And she's the one who's been doing the secret research. We're wasting our time trying to listen in on these other people. It's Torrey who's in back of all this. You know what the computer said the probabilities are."

"They're still probabilities."

"You still have doubts?"

"I still don't have any proof."

"No proof? Then why did she give you the slip today? She's not supposed to know Paris or anybody in it. Where did she go? What did she do? And why isn't she back yet? You just find the answers to those questions, Mize, and I bet you'll have your proof.''

Chapter Five

Diann had no sooner closed her hotel room door behind her than she heard the knock. She checked her watch. It was just after midnight. She knew who was there even before she asked.

"I just wanted to make sure you were all right," Robert's deep voice confirmed through the door.

She answered through the door, having no intention of letting him in. "I'm fine. And tired. And about to go to bed."

"Well, if you're too sleepy to hear about how Kohei Kanemoto died, I certainly understand. Good night."

Diann yanked open the door. She called to Robert's rapidly retreating back. "Wait. You've heard something?"

He turned and slowly made his way back to her. "It can wait if you'd rather not invite me in now."

He stood before her looking just as cool and calm as if he didn't care what her answer would be. But she knew he did. Otherwise he wouldn't be employing such blatant emotional blackmail to get an invitation into her room.

She stepped aside, wondering how he knew that her curiosity wouldn't let her wait until the morning to hear the news. Her tone sounded anything but gracious. "Come on, The bar is over there. You no doubt want a drink, too."

He stepped inside and smiled as she closed the door behind him, all confident, complacent charm and sensuality. "Since you've offered so graciously, how can I refuse?"

Diann shook her head, a rueful smile touching her lips. The man did have a way about him. No denying it. "What can I pour for you?"

He quickly stepped up to the portable bar. "I'll get my own. And I'll mix one for you, too. Something warm and mellow to give you a good night's sleep."

Diann plopped onto the edge of the soft couch. "I don't need anything to put me to sleep. I'm already having a hard time keeping awake."

"Then I'll mix you something to keep you awake long enough to hear what I have to say."

He turned and handed her a cognac, like the one he'd poured for himself. It was delivered with that slight lift to his sensuous lips and the challenging glow in his eyes.

Oh, what the hell. She felt a bit like celebrating tonight. She took the cognac, enjoying the warm brush of his hand against hers as he passed her the glass.

He sat beside her on the couch and clinked her glass with his. He didn't crowd her, but she was very much aware of him nonetheless. This just wasn't the kind of man a woman could ignore.

Physically, she quickly amended.

She swallowed a mouthful of cognac and let the smooth warmth burst down her throat and through her chest. Then she sat back and waited.

He eyed her for a moment before getting to the point. "An autopsy was performed on Kohei tonight. In the opinion of the medical examiner, he died of a heart attack."

Diann nodded. "I knew it had to be something like that."

He was watching her intensely. A dark eyebrow arched. "You *knew?*"

"Well, I knew his death couldn't have been caused by some foul-up in his presentation. He was too good for that.

I still can't believe he was responsible for our all blacking out like that, either.''

"If not Kohei, who?"

Diann waved his question away with an impatient hand. "Not who. What. Some problem in the ventilation system probably."

"Ventilation? You think it might have been inhaled?"

"I don't know what to think. I just seem to remember a..."

"Yes?"

She shook her head. "I could be imagining things. What do you remember just before passing out?"

"One minute I was riding a rocket through space—the next I was waking up and spitting carpet fibers out of my teeth."

"You don't remember smelling anything unusual?"

"A smell? Not really. The sights and sounds had all my attention. Why? What did you smell?"

She took a deep breath, let it out slowly as she tried to focus her memory. "I'm not sure. That's just the problem. You see, I *was* concentrating on the smells. And just before I blacked out I seem to remember a very strange one."

"Can you describe it?"

"No. The only thing I remember is that it was nothing like anything I've ever smelled before."

"What does your chemical background tell you?"

"What do you mean?"

"Well, you must be familiar with the kind of gas that could incapacitate a whole room of people like that."

Diann gave it some careful thought as she sipped her cognac. "Frankly, I don't know of any that work that fast, can knock out a whole roomful of people simultaneously and yet leave no manifest physical problems."

"Other than an annoying buzzing in the ears, you mean."

"Yes. Other than that. But the buzzing stopped an hour or so after I regained consciousness. Are you still experiencing yours?"

"No," he admitted. "But Kohei Kanemoto is dead."

Diann's eyes drew to his, as she tried to interpret the sudden solemn note that had infected the healthy smoothness of his deep tone. "What does that have to do with our passing out? You said yourself the medical examiner ruled that Kohei had a heart attack."

Robert sipped his cognac in a slow, deliberate way, never taking his eyes from hers. "So he did."

Diann felt suddenly that she had gotten lost in this communication exchange. She went over the last few moments of their conversation, trying to find her way. What she came up with was a new question. "Who told you what the medical examiner found? Was it Inspector Pinchot?"

"No. Kohei brother's."

"His brother?"

"He flew in this evening. Kohei's wife reached her brother-in-law in Madrid, where he was staying on business. He's to handle the arrangements of transporting Kohei's body back to Japan for burial."

Diann took another sip of her cognac, letting her eyes rest on the swirling golden liquid. "I didn't know Kohei even had a brother. Or a wife. Or anything about his family, for that matter. Somehow that makes me as sad as his death."

"Why?"

"I admired his rare genius so much. I can describe every one of his innovations in detail. But other than the basic statistics about his age and education from the dossier *Redolence* magazine included on the recipients of the PERFUME awards, I never knew even the most ordinary facts about him as a man. His family, his philosophy, his dreams—those are the kinds of things that really connect us, and I was ignorant of them all. I didn't even know Kohei had heart trouble."

"He didn't."

Diann waded through her own sad thoughts for a moment more before Robert's words sank in. Her eyes jerked back to his. "Did you just say Kohei *didn't* have heart trouble?"

"According to his brother, Kohei had a physical last month that showed his heart was as sound as a twenty-year-old's."

"Then how could he die of a heart attack?"

"Good question."

Diann swept a wayward lock of hair off her forehead as she took another sip of cognac. Memories fluttered through her thoughts like lost butterflies. "This is so strange."

"What is?"

"Kohei dying of a heart attack so suddenly, with no previous indication of heart disease. Kohei was only forty. And Annette was only thirty-five."

"Annette?"

"Annette Prince. She was another diversifier of perfumes. She died of a heart attack after a Las Vegas convention a few months back. She hadn't had any previous heart trouble, either."

"You were friends with her?"

"No. Professional colleagues. She was the only diversifier in the world who could give Kohei any competition. A great talent. I was talking to Kohei about Annette only last night."

"And this morning? What did you talk about then?"

"We just had breakfast together. I was hoping to hear about his presentation, but Kohei didn't have time to discuss it. He had to meet Gabrielle. Quite a coincidence. First Annette dies of a heart attack. And now Kohei. The two most important perfume diversifiers in the world. And two fairly young people without a previous history of heart disease. I wonder what the odds of that happening are?"

"Two million two hundred and twenty-seven to one," Robert quoted quietly.

Diann blinked at his rapid response and deadly calm tone. "What?"

"We both need a refill," he said as he got up and took her glass from her hand. She was surprised to see it empty. He stepped back to the bar.

She called after him. "No more for me, thanks. I've already had more alcohol in the past couple of days than I've had in the past year."

He returned to the couch empty-handed and stood before her, the luscious blue of his eyes close in color to the rich threads in his sweater. He wore an enigmatic expression.

"I'm glad you told me about Annette."

That seemed like a strange thing for him to say. His voice sounded a little different, too. Almost relieved. "Why?"

"I just am."

Diann looked at the ease of his stance, at the glow of mysterious challenge in his eyes. He exuded an innate confidence, as strong and palatable as his sensuality. And nearly as devastating as that slight lift of his lip that he was enticing her with at the moment.

Damn, where had he learned to do that?

He reached out to her. "Perhaps you'd like to show me your view now?"

She slipped her hand into his and let him help her up. "Might as well. It will give me a chance to see it myself. I've been a bit too busy up to now." She walked over to the window and drew back the white percale and beige velvet drape.

An appreciative breath escaped her lips. The place de la Concorde was floodlit before her, alive with its rushing fountains and spinning ovals of traffic. On either side of the dominating obelisk at its center, two fountains of bronze-tailed mermaids and bare-breasted sea nymphs bathed in happy abandon. Eight equally bright, gray-beige statues ringed the square, as though admiring the cavorting ladies at its center and longing to join them.

Robert moved beside her. She felt his warmth as she felt the cognac sizzling in her veins and the magnificent lights of Paris blinding her eyes.

His breath played against her cheek. "I returned the champagne goblet to les Ambassadeurs, as agreed."

A band of warmth wrapped around her neck. "Not exactly. You paid them for it."

She felt the surprise of his slight movement beside her.

"You checked up on me?"

"As you would have checked up on me had the situation been reversed, I'm sure."

His chuckle erupted from deep in his throat. "I should have known. Well, how does it feel to learn you have reformed a thief?"

"I very much doubt I have. You paid for that champagne goblet under duress. I had to threaten you, remember?"

"Hmm. So you did. What if I were to give you my solemn oath that I promise never to steal another champagne goblet?"

She turned to see his expression. His charming sensuality was as breathtaking as the view of the place de la Concorde and far more intoxicating than the cognac in her veins.

She looked away, deciding she was safer watching the view.

"Would you keep such a promise?"

His voice lowered, deep and husky in her ear.

"For you, Diann, I would do many things."

A part of her brain was protesting, telling her she was letting herself get carried away. But its objections were growing fainter with each passing pulse beat.

"Paris is even more magnificent at night than it is by day, isn't it?" she said with a sigh.

The infinitesimal rise in the air temperature registered on her skin, telling her he'd closed the small distance that had remained between them. When his arm encircled her waist, an unmistakable warmth swept through her, stirring her blood, strumming her pulse.

"Paris is like a shiny unexpected promise," he said, his breath feathering her ear. "It seems to say that here you'll find the brightest of your dreams."

His voice whirled around her like a magician's cloak. He smelled so good. He felt so good. She leaned back into the exciting heat of his chest, thrilled to the feel of his hard muscles rippling against her back as he tightened his grip around her waist.

The cognac and the glorious lights of Paris had smoothed out any restricting mental ripples. She refused to think about what he did for a living. She refused to think at all. At this one special moment, looking out at his beautiful city, all she wanted to do was feel.

When his lips found her hair, grazed her cheek, she sighed from the pure physical pleasure it brought. She hadn't given herself much time off from work. She hadn't been able to. Too much urgent work had needed to be done.

But there was nothing urgent to attend to now. And she was standing firmly on the brink of a Paris night, the city of romantic dreams. And behind her, sharing that brink, was a thoroughly handsome, sensuous man, who had made it clear *she* was what he wanted.

She had no intention of getting into anything heavy with him, of course. But surely a kiss wouldn't hurt.

Last night had shown what a sensational kisser he was. She wanted to experience that luscious, delectable thrill again. One more time before she said good-night.

Slowly, deliberately, she turned in his arms to face him, sliding her hands across his chest of smooth iron and over his broad shoulders of warm steel.

Her fingers stroked the back of his neck, slipping through the bold, stray locks of his hair, finding them feather light and cool. She lifted her head and looked full into his eyes. Blue midnight magic glowed back at her. She wondered, if she looked long enough could she get lost in their mysterious depths?

His arms were loosely draped around her waist. He watched her intently. He barely seemed to be breathing.

Confidently, coolly, she leaned against the hard, impressive heat of him. She brushed her lips over his in a light, provocative sweep, intending to pull instantly away and let all those tender, sensuous shimmers glide through her again.

But she never got a chance to pull away.

Suddenly she was scooped up by powerful arms and kissed so fiercely that it tore the breath from her lungs and stirred the very marrow of her bones.

It took an instant. Only an instant. And she was drowning in a mass of emotion so powerful and overflowing she didn't have the senses to understand.

She could only respond. For all she was worth. Her body molded itself to his; her arms pressed against his shoulders; her fingers clutched his hair as small cries of surprise and demand broke through her throat.

And he was both echoing and answering that surprise and those demands, with a power that buckled her knees. She did not know she could feel like this, that she could want like this.

That someone could want her like this.

In a blinding flash she knew that was at the core of this incredible release of feeling. This man would not let himself be taken lightly. His passion tore hers loose, ignited it into a sizzling fervor, incinerated every thought in her head. Instantly. Incurably. Totally without protest.

She couldn't fight it. She didn't want to fight it.

It was he who suddenly broke away. Held her at arm's length with fingers of steel. His eyes burned with the same desire that roared in her belly. His breath came in tortured, ragged gasps, in tandem with her own.

Diann did not understand how he could pull away. Or why he wanted to. She understood even less when he finally sucked in enough breath to speak.

His voice was harsh, raspy, demanding, desperate—nothing like its normal deep, confident tone. "Where did you go when you left Louis Magnen's tour this afternoon?"

She blinked. She couldn't have heard right. That was his question after a moment like the one they'd just shared?

"What?"

"Diann, tell me. The truth. All of it. Now."

Confusion and frustration swirled around in Diann's brain, battling for supremacy. Their conflicting pulls made her mute. For a moment, all she could do was stare.

He shook her shoulders. Hard. As though he could shake the answers out of her. "Diann, tell me!"

Anger—fresh, fast, furious—rushed through her, overriding the confusion and frustration and everything else.

She tried to pull out of his grasp. "Let go of me!"

He stepped back in the face of her anger, instantly releasing her.

She rubbed her shoulders where she could still feel the imprint of his steel fingers.

He took a deep breath. Let it out soundlessly. Then another. And another. Still his voice did not sound normal when he finally spoke. "Did I hurt you?"

He had, but not physically, not the way he'd meant. But how could he have hurt her any other way? People could only hurt you if you cared. Which was why she was very cautious about caring for anyone.

And she certainly didn't care for this man. She wouldn't let herself care for this man. She stopped massaging her shoulders, reluctantly shook her head in answer to his question.

He didn't appear exactly relieved at her denial, but a certain tension drained from those powerful shoulders. Still, his hands curled and uncurled into fists by his side. From anger? Passion? Frustration? All three?

She looked away. She felt like a jumble of raw nerves and racing blood. And confused. So damn confused. As if somehow the Earth had tilted several more degrees on its axis and nothing was ever going to be the same again. She clung to the only thing that felt even vaguely familiar. Anger.

"Just who do you think you are demanding explanations from me, Mize?"

He raked a hand through his hair as something like a choked laugh escaped his throat. "I think I'm the man you should finally be calling 'Robert.' You're one hell of a stubborn woman, Diann. But even you can't still be clinging to last names after kissing me like that."

Diann glared at him for several seconds before she finally broke into a laugh.

It erupted out of some deep chasm of seemingly endless mirth that doubled her over onto the couch. It sounded absolutely hysterical to the still-functioning part of her brain. It probably was. She didn't care.

She let it take control for as long as it would. When the laughter finally subsided, she sat up straight and sighed in relief for the tension it had released.

She looked up to find him taking a seat next to her on the couch. He held out another cognac. She took it, sipped, let the warmth slide down her throat. Her breath steadied into a semblance of normalcy.

"Okay. Robert," she conceded.

His eyes looked smoky as his hand wove around hers, warm and strong and far too exciting.

"Diann, we need to talk."

She slipped away from his touch and the look in his eyes. All of this was happening too fast. Way too fast. Whatever it was.

She didn't want to think about what it was. She fingered the cognac glass nervously. "About what?"

"About so many things I don't know where to start. But you could help immensely if you'd just tell me where you went after the tour this afternoon."

His question was annoying. Very annoying. Particularly since she had no intention of answering it. "Why is it important for you to know?"

"It just is. Diann, talk to me. I've got to know the worst. I've got to know what we have to face."

What was he talking about? He couldn't know about... There was no way he could know that.

She took another sip of the cognac. Not because she needed it. Because she needed time to think. She stared at the glass. "What *we* have to face? I don't know what you're talking about."

"You've got to trust me. Tell me, Diann."

She glanced in his direction. His look was too intense. He must suspect something. But how could he? Had he followed her that afternoon, after all? Had she missed him hiding in the bushes somewhere in back of her? An icy wave of uncertainty washed over her.

Suddenly, tardily, she realized that danger, in many forms, was sitting beside her within that far-too-seductive package. She also realized what she had to do. Carefully she set her glass of cognac on the table. Rose to her feet. Turned to him.

"Look, I got a little carried away this evening. Too much cognac combined with the romantic night lights of Paris. But you should understand that casual affairs are not my style."

He rose beside her, slowly, calmly. But there was nothing slow or calm about the look in his eyes. "They're not mine, either."

Staring at those eyes then, Diann had a sudden feeling she was falling into a bottomless blue of sincerity and if she didn't look away soon she would be lost forever. She looked away.

Her pulse beat in her ears. She could feel the heat of him. He was too close. Way too close. His almond scent wafted around her in a demanding caress. She stared at the beautifully paneled wall over his shoulder and fought for sanity. "My work is the focus of my life. I cannot let myself be sidetracked by... by anything. Besides, I see no reason to take anything that happened tonight seriously."

"No reason to take it seriously?"

The heat of his words brought her eyes back to his face. What she saw there raised goose bumps on her skin. She felt the beginnings of a full-fledged panic making its way up her spine.

Diann had never thought herself the kind of woman who ran from trouble. But this man was trouble, and she fully intended to run from him. At top speed. She quickly made for the door.

His words followed her. "Diann, you can't deny what's happening between us."

Diann reached the door and yanked it open. "Look, I'm a woman who lives for mental challenge. You're a male model. Our ideas and life-styles are light-years apart. There could never be anything between us. Now, I'd appreciate it if you'd leave."

He walked toward her slowly, intently. Diann had never seen a man look at her the way this man was looking at her. The fire in his eyes was so hot the bottoms of her feet had begun to perspire. She swallowed, clutching the knob of the open door and hoping to hell he'd just walk out of her room and bring this totally disturbing interlude to an end.

He didn't. He stopped in front of her. Waited until she raised her eyes to his. Then deliberately he leaned down until they were just a kiss apart.

"There is something already between us, Diann. You know it. I know it. And however much that fact is bothering you, you'll be happy to know it's bothering me a thousand times more."

Diann could hear the truth of those words in his voice and see it in his eyes—full of blue fire and white anger. Her heart was beating so loudly she was sure everyone down the hall and in the other suites had to be hearing it. He was going to kiss her. And heaven help her, she wanted him to.

But he didn't kiss her. He just straightened and walked out.

As HE RETURNED to his room, Robert met Cassel just outside his door.

"You get the bugs in place?" Cassel asked.

"Yes. One's in the phone and one's under the liquor cabinet."

"She's in a suite. What about the bedroom?"

"You're going to have to make do with what you've got for now, Cassel."

"You're slipping, Mize."

Robert shook his head and tried not to grind his teeth as he opened the door to his room and stepped inside with Cassel on his heels. He turned on the light and closed the door behind them.

"Why didn't you use your key and let yourself in?"

"I just got here."

Robert called his next question over his shoulder as he headed for the liquor tray and a drink. He poured a cognac. But his hand was still unsteady and he didn't pick it up. "What's been going on with the other bugs?"

"Magnen called Strunk and made an appointment to see her in the bar. Had something to show her."

"What?"

"I don't know. What little they said over the phone sounded just like the technical jargon of the business. Hard to make sense of it. Hey, if you're not going to drink that cognac, I will."

Robert handed the glass to Cassel. "What else?"

"Conrad keeps calling his wife from Macon. Seems like every hour on the hour. The guy's got it bad."

"Anything else?"

Cassel took a quick sip of the cognac. "A few other conversations in the rooms. Nothing much. What about this afternoon? Could you get anything out of Torrey as to where she went?"

"No."

"Well, I guess we can't expect she's going to spill it on her own."

Robert licked his lips. Incredibly, he could still taste the heat of her on his tongue. "I don't know. I'm beginning to think we've got this all wrong."

Cassel took another sip of the cognac. "What are you talking about?"

Robert began to pace. "Did I tell you she was going to turn me in if I didn't return the champagne goblet she thought I stole?"

"So?"

He stopped in front of Cassel. "Well, doesn't that strike you as odd? To be so concerned about somebody stealing a champagne goblet?"

Cassel squinted up at Robert. "Look, Mize, nobody's said she's a thief."

Robert stuck his hands in his pockets and started to pace again. "It's not just the champagne goblet. It's the way she talks. The things she says. She told me all about Annette Prince dying of a heart attack after the Vegas convention. She even added she thought it strange that both Annette and

Kohei died of heart attacks, when neither had a history of heart trouble."

Cassel's dark eyes seemed to darken even more. "Maybe she suspects you're onto her. Maybe she thinks that by bringing up the Prince woman she'll make herself look innocent."

Robert exhaled a heavy breath as he dropped onto the other end of the small corner sofa. "I don't know, Cassel. She was the only one at the luncheon table who didn't believe Kohei was in back of everyone blacking out and the cause of his own death. And she was pretty vocal about it. You'd think that would be the last thing she'd say if she was guilty, wouldn't you?"

"Just more playacting, Mize, to throw you off the track. You know how good some women are at it."

"Well, she was pretty lousy at it when I asked her where she was this afternoon. She could have lied. She didn't even try. She just looked like she'd rather be boiled in oil than tell me."

"There, that proves it. She's got something big to hide. And we both know what."

Robert rested his elbows on his knees and pressed his palms together. "Do we? I'm not so sure. We could be misinterpreting something here."

"I'm not misinterpreting anything, Mize. Damn, I was afraid of this. You're letting that lady get to you. Just like you let—"

"Back off," Robert interrupted. "No one got to me. The scams got stopped and the money got repaid."

"Hey, buddy, I was there, remember? You fixed it so that the lady couldn't be prosecuted."

"That's all ancient history, Cassel."

"Well, we're dealing with the present now. Mize, I hate to see you getting taken in. Particularly with this one. Are you forgetting what Diann Torrey has done? You'd better not. Because if you're not careful and she thinks you're getting too close, she might just do it to you, too.''

"PLEASE, ROBERT. You must reconsider and give a little speech after your spot is run. It would give the *mesdames* in the audience such a thrill.''

Robert looked at Gabrielle Rife's pleading hazel eyes as he stood with her next to the VCR in the deserted room. She had unbuttoned her stylish suit jacket and the neckline of her blouse was nearly to her waist. She had doused herself with Diann's sensuous HEAT perfume and both the uninhibited sight and scent were making him exceptionally uncomfortable.

If he had known this was why she had asked him to meet her in the Salon Marie-Antoinette before the morning's presentation, he would have found an excuse not to show up.

He took a small step back. "Gabrielle, please understand. I'm not a speaker. I'm a model.''

"*Oui*, and such a model,'' she said as she deliberately ran her hands up his arms to rest them on his shoulders.

Robert knew he was in trouble now. This was not a complication he had forseen. He took another step back. Unfortunately Gabrielle came right with him.

She had a very determined look in her eyes. "Perhaps you could take this shirt off and let the *mesdames* see the magnificent chest in the flesh that they will drool over on the screen.''

"Gabrielle, I don't—''

"Or maybe just a private showing now for me, yes?''

Robert quickly captured Gabrielle's hands as they slipped to his belt. He returned her hands to her side and held them there firmly. "No, Gabrielle. Please understand. You are an attractive lady. Very attractive. But you are a married lady.''

Gabrielle launched herself against him like a heat-seeking missile. She collapsed against his chest, her eyes closed, her

voice breathy. "I am a woman of great needs, Robert. Inhale this wonderful fragrance that surrounds us. When I
watched you on the screen, I knew I had to have it. And
you. Does it not drive you wild?"

It was driving him wild all right, but not the kind of wild
this woman meant. Just as he wondered how in the hell he
was going to get out of this one without a punch to her determined jaw, Louis pushed open the door and came waltzing into the room, a large box tucked under his elegantly
clad arm.

Gabrielle stiffened at the sound of the opening door. Her
eyes flew to the intruder, as did Robert's. Louis stopped
dead in his tracks and glared at the looks on their faces and
the closeness of their bodies.

Then, with a mere twitch of his mustache, he pivoted and
walked from the room. Robert could hear his next comment clearly from the hallway outside.

"Peter, the room is occupied at this time. We will need to
come back later."

"If you insist, Louis. But remember, you promised to
show me."

"I will, Peter. Never fear."

Gabrielle sighed forlornly as the sounds of the men's
footsteps on the gleaming parquet floors retreated. She
straightened. "It is not fair Louis should come. No one was
supposed to be in this room so early."

Robert took advantage of Gabrielle's distraction, released her hands and quickly stepped back. He gave her a
small bow. "That is true, madam. So very true."

And then he retreated from the room just as fast as his
legs would carry him.

ROBERT WASN'T with the rest of the symposium's attendees
when they collected just before ten in the Salon Marie-
Antoinette.

Diann told herself she was glad. She felt embarrassed about her feelings and responses toward him the night before. She told herself that if she never saw him again it would be too soon.

Helena, Peter and Louis took their places at the head table with her, while Gabrielle flitted around the other tables, greeting people and generally playing hostess.

"Everything okay, Diann? You're wearing the strangest expression."

Diann turned to Peter and tried to put a smile on her face. "Everything's fine."

He moved closer and rested a hand on her arm as he sent Louis a stormy look. "Glad to hear it. I was very angry at Louis for letting you leave by yourself yesterday when you were ill. You should have had someone to escort you back to the hotel."

Louis, who sat on Diann's other side, ignored Peter's look and serenely sipped his coffee.

Diann turned back to Peter. "I didn't want anyone along, Peter. Louis was a real gentleman to do as I asked."

"*Ja,*" Helena chimed in. "A real gentleman is a man who thinks of the woman's desires."

Peter frowned at Helena and turned back to Diann. "I can't imagine you desired finding your way back to the hotel alone when you didn't feel well?"

"Would you have wanted an escort if the situation had been reversed?"

Peter looked a bit taken aback. "I'm a man. I don't need my hand held."

"And I'm a woman, and I don't need my hand held, either, Peter. I thank you for your concern because I know your heart's in the right place. But too often men seek to second-guess a woman needs, when all they really need to do is listen to what she says."

"Ja!" Helena chorused enthusiastically. She raised her water glass in the fashion of a toast. Diann tipped her own water glass and took a swallow, glad to have an ally.

Louis smiled and shifted his shoulders in an elegant shrug.

Peter leaned back, looking uncomfortable. "Well, if I'm guilty of a breach of the new feminine etiquette, Mize is, too. He even left our tour to try to find you. By the way, where is Mize?"

"I have no idea," Diann said. Then, against every mental and emotional caution, she found herself looking for him as she studied the other tables. The blackout episode had deterred surprisingly few attendees. The room was nearly full.

But Robert wasn't in it. Where was he? And why in the hell did she care?

As she glared around, she caught the eyes of the copper-haired gentleman she'd seen at the first evening's dinner. He raised an inquiring eyebrow at her and Diann quickly looked away. The last thing she needed was to encourage a convention Lothario. Gabrielle approached the podium and began the morning's introduction.

Diann watched Gabrielle, but her thoughts wandered.

As it had nearly all night long, Robert's face flashed into her mind's eye as his words echoed in her ears. *"There is something already between us . . . it's bothering me a thousand times more."*

And every time she thought about those words, Diann's heart beat a little faster. Had he meant them? Was he really a man who didn't have casual affairs? Could she believe—

Diann suddenly came to attention as Gabrielle's last words registered on her wandering thoughts.

"And now, *mesdames* and *messieurs,* what you have all been waiting for—Man to Woman's sensational new TV advertisement. Projectionist, if you will, please . . ."

The lights were dimmed slightly in the front of the room as a gigantic thirty-foot projection screen on casters was rolled into place. Gradually images began to take shape on the screen as the percussion instruments of an entire orchestra began to play a suggestive beat.

The first shot of him was a sweep of his bare, strong, well-formed feet, spread apart on shimmering sands. The illuminating light was golden, showing off his tanned, wet flesh like gleaming bronze as the camera circled around and up to take in the rest of him—flashing muscular calves, sturdy knees, slick rock-hard thighs, all beading with moisture.

The suggestive beat quickened. Diann swallowed.

The camera swung higher. Robert held a woman in his arms as he stood on those sands under the golden light of a hot sun with a cool blue ocean lapping at their feet. But it was very hard to see the woman in front of him and Diann didn't really try. Not when the back of him was being so sensually displayed.

He had it to display and then some. In circles that spun up to his windblown, deep-brown crown of hair and then down again, the camera exposed the masculine muscled strength of his bronzed shoulders, back, buns—as they flexed, glistened, rippled, enticed and enthralled with each exploring sweep.

A sigh of pure feminine pleasure erupted around the room. Diann took a deep breath, determined as hell not to contribute to it, although she was afraid she already had.

As the beat built to a crescendo, Robert's gleaming body broke apart from the woman, who faded into nothingness as he turned to look directly into the camera circling overhead. It moved in on him for a close-up.

He was naked, gloriously naked, muscles in his magnificent bronzed chest rippling, beads of water defining every sinewy contour. Below the waist he was in shadow except for the flick of shine from his superb muscular thighs. Diann's eyes followed the camera as it traveled up the perfect symmetry of that massive chest wall, past the strong neck to the chiseled face and thick, loosely curled hair.

Diann could feel his eyes looking at her—just at her—from that projection screen, exactly as she had felt him do three weeks before when she'd first seen the spot. And the night before when he stood over her in her room.

He wasn't smiling. The left side of his lip curled upward as that mysterious glow shone forth from the blue heat of his eyes.

The beat stopped on that incredible look. Diann felt her heart stop, as well.

As spectacular as his body was, Diann knew it was the sensual power of the man behind that look that made this commercial so hot.

The room was suddenly still as the women sucked in their collective breaths. A red perfume bottle appeared in the corner of the screen, shaped like a glowing flame. A feminine voice, low and breathy, sighed, "When all you want between you and *him* is HEAT."

And then the screen image faded and the lights came back on in the salon. Another stunned silence followed. A second later it was shattered by the spontaneous applause echoing around the room. Diann knew it was the women's hands that were behind its thunderous volume when they came as one to their feet in a standing ovation.

She remained seated, irritated in a way she'd never been irritated before. Robert Mize had become the sexual heart-throb of thousands—maybe millions—of women since that commercial had begun to air. And judging by its success, he was only getting started in a very lucrative career.

He was a commodity—soon to be selling himself to the highest bidder. There was nothing exclusive about him or about the way he looked at her. How could there be? He now belonged to the world of women's fantasies. Diann fought with sadness, anger and a deep well of disappointment.

And meanwhile the women in the room went wild. It took several very long minutes for Gabrielle to quiet them. Finally the women sat down and Gabrielle smiled.

"I'm glad you've enjoyed your morning's appetizer, *mesdames*. And now it is my pleasure to introduce to you the Fragrance Fraternity's recipient of the PACKAGER Award. He is France's own Louis Magnen and he will show you the absolute newest in innovative packaging. *Mesdames* and *messieurs,* please give Monsieur Magnen a warm welcome."

Louis took the podium to enthusiastic applause. He looked as sleek and elegant as a well-carved sculpture in his dark formal suit.

He signaled the portly, bushy-haired hotel attendant to dim the lights. A nervous rustle accompanied his direction as the audience was forcibly reminded of their experience in the dark in this very room the day before.

Fortunately for everyone's relief, the lights did not go out completely.

"*Mesdames* and *messieurs,* La Belle's Perfumes takes this opportunity to introduce you to a new packaging breakthrough along with the launch of a new fragrance."

Louis turned his attention to the large projection screen behind him. Using a remote control in his hand, he began a video tape, with the only background sound a gentle Bach played on an exuberant harpsichord.

Lovely, glowing perfume bottles of all shapes and sizes appeared on the screen, beautifully draped in satin and velvet.

Louis did his own announcing, his rich, liquid French accent adding elegance to every word. "Perfume has historically been packaged in exquisite and graceful glass bottles, with the most exclusive and expensive fragrances housed in crystal. But the choice of glass or crystal has been solely for the beauty of a fragrance's presentation. As a vehicle for preserving a perfume's essence, neither container is particularly suitable."

The video tape now focused on one of the bottles, a spectacular replication of the Eiffel Tower in black and gold. Invisible hands removed its cap.

"Exposing a fragrance to light and air are the two quickest ways to dissipate its energy and vitality. Even a black bottle, such as the one you see now, lets light in to act chemically on the fragrance within. This is why few perfumes can last more than six months after purchase. And why most begin to lose their original harmony of notes right after the seal is broken."

The perfume bottle faded and the next images that emerged were those of a conveyer belt and skinny spaghetti strands of what looked like a translucent material being moved quickly along.

"What you are seeing now is a special brand of polymers—plastic—the stuff of which our modern societies cannot do without. But this is not the kind of mundane, uninteresting plastic you are used to seeing. This is a very special plastic."

The film showed the thread-thin fibers being woven together in glistening, translucent strands. Magically, the individual strands formed into lovely crystal containers.

"Yes, *mesdames* and *messieurs,*" Louis said. "They look like crystal. They can be made to feel heavy like crystal. But these containers are plastic. Their seals are so tight that when their elegant caps are replaced, air cannot seep in. Their fibers are so dense that harmful light cannot penetrate, so the delicate fragrance will not be dissipated. And they can be formed into any shape, any size, any color."

As Louis said the words, the delicate fibers amassed at incredible speed to form a heart, then a diamond ring, then another Eiffel tower, black and gold and a dozen more dazzling colors. These objects were far more beautiful and elegant than their glass counterparts.

An appreciative murmur greeted the visual marvels.

"And yet with the ability to protect the fragrance within, to fashion itself into every form imaginable, to exist in more colors than even nature's rainbow, that is not the end to this amazing new polymer. Let me demonstrate."

The lights came back up as the tape ended. A dozen very attractive young women clad in harem pants, their outfits reminding Diann of Barbara Eden's in the "I Dream of Jeannie" series, moved among the salon's tables, depositing exquisite golden "bottles" in the shape of an Aladdin's lamp. They performed their distribution quickly and then stepped to the sides of the room.

Like the other attendees, Diann found herself picking up the lamp, feeling its weight and admiring the beauty of its glow, which competed with the finest crystal.

"No, they are not real crystal lamps, *mesdames* and *messieurs*. They are the new polymer. But I challenge you to tell the difference."

Diann couldn't. She marveled at Louis's sparkling, beautiful, palm-size container.

And then the scent drifted to her—very sophisticated, with the upscale notes of leather and sandalwood. She checked the seal, but found it intact. She brought the bottle to her nose and could barely believe what her senses were telling her. The fragrance was coming from the plastic container.

"Yes, *mesdames* and *messieurs*," Louis confirmed from the podium. "As some of you have already discovered, this polymer also accepts scent. With La Belle's special process, the fragrance of a perfume can be woven into the very fibers of its container. Now when a woman shops for a fragrance, she can pick up the container and know what is inside," he continued. "And there is even more. You have in your hands La Belle's newest fragrance sensation, GENIE, in its container of scent-saturated polymer, impervious to light and tightly sealed to protect its essence. Now I'm going to show you how to release your GENIE so you can enjoy its liquid potion inside.''

The audience murmured in excitement as a gigantic replica of the golden Aladdin's lamp perfume container was rolled to the front of the room. The replica was nearly six feet long and four feet wide and was sitting on a pedestal three feet high.

Louis signaled for the lights to be dimmed again and everyone quieted. Diann didn't know what to expect. But she did know that Louis Magnen's achievement in packaging had already surpassed anything she had expected.

Louis paused deliberately, but Diann saw his mustache quiver at the edges as his own excitement got the better of him.

Slowly he made his way to the gigantic Aladdin's lamp. He rubbed the palm of his hand on the side of the lamp, then cut the seal and lifted the lamp's lid. From out of the spout of the lamp came an enormous, glowing, diaphanous genie, turbaned and round faced, with arms folded over a sequined vest, red trousers and golden curled-toed slippers. He was visible for several seconds before he dissipated into thin air.

The audience broke out in deafening applause, so deafening, in fact, that it took several seconds for the screeching to be heard.

But once it was, the clapping died an instant death.

Diann's eyes immediately flew to one of the young women clad in harem pants. Her mouth twisted with her scream. Her hand shook as she pointed.

But not at the gigantic golden Aladdin's lamp.

No, she was pointing at its pedestal, where Louis Magnen now slumped in a lifeless heap.

Chapter Six

Robert watched Helena Strunk stride up to the late luncheon. "I have checked with the desk," she announced, several decibels louder than necessary. "Nearly a fourth of the attendees are checking out tomorrow morning. Several are not waiting for tomorrow. They check out right now."

She sank into her chair with an audible plop, then reached for a tissue.

Gabrielle sobbed quietly.

Robert looked around at the diminished attendance at the luncheon in the darkly paneled l'Obélisque restaurant.

He didn't much blame those who had bailed out early. A codirector collapsing the first night, followed by the sudden deaths of the first two speakers, weren't exactly the kinds of activities they'd signed up to see. He suspected those who remained did so only because of the excellence of the presentations.

And maybe the fact that they had paid in advance and the room and conference fees were not refundable.

Robert studied Diann as she sat quietly beside him. She rubbed the small Aladdin's lamp of GENIE perfume, broke the seal and then opened the top to watch the miniature genie emerge momentarily in a diaphanous wisp.

Helena must have been watching, also, because she leaned forward, her tone surprised and upset. "The small ones have the genie, too? Inspector Pinchot confiscated my lamp of Louis's new perfume. I thought he was confiscating everyone's.''

Diann exhaled heavily. "He didn't ask for mine." She rubbed the side of the bottle again and opened the top, but the genie didn't appear the second time.

"It only works when the bottle is first opened," Robert said.

She looked at him briefly. "You tested yours?"

"Yes."

She looked back at the palm-size golden container. Robert had the fleeting impression that she was making herself focus on it and it was taking some effort.

"That would have to be the way it works, of course."

He touched her forearm with a quick stroke, wanting to bring her attention back from wherever her mind really dwelled. She didn't respond to his touch.

"Since you seem to understand it, Diann, maybe you can explain it to me."

Her nod was subdued. "The gases used to create the genie image must be trapped by the original seal. When the bottle's seal is broken, the gases escape and form the genie's image for that instant in time before they dissipate."

"You know what the gases are?" Peter asked from across the table.

She sighed as though tired. "Probably a set of everyday common chemicals having distinctive colors. But the idea and its perfect execution are brilliant. I've never seen anything like it or anything like these containers."

Peter shook his head. Not a strand of his straight blond hair moved. "Poor Louis. Such a waste of talent. I'm surprised the French police are letting anyone check out. After the grilling I took from Inspector Pinchot this morning, I had the feeling he thought I was a part of some conspiracy to murder off the competition."

Diann glanced at Peter. "I know what you mean. He had me describing every minute I ever spent with Louis over the past few years. Still, I suppose he must think it strange that two of our presenters at this symposium have died. Frankly, I think it's beyond strange myself. What could have possibly killed Louis?"

"They don't know yet," Robert said. "All they know is that, like Kohei, there's not a mark on him."

Peter flashed Robert a frown as though to say no one needed the memory jogger. The table grew uncomfortably quiet. Robert studied the people before him, the tension in the air almost palpable.

On the first night there had been seven. Now there were four. He was forcibly reminded of Agatha Christie's *Ten Little Indians* and the way that countdown had unfolded.

He looked at Diann, white-faced beside him. He'd watched her from his position at the back of the Salon Marie-Antoinette during Louis Magnen's presentation. She'd been one of the first to run to Louis's side. Her facial features had remained composed through the summons for the doctor and the pronouncement of death, but he'd noted the perceptible shaking of her hands.

They were still trembling, although she had made every effort to disguise it as she continued to finger the lamp-shaped perfume bottle. She was quietly, resolutely, functioning.

The other two women at this table took Louis's death far differently. Gabrielle's cheeks were red, constantly stained with alternating quiet and noisy tears. Helena's complexion was almost purple, her expression a monument to anger as she periodically attended to her runny nose.

And then there was Peter Campbell, displaying a sangfroid that upheld his stiff-upper-lip national reputation and then some.

Robert's eyes wandered back to Diann's face. Her normal spark seemed to have retreated into some quiet, shocked cell. Could she possibly be this good an actress? More and more he was having trouble believing it. They had to be wrong about her. They just had to be. Or was he just being a fool?

She reached across her untouched plate of food for a glass of water. Her hand wobbled as she brought it to her lips. She spilled some on the tablecloth.

He had a sudden urge to put his arms around her and just hold her close. He wondered what her response would be if he gave in to the urge. Would she let him? Or would she throw the water in his face?

"Legionnaires' disease!" Gabrielle proclaimed suddenly and loudly, tearing Robert's attention away.

He'd made sure he was sitting as far away from Gabrielle as possible on the other side of the table. Now he looked over at her in interest. "Legionnaires' disease?"

"Yes, Robert, you have heard of it, no?"

"I have heard of it. It was that strange, deadly ailment that attacked all those conventioneers decades ago."

Helena's interest seemed to peak. "A convention disease? There is such a thing?"

"It occurred at the American Legion Convention in Philadelphia in July of 1976," Diann explained. "More than thirty people died."

"Yes, yes," Gabrielle said. "That is it! I do not remember what caused these deaths, but I remember Conrad told me about the many people who got ill and died at this convention."

"What caused the illness?" Helena asked.

"A previously unknown strain of bacteria," Diann said without hesitation. "It had developed in the central air-conditioning that served the hotel they were staying at in Philadelphia. They inhaled the bacteria into their respiratory systems, and it ended up invading their white blood cells."

"I seem to remember reading about that now," Peter said as he turned to Diann. "But I can't remember the specifics. Did everyone who was infected die?"

"No. More than two hundred people were infected. The mortality rate in Philadelphia and at the other places it broke out, was between fifteen and twenty percent."

Robert was finding it a bit surprising how knowledgeable about this disease Diann was. She had to be around twelve when it happened. And she was a chemist, not a doctor. Where had she learned such detail?

Gabrielle was nodding vigorously. "And something here in the ventilation system is attacking us. That is our explanation, no?"

Peter toyed with a golden ring on his pinky finger. "Except Kohei had a heart attack."

Gabrielle waved her hands. "And what brought on this heart attack? Could these bacteria not be the cause? Conrad collapses. We black out. Kohei dies. Louis dies. Diann, could this Legionnaires' disease not have found us here?"

Diann's brow furrowed. "Not that precise disease. They don't show the same symptoms. But I suppose a new causative agent is always a possibility. Bacteria and viruses are mutating all the time."

"Then it is possible a new one is here in this hotel," Helena said. "This is logical. A new convention disease is responsible for the deaths."

"Well, if you're right," Peter said, "then the most likely place for the bacteria or virus to be concentrating is in the Salon Marie-Antoinette, where we blacked out and both Kohei and Louis died. You realize that, don't you?"

From the widening of Helena's eyes, Robert could see she had not thought of that. She straightened her shoulders. "I will not step foot in that salon tomorrow. I will give no presentation. Gabrielle, I am going home!"

Gabrielle waved her hands to get Helena back in her chair. "Do you think I would let you go into that room? No one will go in there until we are sure. But you must not desert me. Please, Helena, Peter, Diann. I will arrange for us to move to another hotel if necessary. But the symposium must go on. I have worked so hard to make it a success. And none of you have yet given your presentations, for which I know you have worked so hard. Please."

She brought her handkerchief to her eyes and wiped away a fresh flurry of tears. Robert watched Diann, Helena and Peter all exchange looks that seemed to halt the idea of an exodus.

Then Diann leaned toward the crying woman. "Gabrielle, if you're right about some kind of a bacteria being behind these deaths, then moving to another hotel is not enough. We can't just abandon whoever might follow to their fate. If these deaths are being caused by a previously unknown agent in the air or water or food, we have a duty to call Inspector Pinchot and ask him to check the hotel."

"*Ja.* Before anybody else dies," Helena said, nodding furiously enough to lift the straight ginger strands of her hair.

Gabrielle was on her feet before Helena's short hair had had a chance to settle back into place. "You are right. The authorities must be told. I will do this. Right now. Peter, you will come with me?"

Peter rose and smiled. "Of course, Gabrielle."

He held out his arm to her, and Gabrielle tucked her hand inside it with a reciprocating smile on her face.

"I will come, too," Helena said as she rose to her feet, her ever-ready tissue tightly balled in her right hand.

Gabrielle looked back at her with a flash of irritation that quickly smoothed into a smile. "*Oui.* A force of numbers. We take on this inspector."

As soon as they left, Robert directed his attention to Diann. She sipped her coffee quietly. Her intent expression told him her thoughts were again far away.

"So you really think Kohei's and Louis's deaths are related to a bacteria like that found to be responsible for Legionnaires' disease?"

She eased her cup back onto its saucer like a glider coming in for a tricky landing. "Actually, it seems a logical explanation."

Her voice hesitated, as had her movements. Her face sported a small frown.

"Except?" he prompted.

"Except if it is some bacterial agent, why have only Kohei and Louis been infected? And if it is localized in the Salon Marie-Antoinette, why did Conrad collapse in the dining room?"

He smiled at her. "Good questions, Diann. So what do you think are the answers?"

"I don't have any answers. Just questions." Her eyes flipped to his nervously. "Look, I'm not feeling too well. I think I'll go up to my room and lie down for a while."

She scooted her chair back and stood. Robert rose with her. "I'll walk you up."

"Thank you, but no."

"There's something we need to discuss."

She turned from the table and toward the door of the restaurant. "I said what I had to say last night."

Robert moved alongside her. "Then I'll do all the talking."

But he didn't get a chance to say anything. There were other people on the elevator as they rode up. There were other people milling about the hallway to her suite.

"I thought you wanted to talk," Diann said as they reached the door to her suite.

"What I have to say to you I'd like to say in private. Invite me in."

"No."

He moved closer, resting his hands lightly on her shoulders.

Her eyes remained unyielding. He could feel the warmth of her through his hands, her vanilla-icing scent bringing back the alluring memories of her taste and feel in his arms.

"I won't stay long. Just a couple of things I wanted to say. Then I was rather hoping there were a couple of things you might want to say."

She studied him. He could see her fighting to keep her scrutiny detached. He could see her failing.

Finally she sighed. "I have nothing to say."

She was too close to resist and Robert just didn't feel like resisting anymore. "Nothing, Diann?" he asked before leaning down to kiss her.

For an instant her lips remained cool beneath his light pressure. But in the next they melted into his with a longing sigh that whipped his heartbeat into double time. He was right about her, how she felt, who she was. He could feel just how right by the rush of heat through his veins.

But when he tried to deepen the kiss and gather her into his arms, he suddenly felt her restraining hands on his shoulders as she shoved him back.

She looked a bit desperate. She sounded quite a bit desperate. "No. You said you were a thousand times more bothered than I was by what you imagine to be between us. If it bothers you so much, why don't you act like it and leave me alone?"

This time, her eyes said she meant it. He couldn't be sure if her reluctance to just let things happen came from the secret she kept or was because she was still fighting the battle of what he did for a living. He conceded it might be both.

He ran his hands lightly up and over her shoulders. "Diann, haven't you figured it out yet? I'm so bothered by what's between us I can't stay away from you."

She took a deep breath and pulled back. "You'll have to," she said as she escaped into her room and quickly closed the door behind her.

DIANN WAITED thirty minutes before leaving her room again. She'd changed from her conference business dress of that morning into a pair of walking shoes, black slacks and a black sweater. She'd shoved her arms into a knee-length raincoat, also black. She'd bundled her hair on top of her head and secured it with a comb.

She took the grand staircase down to the lobby and scurried through it, carefully scanning behind her to be sure that no one followed. Then she heard a familiar laugh coming from the bar. With increasing curiously, Diann crept up to its entrance and looked inside.

The Hôtel de Crillon's bar combined rich wood paneling, red velvet stools and gleaming cracked glass into a swirl of up-to-date elegance. At first she thought it was deserted. Then her eyes caught a flash of glass and she heard the unmistakable clinking of a toast.

Their table fit into the darkest corner. Peter's arm encircled Gabrielle's shoulders as he whispered something into her ear. She laughed again and took a sip of her drink. Peter drew out a vial of perfume, anointed Gabrielle's neck and buried his head in the fragrance. Gabrielle sighed and leaned against the chair's back.

Diann withdrew, troubled. There was nothing platonic about that scene she'd just witnessed. She tried to remind herself that they were adults and she had no business judging them.

She bit her lip, wishing fervently that her curiosity had not led her to look inside that bar. When she remembered the sound of love in Conrad's voice when he spoke about Gabrielle, she started feeling even worse. How could Gabrielle do this to him?

Diann scurried through the lobby of the Hôtel de Crillon, more concerned now in getting as far away as possible from that scene in the bar than she was about concealment. At her request, the doorman quickly secured a taxi for her.

She showed the driver the address Dr. Béraud had written down in French for her, knowing she'd only massacre the pronunciation if she tried reading it aloud. Her taxi driver nodded and gave the slip of paper back to her.

Diann leaned against the seat of the taxi. All in all, it had been a pretty rotten day. And finding out about Peter and Gabrielle hadn't improved it.

Kohei's death had been bad enough, but she'd never seen someone die right before her eyes. She took a deep breath and tried to dispel the image of Louis's lifeless form. It seemed impossible that she'd never again see the light of discovery in Kohei's eyes or watch Louis's thin mustache twitch.

The sad pain lumped in her throat and wouldn't dislodge. No matter how many times one was forced to face death, it just never seemed to get any easier.

Were Peter's and Gabrielle's abominable behavior simply their way of coping with their own shock?

"Well, if it is, it's a crummy way," she announced to the interior of the taxi. The driver flashed her a curious glance in his rearview mirror and then looked away again, executing a typical French shrug at the crazy American woman talking to herself.

It was at times like this that Diann wished she could just have a good cry and release her feelings.

But she couldn't. She had taught herself not to cry at too young an age to go back to it now. She would cope in the only way she had ever coped—by fighting what she could and trying to accept what she could do nothing about.

She gazed out the window. The sky was gray over a persistent drizzle. Even Paris's charm seemed a bit soggy around the edges. She closed her eyes and tried to think of something else. Immediately Robert Mize's face materialized, his blue eyes a study in spring sunshine. He was smiling at her. She could almost feel the warmth of his arms. "I can't stay away from you," he was saying.

His words had sounded so sincere. Diann wanted to believe them. But even if she could let herself believe them, he was still only a model. And a petty thief. And happy to be both.

So she was physically attracted to him. Hell, she'd have to be dead not to be physically attracted to the man. That didn't mean she had to have an affair with him that couldn't go anywhere. That wasn't who she was.

Diann deliberately opened her eyes and sat up. She knew who she was. She was a woman who was damn careful about whom she became involved with. She was a woman in control of her emotions. She was a woman with important work to do. And she had no time for mistakes.

So she'd slipped. A mere mad moment or two. She'd let Paris induce too romantic a mood. Well, not anymore. She would reclaim her control. This would end. Here. Now.

She rolled down her window and let in the cool, rain-swept breeze, as though daring the rainy Paris afternoon to disagree with her decision.

Unfortunately it was at that moment that a passing taxi's tires found a puddle of water and spun it up and through her open window. Diann gasped in surprise at her unexpected face washing. Quickly she rolled up her window and dived for the tissue in her purse.

"YOU'VE DONE IT, Diann," Dr. Béraud said as he rose from the stool in his makeshift home lab, his eyes twinkling at her. "Look at those mice. Before inhaling your formula they couldn't even smell the cheese, much less remember their way to it. And I had run several of them through at least a dozen times. Now look at them."

Diann was looking. And smiling, as she had with the hundreds of similar experiments she had performed. And knowing that no matter how many more she performed, she would still be smiling.

Dr. Béraud removed his reading glasses and rubbed the bridge of his nose. "They learn these mazes easily now. This one with the wobbly gait is Moses. His age is equivalent to an eighty-year-old man. Yet look at him go!"

Diann laughed at the animation in her former professor's voice. "The formula doesn't improve their physical capabilities."

"I disagree, Diann. Can you imagine how physically disabling it must be to have your memories and thoughts so clouded? To start out to go somewhere and stop because you're not able to even keep the thought of where you were going in your head?"

"Yes, I can imagine it," Diann said quietly.

Dr. Béraud looked away from the scurrying white mice in the several mazes cluttering the tables of his lab. His gaze went to Diann's face. What he read there had him immediately coming to her side. He took off his glasses and wrapped his arm around her waist.

"I forget sometimes."

She patted his arm. "I forget sometimes, too. When I'm lucky."

She watched Moses wobble gingerly around the last corner to claim his cheese prize. She had watched similar triumphs in the past few months. But the thrill always felt fresh and new.

"When are you going to publish?" Dr. Béraud asked.

"I'm putting the article together as soon as I get back. I wish you'd let me put your name on it as a coauthor. I never would have gotten to the top floor of this research if I hadn't been using your mental escalator."

"Thank you, Diann, for wanting to let me share in your achievement. But even if I thought it justified—"

"You can't have any question about that. You began this line of inquiry. I remember the day in class when you postulated the theory and asked for lab assistants to help you in testing out the formulas of your research. You would have done it all if you hadn't been forced to leave the university and lose access to all the valuable equipment and computer analysis."

"I may have done it. I'd like to think I would have. But you are the one who did it, Diann. Take the strokes coming to you. You have earned them. Remember, I had five lab assistants. You and you alone persisted."

Diann exhaled a heavy breath. "Good thing I didn't know how long it would take or my impatience probably would have defeated me."

She looked back at Moses, munching happily on his cheese. "There's still such a long way to go yet. And so many who are waiting. I feel the weight of each minute."

"It will go more quickly now."

"I hope so. My salary from Man to Woman has barely been sufficient to keep me going. You know how expensive the necessary equipment is. If I hadn't been able to use MW's computers and lab at night and on weekends, I never could have done it."

"But you have done it. Once you publish there'll be half a dozen drug companies clamoring to fund your double-blind studies. Diann, everything you've worked for these past eight years is about to pay off. I'd wish you'd look a little happier about it."

Diann eased the frown from her face and adopted a smile. "You're right. As a very erudite professor of chemistry once told me, 'When you find good in your life, have the sense to celebrate it.'"

Dr. Béraud's smile expanded tenfold. "There is nothing better for a teacher than to find a bright, attentive student. Come, we will eat the stew I put on for us and drink a bottle of Beaujolais I have been saving. The time has come to tell me all about this NOSE Award being given to you by the perfume industry."

DIANN TALKED on and on about her work at MW as they ate
Dr. Béraud's mediocre stew and drank his excellent wine.
She avoided mentioning the deaths that had occurred at the
convention. No reason to burden him with them. Actually,
being engaged with a mind that could understand the de-
tails of her work had enabled her to put aside the sadness of
those deaths for a while. She was thankful for the respite.

As she related some of the more comical events on the
job, she got a chuckle or two from Dr. Béraud. But after a
while the responses stopped and Diann suddenly heard a
snore coming from beside her. She looked over to see that
Dr. Béraud's unshaven chin had fallen onto his chest.

Her eyes flew to the watch on her wrist. Nearly nine
o'clock. Not exactly late. But she knew Dr. Béraud had
spent the prior night awake, testing out her formula over
and over again to be sure of its consistency. She should have
been more sensitive to his exhaustion and left long before
this.

His empty wineglass dangled from his hand. She gently
removed it and then raised his feet to the lumpy, threadbare
couch so that he could sleep more comfortably. She ducked
into the small bedroom and brought out a blanket and pil-
low, slipping the former over him and the latter beneath his
head.

She grabbed a pencil and paper and scribbled a quick note
promising to call before she left Paris.

Then she turned toward the telephone. And hesitated. She
needed a taxi, but she had no idea what number to call. Dr.
Béraud had summoned one the evening before. Had he left
the number near the phone?

She searched the pieces of paper there, but no telephone
number emerged. The directory was all in French, so that
wouldn't help. Well, what now?

She could wake him, of course. But she hated the idea.
She could spend the night, but if he woke up and wanted his
bed, she'd be in it and inconveniencing him.

She tried to remember their taxi trip from the Luxembourg Gardens the day before. There seemed to be so many twists and turns down small streets. She hadn't paid much attention, being engrossed totally in telling Dr. Béraud about her experiments.

But she did remember the neighborhood bakery where they had stopped for bread. They'd walked to the apartment from there. Just two blocks over and one down. She could find that. And she was sure that with a little luck she could communicate to the proprietor her need for a taxi and he could make the call for her.

She lifted her raincoat from the coatrack by the door and slipped her arms inside. She tucked her purse beneath her arm. Then with a final blown kiss toward the resting head of white hair, she let herself quietly out of the small apartment.

It was chilly and rainy once she exited into the inner courtyard of the respectable, but far from elegant, Left Bank apartment complex. Lights and the muffled noises from television and kids and music flowed down from the units circling its courtyard. She hurried to the heavy doors leading onto the city street. Cars skidded by, splashing water against the small stone sidewalk.

A few other pedestrians braved the weather, no doubt on their way home. She gave herself a moment to get her bearings. Then she brought the hood of the raincoat over her head and set off confidently in the direction she was sure would take her to the bakery.

But she didn't find the bakery two streets down and one over. She began to lose her confidence. She searched her memory, trying to determine where she had gone wrong. Was it three down? She walked another block. Maybe it was two over? Or three? She tried every combination she could think of.

When after twenty minutes she still had not found the bakery, she gave up. Well, nothing to do but to go back to

Dr. Béraud's apartment, wake him up and ask him to call a taxi.

She turned and began to retrace her steps. But it wasn't easy. She's tried so many different turns on the dark streets in an attempt to find the bakery that her direction was off. After thirty minutes she admitted to herself she was lost.

Great. Completely lost at night in a foreign city where she didn't know the language. Could it be worse?

A deluge seemed to open above Diann and the rain poured down with a vengeance. Yes, it could be worse.

Her feet felt like ice within her thoroughly soaked shoes. She wished with all her heart that she hadn't left Dr. Béraud's tiny, cozy apartment. Still, wishing wasn't going to make it happen.

She looked up past the roofs of the buildings, trying to see the reflected glow that would tell her in what direction the well-lit center of the City of Light lay.

There. Behind her. A perceptible lightening of the sky. She dug her hands into the deep pockets of her raincoat, lowered her head so that the hood could keep her face dry and set off again, walking as briskly as she could.

She covered blocks and blocks, looking up periodically to check the direction of the faint haze of reflected light. But it seemed to change direction on her and she found herself weaving through darker and darker streets.

Diann didn't have to be a resident of Paris to know she had somehow stumbled into one of its shabbier sections. The broken alleys and smells of garbage were more than enough to bring that forcibly to her attention.

She nearly jumped out of her skin when a cat suddenly flashed past, no doubt on the trail of a meal or his lady love. She quieted her nerves only with a determined effort.

Another block and she looked up again to catch sight of the reflected lights. And bit her lip in frustration. Damn. Now they seemed to be behind her!

She had to admit it. She was hopelessly lost. Well, nothing to do but approach the very next person she met and do her best to ask for directions.

Only there hadn't been anyone else on the streets for blocks now. She stopped under a dim street lamp to catch her breath. The rain beat steadily down on her. She seriously considered going back in the direction she'd just come. At least back there she'd seen a few pedestrians she could approach for assistance. And right now finding a person familiar with the terrain was number one in importance.

She was just turning around, when from out of the corner of her eye she saw a shadowy figure slip out of a darkened doorway and stealthily begin to cross the street toward her. Then another shadowy figure disengaged itself from the blackness of a building on the other side of her and headed in her direction.

Diann stiffened in alarm. A second before she had been hoping to see someone. Now she wished most fervently she was once more alone on these streets.

Everything about the way these figures moved toward her told her she was their prey. She tasted panic, sharp and acidic, burning in her throat.

Her first impulse was to run. But a deeper instinct told her they could easily outrun her and she wouldn't get far. She was better off staying where she was and facing them. At least she was beneath the dim light. Those who preyed on others did not like the light.

So she stood her ground, grasping her purse in her hand and raising it like a weapon and getting ready to fight like hell and scream bloody murder.

She knew her instincts were right when the shadowy figures suddenly stopped in their positions on either side of her. She could see the flash of their eyes—dark animal eyes—assessing her as they exchanged glances in some quiet communication.

She held her breath. And then felt it ripping through her chest when they started toward her again.

Because that was when she saw the knives in their hands.

They didn't care about the light. They didn't care that she would stand and defend herself. They probably knew her screams would bring no one to this dark, deserted alley.

Diann went rigid with fear. And when she opened her mouth to scream, absolutely nothing came out.

Chapter Seven

Robert's heart pounded as he raced into the lamplight, stopping in front of Diann to face the two street thugs. He was larger—quite a bit larger—than either of them, and he let them see that. Of course, there were two of them, and the knives in their hands evened up the score and then some. He put as much menace into his voice as possible. "Get lost. Now."

They laughed, and he heard the bold high notes of youthful stupidity in those laughs. Then they stopped laughing and vulgarly bragged about what they were going to do to him if he didn't step aside.

Robert answered their threats with the only form of communication he knew these two would understand. With lightning-fast reflexes, he kicked the knife out of the hand of the thug on the left and punched him in the stomach. Then he swung around and put his fist in the face of the thug on the right.

When the man landed on the grit of the wet alley, Robert stepped on his hand. The creep cursed and then dropped the knife. Robert swung down and picked up both knives before either thug recovered. When they did a moment later, they scrambled to their feet and raced away, disappearing again into the darkened alleyways.

Robert only paused long enough to assure himself of their total retreat before turning to face Diann.

Her face was ashen beneath the light of the street lamp. She still held her purse as though she was prepared to use it as a weapon, despite the fact that she was visibly shaking all over.

"Diann, are you all right?"

Her response was barely loud enough to reach his ears. "Robert? I can't believe it's you."

He reached for her arm and urged her forward and away.

He doubted the two thugs would be sticking around, but on the other hand, he wasn't into taking any chances. If they rounded up an additional acquaintance and some more knives, they might also round up the additional courage to come back.

She moved quickly beside him, saying nothing more, but he could feel her trembling. He kept his hand securely under her elbow until they were many blocks away and had reentered a more acceptable residential area.

Not that there were any safe areas anymore, anywhere in the world, he reminded himself. He kept a look out as he headed for the side street where he'd parked his rented Peugeot.

Only when he'd reached it did he withdraw his hand from her elbow to insert the key into the door lock. "There's a police station just a few blocks away."

Immediately she clutched his arm. "Please. I can't go to the police. They'll ask why I was here."

He turned to her. She was trying to sound calm and controlled, but she was as pale as a whisper and trembling visibly. A sudden pressure inside his chest pushed against his heart like a vise.

He reached for her and wrapped his arms around her, bringing her close. He held her trembling form firmly, stroking her hair tenderly, irritated to find his own hand shaking as he cursed long and hard in French.

When he thought of what might have happened to her had he caught up to her even a second or two later, the curses got more elaborate and vehement.

Finally she stopped trembling and he realized he had stopped cursing. Still he continued to hold her closely. Gradually the vise around his heart eased. She felt so good and safe in his arms. They were both getting soaked. But at that moment all he wanted to do was hold her to him.

Finally she stirred and looked up into his face. "Can we go back to the hotel now?"

He released his tight hold on her and stiffly stepped back to unlock the passenger door to the Peugeot. He handled her inside and quickly locked the passenger door behind her. Then he circled around the Peugeot and let himself into the driver's seat.

He gunned the engine, tore away from the curb. They were halfway back to the Hôtel de Crillon before she spoke again. "You were following me."

No point in denying it. It wasn't as though there was any other explanation for his being in that alley.

"Yes."

"Why?"

"We've both got questions that need answering, Diann. I'd rather be in warmer, dryer clothes before we start. We'll be at the hotel soon. Then we'll get a few things straight, you and I."

After that ominous proclamation, she turned from him and let the matter drop.

He left her at the door of her hotel room, promising her he'd be back soon. Then he went to his room and had a quick shower and change. He picked up the phone and dialed Cassel's number.

"It's me. I'm back."

"About time you checked in. I was getting worried. What happened?"

"She got herself lost."

"What?"

"I'll explain later. I'm going to meet with her now, and I think I'll finally be getting some answers. Anything urgent come up while I was gone?"

"The autopsy on Louis Magnen came in. The medical examiner is calling his death a heart attack."

"Well, it's not like we weren't expecting it. Anything else?"

"The lab tests came back on the stuff in those two vials from her luggage."

"And?"

"One's definitely just a perfume, although it has some interesting properties. The other's a real puzzle. The lab boys can't figure what it's supposed to be. But it doesn't seem to be harmful—at least not in liquid, solid or gaseous form."

Robert laughed. "Is there another form?"

"Okay. It doesn't seem to be harmful period. But that doesn't mean that it might not be when mixed with something else."

"Give it up, Cassel. We've been wrong about the lady. I'm sure of it. Anything come through on the bugs?"

"I've got three taped conversations I think you should hear. They could be nothing. Then again—"

"Then again they could be something. Look, find out if Gabrielle Rife is moving the symposium attendees to another hotel the way she talked about this afternoon. Then meet me back in my room in an hour with the tapes. Let yourself in if I'm not here."

"Tonight?"

"Sorry to postpone your beauty sleep, but I want to go over those tapes in detail. We've missed something. And I intend to find it."

DIANN OPENED the door to Robert's knock, feeling a lot better after taking a hot shower and pulling on some comfortable dry jeans and a sweater. There was a lot to be said for creature comforts restoring one's equilibrium.

As always he looked wonderful. But he'd never look as good to her as he did when she saw him appear on that dark street, standing between her and those two awful creatures with the knives. Involuntarily she shivered and rubbed at her arms, trying to erase the icy bumps that had suddenly popped out on them.

"I've ordered some hot chocolate. For two. If you'd rather something intoxicating, you know where it is."

"No, thanks. You'll do."

His smile was strong and solid. As he was. Diann took a deep, steadying breath, trying not to read too much into his remarks, trying to maintain her carefully reengaged equilibrium.

There was something she had to say and she was having a hard time getting it out, an unusual situation for a woman of her outspoken tendencies. She deliberately turned away from him and eased herself onto the couch, curling a leg beneath her.

"Robert, what you did tonight was so very brave. I haven't thanked you because frankly words seem sort of inadequate."

He sat down beside her, and for the first time Diann saw a look of discomfort flash across his face. His tone was almost gruff.

"You're all right. That's good enough for me. Although you were a perfect idiot to be walking the streets of a city, any city, at night alone. Now, will you please tell me why you were so stupid as to leave your friend's place without first letting him call you a taxi?"

Diann started at his words, totally taken aback. Her voice rose an octave. "You know about Dr....about my friend?"

He looked at her for a long, steady moment before speaking. "'Doctor,' is it? The older ladies living in his apartment complex said his name was Fouché, but they didn't say anything about his being a doctor.''

"You asked them about him?"

"I wanted to know whose apartment you disappeared into this afternoon. His neighbors are very interested in the secretive Fouché. They want to know why such a handsome bachelor in his seventies doesn't have a wife. If he's a relative, you should warn him those ladies are out to get him.''

Diann sank into the cushions with a sigh. So he didn't *really* know. She felt an enormous weight lifting off her shoulders. "They're out of luck. My friend has been married to his work for a long time now.''

"What work?"

Diann bit her lip. "I owe you. I know that.''

His hands found hers and encircled them in their warmth. "I don't want you to tell me because you think you owe me something. You don't. Only a real louse would expect something in return for helping a woman—or a man, for that matter—from being attacked by some street thugs.''

She smiled. This man had some solid good qualities beneath his solid good looks. Had she really once only defined him in terms of the male-model role he performed? How young and foolish she had been.

"Robert, believe me, if it were just my secret, I'd tell you in a second. But to betray a confidence—''

"Would you be betraying a confidence? Or would you just be sharing a confidence with a friend?''

Diann sat forward and studied his face. There was no sexy tilt to those full lips. No challenging, mysterious glow in those blue eyes. Just a straight, serious look that Diann found could be equally as devastating.

She sat back, the lingering questions in her mind answered. "Dr. Béraud was a professor of mine at Cornell, a brilliant man and a wonderful teacher. He was quite respected in chemical circles as a researcher, as well. Then eight years ago his car was involved in a hit-and-run accident involving a pedestrian.''

"Was anyone hurt?"

"A university student was killed. There were witnesses who got the license-plate number of the car. Within hours the police were at Dr. Béraud's door with a warrant. They found the car with its dented fender in his garage, an open bottle of whiskey on the passenger's seat. He was arrested."

"Was he convicted?"

"No. He drew out what little he had in savings and jumped bail, flying here to France, where his elder sister, Marie Fouché, lived. She helped him hide out until she died a couple of years ago. He adopted her married name, Fouché. The little money his sister left him is what sustains him."

Robert was silent for a moment. Then he shook his head. "Diann, the man caused the death of another, intentional or not. Just because he's an elderly scholar, that doesn't make him immune to the law. Béraud should have faced up to what he had done."

"But that's just it, Robert. He didn't do it."

"But you just told me that his car—"

"Exactly. His *car* was involved. Not him. You see, Dr. Béraud has a son, Roth. Roth's mother died when he was six and Dr. Béraud raised him alone. It was because of Roth that Dr. Béraud took a job as a teacher, instead of devoting his life to research, as was his dream. He wanted more regular hours so he could be with Roth as much as possible. Not that it did much good."

"Are you saying that it was Béraud's son, Roth, who hit the pedestrian with his father's car?"

"Yes."

"But why didn't Béraud just tell the police that?"

"And send his only son, who he's convinced himself he failed, to prison? No. He accepted disgrace, and he would have even accepted prison, rather than turn Roth in. And believe me, prison would have torn the soul from him."

"If this son was worth anything, he should have come forward and cleared his father."

"I agree. And Dr. Béraud is convinced Roth would have if the matter had made it to trial. He didn't want Roth to confess. He wanted to give Roth another chance to straighten out his life. That's why Béraud jumped bail and fled to France and has been hiding out ever since."

"What happened to Roth?"

"The incident appeared to sober him up a bit. He's married now. Works as an assistant manager in a New Jersey grocery store. If he's still drinking, at least he's had the sense not to mix it with driving."

"How did you learn all of this? Did Béraud tell you?"

"No. I was one of his research assistants at the time it happened. I had been to Dr. Béraud's home and met Roth. Seen the way he drank. And drove. The moment I heard about the hit-and-run, I knew who was really behind that wheel."

"And you didn't tell the police?"

"I went to Roth first to give him a chance to confess. I told him I would tell if he didn't. He begged me to speak with his father first. I did the moment Roth had secured Dr. Béraud's bail. Dr. Béraud told me to say nothing. He told me if I did accuse Roth, he'd openly confess to the hit-and-run. I had only suspicion to offer the police. Against an unsolicited confession, I had no illusions who they'd believe."

"So you kept quiet?"

"No, I was a stubborn, hardheaded twenty-two-year-old who didn't know how to keep quiet about such an injustice. I wasn't about to let a man of Dr. Béraud's caliber suffer for the sins of a son who I had judged as worthless, anyway. But while I was sitting with the police, trying to convince them of Dr. Béraud's innocence, Dr. Béraud jumped bail and fled. After that, the police wouldn't listen to a thing I had to say."

"How did you find Béraud?"

"I knew he'd head for France. While I was working as his assistant, he'd told me about his sister in Paris and how he planned to visit her someday. He always said that if he ever retired, it would be to Paris. I went through his desk at the university before the police got to it and took out all the letters with his sister's married name and return address on them."

"You kept evidence from the police?"

"It was only evidence that would lead them to an innocent man. My conscience is clear. Anyhow, a year later when things died down, I wrote to Dr. Béraud at her name and address. He answered using Fouché on the return address for safety and we've been keeping up a correspondence ever since."

"About what?"

"Mostly about Roth and how he's doing."

"Doesn't Béraud's own son write to him?"

"No. Nor does he call. Roth knows where his father is, of course. But since Dr. Béraud left the States, his son hasn't so much as sent him a postcard. When I let myself think about it, I still get angry. Roth wasn't worth a brilliant man giving up his reputation and career. I'll never understand how Dr. Béraud could have been such a fool to do it, but then, I've never been a parent."

"Why were you so secretive about visiting Dr. Béraud? Surely you didn't expect the New Jersey police to follow you here."

"They did suspect I'd helped Dr. Béraud get away because I believed him innocent. They checked my telephone calls and mail for a long while afterward."

"But surely not still."

"No. It isn't the police who makes me cautious. The family of the hit-and-run victim had offered a substantial reward for any information that leads to Dr. Béraud's capture. I couldn't take the chance of anyone finding out where he was and being tempted to claim that reward.''

"But you're taking the chance with me now."

She looked at him straight. "Any man who would put his life on the line to protect someone else like you protected me tonight isn't the kind of man who would turn in an innocent person for money or any other reason."

He smiled at her then, and the genuine warmth of that smile had Diann's heart cartwheeling inside her chest.

"So you visited Béraud on the sly when you got to Paris to give him a face-to-face update on his son."

"Well, that and to tell him about my experiments, of course."

Robert's smile faded. "Your *experiments?*"

Diann started at the knock on the door. She didn't realize how jumpy she still was after her harrowing experience. Of course she knew it was just room service with the hot chocolate she'd ordered. She got up to let in the waiter and found Robert had gotten up with her.

"I'll get it," he offered, and headed for the door.

She sat down again and thought nothing more of it, until she noticed how carefully he asked who it was first. And even after the waiter had identified himself, Robert still opened the door slowly and cautiously. It seemed she wasn't the only one who was still nervous.

Or was it nerves? Several things that had been bothering her about Robert seemed to coalesce at that moment into one very large question mark. When the waiter had left, Diann handed Robert his cup of chocolate from the tray. "Why did you follow me this afternoon?"

He sat down beside her and took a sip of the hot chocolate. "I'll explain in a moment. But first, I'd like to know about these experiments you discussed with Dr. Béraud."

He'd brought up the one subject that could divert her. Temporarily. She leaned forward eagerly. "They all began eight years ago when I was one of Dr. Béraud's laboratory assistants. We were working on a theory he had about Alzheimer's disease. When Dr. Béraud was forced to leave the university and his work because of the false criminal charges, I kept on with the experiments.''

"Even while you've been working at MW?"

"Yes. In my off-hours only, of course. And I've made every effort to keep them secret. I had to be sure my results were accurate and consistent, you see.''

"Actually, I don't see. What kind of experiments were these?''

"To describe them properly, I have to give you a bit of background first. Have you heard of Alzheimer's disease?''

He nodded. "The disease that leads to mental deterioration?''

"More precisely, it's a progressive degenerative brain disorder of plaque buildup leading to cognitive impairment, which most often strikes the elderly, although it can and does strike individuals in their fifties and younger— hardly what anyone would call 'elderly.' ''

"And your experiments have something to do with Alzheimer's?''

"They have everything to do with it. Those who get Alzheimer's disease seem to have an early warning symptom. Before any mental deterioration is evidenced, these people experience a significant loss of the sense of smell.''

"A loss of the sense of smell? This has been documented?''

"For a long time now. And Dr. Béraud postulated that if a loss in the sense of smell was an early warning symptom, then perhaps that meant that the olfactory area of the brain was one of the first areas attacked by Alzheimer's. He believed efforts to restore its function might help to pinpoint what chemicals would be effective in combating the buildup of plaque throughout the brain.''

"That's an interesting theory. Any validity to it?"

Diann had trouble keeping the smile from her lips. "You could say so, since I've proved it's true."

Robert put down his cup of hot chocolate and turned to face her. "Are you saying you've found a way to stimulate the olfactory sense in Alzheimer's patients?"

"Only the white mice patients so far. But it works, Robert. Qualifiably and consistently. It works!"

ROBERT COULD SEE the excitement in her eyes and hear the joy in her voice. So this was what all those secret experiments were about. When he thought of the interpretation the organization had given them, he felt like laughing.

"Okay, Diann. I can see you're just bursting to tell me. How do you reestablish the smell function in these patients?"

"By using a substance I've developed in the lab called secretase noetic inhalant, formula five hundred—or SNIFF, for short. Secretase is an enzyme that slices up plaque. I've found a way for secretase to be inhaled directly into the brain's olfactory center, where it can free the nerve cells of the plaque. Actually, all my work discovering new perfume scents gave me the breakthrough I needed."

"Did it, now?"

She hardly seemed to be noticing him anymore. Her eyes shone with discovery. "The important impact of scent on the brain gave me the key. Other researchers have pursued the ingestion or injection of secretase, but I began to realize that it's the nose that's our direct route to the brain."

"So Alzheimer's patients will inhale your SNIFF?"

"Yes. It takes just a few hours for them to start showing that their sense of smell is returning. And the effects of exposure seem to be cumulative."

"Meaning their sense of smell improves with each inhalation?"

She looked exceptionally pleased at his quick understanding. "And what's more, the mental deterioration of Alzheimer's doesn't manifest itself. When the mice finally die, it's from old age. A ripe, *lucid* old age."

"You're sure the loss of the sense of smell in the mice you tested was due to Alzheimer's and not something else?"

"Oh, yes. I've also tried the formula on mice that have the actual mental deterioration symptoms of Alzheimer's and they show an improvement not only in their sense of smell, but in their mental clarity, as well. This seems to indicate that the secretase is also getting into other parts of the brain and breaking up the plaque."

"So your formula may be able to not only prevent Alzheimer's but also arrest its further spread, even after the disease has begun? And maybe even reverse some of the deterioration?"

She nearly bounced in her seat. "That's what I'm hoping. I won't know, of course, until I get these results with the white mice published and secure a grant for the studies with human volunteers who have the disease. But it's so promising!"

Robert looked at the shine on her face. She literally glowed from within. "Diann, I once made disparaging comments about your wasting your talent and education developing perfumes. Why didn't you explain this to me then?"

"Because I don't feel defensive about my job at MW. I think developing wonderful perfumes for people is a very worthy occupation all by itself. Yes, my research into arresting Alzheimer's is uppermost in importance. Once I get the funding, it will become my twenty-four-hours-a-day focus. But I consider my efforts to develop fragrances that lift the spirits and the hearts of both men and women time well spent, too."

And she meant it. He could see that in her eyes.

"I now understand why you laughed at me when I unfavorably compared your efforts with those of your Cornell classmate."

"I wasn't laughing at you, Robert. On the contrary. I was laughing at myself for underestimating your mental weapons. You had wielded them pretty effectively against me then. You see, I hadn't expected a whole lot of mental challenge from a male model. But then, you're not just a male model, are you?"

She was wearing an interesting expression. Robert decided to find out everything he could about what was behind it before admitting to anything. "Why do you say that?"

"Oh, your appearance had me fooled at first. And you played your part so convincingly. But a man like you doesn't follow a woman around because he's smitten with her. You've been following me around for a totally different reason. What is it?"

Robert slowly reached into his pocket and pulled out his wallet. He opened it to his identification and passed it to her. She looked at it and frowned.

"Worldwide Life and Casualty? Philadelphia? An insurance investigator?"

He laughed at the surprise filling her voice. "Still not cerebral enough for you, Diann? Am I going to have to razzle-dazzle you with my many exploits outwitting the bad and brilliant schemers of insurance fraud?"

Her mouth formed a good-natured grin as she handed back the ID. "How long have you been an insurance investigator?"

"Ever since I got my M.B.A. from Harvard."

She shook her head despairingly. "And you misled me into thinking you'd frittered away your chance at an education by going from school to school."

"Actually, I did gather my B.A. credits from several institutions before getting admitted to Harvard's graduate program. So you see, I didn't lie to you, Diann."

"You told me you played professional baseball last year, remember?"

"I did. I was on an undercover assignment. We suspected some members of a baseball team to be running an insurance scam. We were right."

"And that's why you became a male model for MW! You're undercover again on another case!"

"Yes."

"But who could you be after at MW?"

He kept staring meaningfully at her face and watched the truth finally pop into those expressive eyes. She literally jumped off the couch.

"Me? You suspect me of insurance fraud? Are you crazy? Other than what's mandatory by law on my beat-up 1978 Buick, I don't even have a scrap of insurance. And I've never filed a claim."

He eased her back into her seat with a patient gesture. "Diann, I couldn't care less about your car insurance. I'm the manager for Worldwide's creative-arts division. We don't investigate any claim that's less than five hundred thousand dollars."

"A half million? Now I know you must be crazy. I don't even have a hundred dollars in life insurance."

"None you pay the premiums on, that's true. But your company holds a million-dollar policy on you and your educated nose."

He could see the information register with some surprise.

"It does? I never knew."

"It's standard procedure for companies that employ those with special, intangible talents to protect their investment against unexpected disability or loss."

"Okay. I suppose that makes sense. But I still don't understand why you've been following me."

"The reasons might start getting clearer when I tell you that your company isn't the only one that insures its perfume stars. Every nominee and finalist for the Fragrance Fraternity's PERFUME awards has a hefty policy from our company."

The intelligence in her eyes was working. "Including Kohei and Louis?"

"Yes. Worldwide will be paying off million-dollar policies on each."

Her brow furrowed. "But you can't be here because of their deaths. You joined MW's staff more than a month ago."

"Yes, I did. Right after the first two deaths."

Her pupils expanded visibly. "The *first* two deaths? What first two deaths?"

"The first was Terrence Wonnacott, a Canadian perfume packager. You met him when you attended that convention nine months ago in Toronto."

"You mean Terry. Yes, I remember Terry very well. He's dead?"

"He got into his car to drive home from that convention the afternoon it broke up and never even managed to lift the key into the ignition. A parking-lot attendant found him slumped over the wheel that night."

Her face grew sad. "I'm so sorry to hear it. He seemed like such a nice person, and so bright. I remember Gabrielle had taken a real fancy to his use of silk-and-satin bows on his special bottles. Had he been ill?"

"No, he was in great health, according to his doctor. He just suddenly suffered a massive heart attack. His company had a policy on him for a half million, which of course we paid."

Diann looked uncomfortable. Very uncomfortable. He watched her eyebrows draw together. "The second death was Annette Prince in Las Vegas a couple of months ago, wasn't it?"

"Yes. Her policy was for three-quarters of a million. That was when the computer alerted us that something was wrong. The probabilities went out of range when two young people, both associated with the perfume industry, had sudden fatal heart attacks without any previous heart problems."

Diann nodded. "'Two million two hundred and twenty-seven to one,' you quoted to me when I wondered what the odds were for Kohei and Annette to both have sudden heart attacks. Were those really the odds of it happening by chance?"

She had a good memory. He wasn't surprised. "Those were the odds of all three—Terry, Annette and Kohei—having heart attacks happening by chance. But then Louis had his heart attack, and now the odds are so astronomical the computer won't even quote them."

She took a deep breath and let it out audibly. "Four people with sudden heart attacks. It's unbelievable. There must be some agent that—"

"Before you start talking about some bacterial agent again, let me assure you that the computer has already explored that possibility. The odds on it are just as astronomical as these deaths occurring naturally. There's only one explanation for these deaths and that is deliberate and calculated murder by a means and person unknown."

Her spine straightened perceptively. "Murder?"

"Yes, Diann. Multiple murder. I'm on the trail of a serial killer. One whose victims are the top stars of the perfume industry."

She reached for her chocolate and drank the lukewarm dregs. From the look of shock on her face, he was sure she tasted nothing.

"Why haven't the police been told? Why aren't they here?"

"I did notify the Canadian and American police after Annette Prince's death brought the possibilities of murder to our attention. But neither police force was eager to open murder investigations into deaths that had already been labeled natural. In short, they chose not to believe us."

"But they have to believe you now. Two more people have died!"

"In a foreign country under foreign police jurisdiction. We faxed them the information immediately."

"What did they say?"

"Nothing yet. But I don't have a lot of hopes, Diann. Neither the autopsy on Terry Wonnacott nor the one on Annette Prince showed any foreign substance on the toxicology screens. Even if the police in Toronto and Las Vegas believed us, they might not be able to do anything."

"What about the FBI?"

"Two deaths do not a serial killer make, according to the FBI. And even though we now have four, the FBI does not get involved in investigating the deaths of foreign nationals in foreign countries. Other than Annette Prince, all the other deaths have been outside their jurisdiction."

"So Worldwide Insurance is the only organization investigating. Because of their insurance losses?"

"We're the only ones in the unique position of seeing the pattern behind these deaths."

"Does Inspector Pinchot know who you really represent?"

"This is a touchy situation for us, Diann. Worldwide may operate worldwide, but we are an American company. We are not licensed to investigate in a foreign country. Our investigators have found themselves dumped in jail for conducting undercover operations before. If Inspector Pinchot knew my real position, I'd probably be one of those investigators who found himself on the other side of the bars."

"But don't you feel partly responsible for Kohei's death and Louis's because you didn't tell Inspector Pinchot they could happen?"

"Diann, two weeks ago I had my office send the Eighth Arrondissement a full report of Worldwide's suspicions concerning a possible attempt on the lives of attendees to this symposium."

"What's the Eighth Arrondissement?"

"The district police in charge of the area around the hotel, the force Inspector Pinchot heads. That's why Inspector Pinchot was suspicious of the first death and on the scene so quickly."

"Yes, he was suspicious, wasn't he?"

"We couldn't get the authorities to exhume Terry and Annette to conduct more extensive lab tests. I was hoping the autopsies Inspector Pinchot ordered performed on Kohei and Louis would point to some foreign agent in the bloodstream, lungs or intestinal tract. But neither has. And without proof of a murder, even the suspicious Inspector Pinchot cannot conduct a more extensive investigation."

By watching her eyes, he could see her absorbing the facts and trying to make sense out of them. She was quiet for several moments before speaking again.

"A killer on the loose! This is . . . bizarre, dreadful! With all your computer power, have you been able to come up with some suspects?"

"We came up with one very promising suspect. She was at all the conventions. She spent time alone with all the victims prior to their demise. She was a chemist, so she had the capability of selecting, or maybe even producing, an agent that could kill by mimicking a heart attack and not leave a trace. And last but not least, she was conducting suspicious, ultrasecret experiments after hours that no one else knew about."

He saw the message sweep through her in waves of disbelief. Her voice echoed that disbelief. "Dear sweet heavens. So that's the reason you were following me. You thought I was murdering my colleagues!"

Chapter Eight

"Sorry," Robert said. "But at first you fit the guilty profile pretty well, especially when you slipped off to see Dr. Béraud without telling anyone where you were going. You had opportunity and we had every reason to suspect you had developed the means while you were conducting those secret experiments."

Diann shook her head in disbelief and hurt. All this time he'd been pursuing her only because he thought her a murderess. Not exactly a comforting testament to her feminine charms.

She took a deep breath and let it out slowly. "Your whole reason for joining MW was to get close to me so you could find out what I was up to. No wonder you said you'd been trying to meet me for a long time."

"Yes."

"You were following me when we first met on the Champs-Élysées. You didn't just happen along."

"Yes."

"And the reason you said you were going to stay close to me was that you were waiting for me to slip up so you could catch me trying to murder someone."

"Yes."

Diann felt a sad little pain of fallen hope in her chest, which surprised her. She didn't realize she was harboring any hope.

She took a deep breath of reality and faced him, trying to keep the disappointment out of her voice. "What motive could I possibly have had?"

She hadn't succeeded. A definite hurt underlay the matter-of-fact edges she'd carefully given to her words.

He found her hands and clasped his around them. "We weren't even trying to think about motive. Motives for serial killing can be totally off the wall, as any FBI profiler will tell you."

She laughed, but it wasn't a happy sound. "Well, I suppose you wouldn't be telling me all this if you still imagined I was a cold-blooded killer."

"No. I had trouble imagining that from the first. A lot of trouble. Since the moment I saw you, Diann, a part of me has been fighting to believe you innocent. Despite what the probabilities said or the evidence seemed to indicate, I knew no one who looks like you and walks like you and talks like you could be anything but genuine."

She glanced up at him, read the message on his face and smiled inwardly. Score one for feminine charms, after all. A perceptible tension released itself from her shoulders. "I hope you've got another suspect now that you've lost me."

He released her hands and leaned into the couch. "The only other people who were at all the other conventions and who are still alive are Helena Strunk, Peter Campbell, Gabrielle Rife and Conrad Rife."

Diann tried to picture those four people in the role of murderer. She shook her head. "No, there has to be someone else."

"We've been very careful about checking out everyone else attending this symposium. Trust me. Those are the only ones besides yourself."

"But Conrad was stricken, too."

"He did suffer a heart attack, it's true. But if someone was trying to get him at the banquet, they messed up on the dosage of whatever they're using. Or maybe his heart medication prevented it from being fatal."

A few more lights were switched on in Diann's brain. "And that's why you took the champagne goblet. You're not a petty thief at all. You wanted to check it to be sure Conrad hadn't been poisoned."

He smiled as he raised a finger to stroke her cheek. "Disappointed I don't need redeeming?"

She smiled back, a wicked light in her eyes. "Don't you? I still had to bully you into paying for it."

He laughed in that honest, throaty way again and Diann felt it bubbling in her blood like a vintage champagne. He leaned forward and gave her cheek a quick kiss. "You'd best stay close to watch my every sticky-fingered move from now on."

Diann felt his brief touch like a hot brand on her cheek. Her breath seemed to get stuck in her lungs. *Take it lightly,* she cautioned herself. *You're only an assignment for him.*

He leaned back, his brow puckering as he contemplated their mystery, totally unaware of what havoc he'd just unleashed inside her. "Whether Conrad was an intended victim or not, we may never know. But at least he's safe at home in Macon. Which means that it's just you four left. And one of you is killing off the others."

Diann got up off the couch and began to pace the room, both to cool off her sudden temperature rise and to consider the message in his words. "No. I'm sorry. But it's too fantastic. I've known Helena, Peter and Gabrielle for years. To think that one of them could be a murderer— No. I just can't accept it."

Robert got up and went to stand beside her. "Try to be objective, Diann. What do you really know about these people? You say you've known them for years, but don't you really mean you've seen them two or three times a year at industry functions? And for what? A few days at the most? And you discuss what's new in the business, not who they are or even anything very personal. You said yourself you knew nothing about Kohei's family life.''

Diann took another deep breath as she felt the warmth of Robert's nearness invade her. She let the breath out slowly, almost carefully. ''It's true I don't know a whole lot about their personal lives.''

She frowned. ''But, damn it, Robert. They're intelligent, professional people. And they all love our industry. Even if they didn't care about the individuals involved, the loss of the irreplaceable talents of Terry, Annette, Kohei and Louis is devastating. None of them could have wanted that.''

''On the surface that may be the way it seems. But, Diann, the facts are rather hard to refute. It's one of them. It's got to be.''

''But which one?''

''Maybe you can help me decide. Come. Sit down. Tell me everything you know about them. Start with Helena. What kind of a woman is she?''

Diann did as he urged and reclaimed her seat on the couch. She tried to put her impressions of Helena into words. ''Tough, Smart.''

''Personally?''

''Professionally. We've both already agreed I don't know much about these people personally.''

''Right. So what else do you know about Helena professionally?''

''She's absolutely sensational at precision blending.''

''Why is that important?''

''Well, once a 'nose' like me develops a perfume formula, it's up to the company's blenders to be able to accurately reproduce that formula, and that's not an easy job.''

''Why not?''

''Most of the ingredients of a perfume come from the flowers, the fruit, the leaves, the stems, the roots of plants.''

"Hold it there for a minute. Give me some examples of these ingredients."

"The oils that give perfume its fragrance, the alcohol that acts as a base and helps to release the fragrance as it evaporates, the fixing agent that helps to lessen the volatility of the oils so that all of the fragrance does not leave the bottle after one opening—those are the basic components. But there are literally thousands of ingredients that can be used."

"Okay. Suffice it to say that many come from plants. So what does that tell me?"

"Well, you've no doubt heard that grapes used to make wine have good and bad years, depending on the rain and sun and soil conditions in which the grapes have been grown. This is true, too, of perfume ingredients."

"So a particular perfume can have good and bad years?"

"Wine grapes can be tracked by good or bad years. A perfume's fragrance can differ perceptively from one batch of blended ingredients to the next."

"Are you saying that two bottles of the same perfume from the same bottling plant can differ?"

"If the ingredients don't come from exactly the same plants grown in the same area during the same season, yes. With at least two to three hundred ingredients in a quality perfume, variation is the rule, not the exception."

"What's done to ensure consistency?"

"The best perfumers have many quality-control steps to try to minimize deviations. But Helena Strunk has no peers in her ability to achieve this consistency. Every bottle of Mit Luv's perfume is blended in such a way as to be absolutely accurate to the original fragrance. The scent you try on in the store is the one you take home. No exceptions."

"Do you think she's developed some chemical that helps her to achieve that consistency?"

"I can't imagine how a single chemical could do it. I would be more inclined to believe she's discovered a purification process, something that eliminates the possible presence of microscopic mildew or other active microorganisms from the plant part absolutes that could adversely affect the quality of scent.''

''Absolutes?''

''An absolute is an ultrarefined essential oil. For example, it takes seven hundred fifty kilograms of jasmine petals to make just one kilogram of absolute. Of course, some labs have learned to create some remarkable aldehydic fragrances.''

''Aldehydic? What are those?''

''Synthetic substitutions that approximate nature's originals. Although frowned upon by master perfumers, who consider themselves purists, synthetics combined with natural plant absolutes can make very pleasing and effective perfumes.''

''And Helena would have to know some chemistry to come up with these aldehydics?''

''She would be involved, yes.''

''Then that means she might know enough chemistry to have discovered something that kills by stopping the heart.''

''Is that how they all died?''

''According to all the autopsies.''

''No blockage? Hemorrhage?''

''None. Their hearts just stopped beating. The pathologists my company consults with can't offer an explanation. If there's an agent causing these heart attacks, and there must be one, it resists detection in an autopsy. And it leaves no evidence of damage to the heart muscles or vessels.''

''So that's why you think it's new and were so suspicious of my experiments.''

''Yes. And now I'm looking toward someone else who may have discovered such an agent. Will we learn how Helena manages her purification process in her presentation tomorrow?''

"If she presents tomorrow after all this trouble, you can be sure you won't learn about how she does it. That's a trade secret."

"Too bad. All right. Let's look at it from another angle. Who would benefit from learning the trade secrets of any of the perfume stars?"

"A competing perfume company. MW would love to learn how Helena blends so perfectly. Just as it will do its best, I'm sure, to analyze Louis's beautiful new scent-infused polymer containers. And, if they could get a hold of them, Kohei's scented earrings and his research on scent as a mental stimulator in the workplace."

"Does MW or any of the other perfume companies employ spies?"

"Robert, I don't know. Maybe. But if MW does, no one's ever mentioned it to me. I pretty much spend all my time in the lab."

"Yes, I can attest to that. You don't even leave it for lunch."

His words surprised her. She turned to him. "No, I don't. How did you know that?"

"Because I parked my behind outside that lab door for several days waiting for you to leave so I could bump into you and introduce myself. I missed several meals."

She smiled. "Serves you right for thinking I could be a murderer. So now what's next?"

"What do you know about Peter Campbell?"

"He's sophisticated and intelligent and full of understated English charm."

"That professional or personal knowledge?"

Diann smiled. "How about both?"

Robert looked down at his slacks to finger a nonexistent piece of lint. His voice was perfectly even—too perfectly even. "How personal have you gotten to know him?"

At that moment Diann decided that it was too bad she was so straightforward. If she had been a more devious woman, she could have had some fun with the jealousy she sensed sizzling just below Robert's calm surface. That he could be jealous gave her an excited little thrill.

Point two for feminine charms.

"Actually, I haven't gotten to know Peter personally."

Diann watched as the tension that had been growing in Robert's shoulders relaxed. "So what does Peter Campbell have to offer professionally?"

"Peter is amazing for his ability to distribute Regal Bouquet's products. Everywhere you go, there they are. Even in the bathroom in my suite here I found a complimentary quarter ounce of ROYALTY, one of their top fragrances. When you remember France is the perfume capital of the world and the Hôtel de Crillon a totally French-owned hotel, the significance of Peter's having gotten one of his company's perfumes to grace its elegant tile baths begins to bring home how effective a distributor he is."

"So could someone be killing off these people to get hold of their secrets?"

"Killing them isn't going to help a competitor gain access to their secrets, Robert. I suppose you could stretch it and say that one of the perfume companies could theoretically benefit if the stars from all the others were killed. But these companies we're dealing with are multibillion-dollar entities. Individuals—even such talented stars as are present at this conference—can eventually be replaced. The corporate gurus outthink, outmaneuver, out-R-and-D their competitors. They don't go out and murder them."

"Well, someone is doing just that. If it isn't someone from the perfume companies, that just leaves us with one other possibility. What can you tell me about Gabrielle and Conrad Rife?"

"You can't really suspect Gabrielle or Conrad."

"Since Conrad was in Macon when both Kohei and Louis died, I admit he's off the hook. But Gabrielle isn't. Tell me about her."

His look was straight, strong, decisive. Diann felt the power of the man, focused and unyielding. For many reasons she was profoundly glad she was no longer his suspect.

"Gabrielle is a woman who's always been in love with perfume. She tried starting her own perfume company, but although she's quite good at organization, she couldn't lure the talent she wanted away from the established firms. Being a perfectionist like the rest of us, she finally gave up the effort in total frustration."

"She ever try to recruit you?"

"Oh, yes. Quite strongly, as a matter of fact."

"But you weren't tempted?"

"No. MW gave me my start. They recognized my talent and promoted me very quickly. I owed them my loyalty. Besides, I had my experiments going with SNIFF. Disrupting them by moving to another company could have cost me time, and I've always considered time too precious to lose."

"Do you know if Gabrielle tried to recruit any of the other winners of the PERFUME awards?"

"Oh, I'm sure she tried to recruit them all."

"To no avail, apparently."

"Well, you can't blame them. Moving to a new company would have been a gamble. If Gabrielle's venture failed— which it did—it's not like they could go back to the job they left. Perfume companies consider an employee who takes his or her expertise elsewhere a traitor."

"So what did Gabrielle do after her company failed?"

"That's when she talked Conrad into forming the Fragrance Fraternity and its literary arm, *Redolence* magazine. Frankly, I think she's happier in her new role. She has a professional staff who run the magazine. She focuses her energy on her monthly column, 'Rife with *Redolence*,' in which she tastefully highlights the glamour and glitz associated with perfume."

"Like?"

"Oh, like what fragrances the rich and famous prefer and why. Conrad and she travel in some pretty exclusive circles."

"And the magazine is the industry's trade journal."

"There are others, but *Redolence* is the most respected and sets the industry standard."

"Did Gabrielle select you and the others to receive the PERFUME awards?"

"Not personally. Her magazine staff does that. Although I'm sure she has the ultimate veto should she disagree."

"And Conrad? How does he fit in?"

"He's her financial and emotional support. He tries to be at her side at every function, even with a demanding recycling business."

"His financial statements show he's expanding significantly every year. I didn't realize how much money there was in waste recycling until I got a look at his healthy balance sheets. The Rifes are millionaires many times over."

Diann paused to think that one over. "Doesn't surprise me. Have you done background checks on everyone?"

"Everyone who is suspect."

"Then you must already know about Helena, Peter and Gabrielle. Why are you asking me?"

"You're an insider to the business. I thought your perceptions might bring to light something I've missed."

"Have they?"

"I'm getting a better understanding of the perfume business and why these people are stars."

Diann didn't want to ask her next question, particularly since she already knew what the answer would be. But as always, her curiosity got the best of her.

"You've done a background check on me, too, haven't you?"

He looked suddenly uncomfortable. "Yes."

Diann lifted her chin defiantly. "So what did you learn?"

"Your father and mother were divorced when you were fifteen. Your father was awarded custody of you and your thirteen-year-old sister, Connie. You went away to college when you were eighteen. You were an honor student all the way through. You started working for MW while you were still in school getting your advanced degrees. You stayed with them after graduation. You work hard, too hard."

Diann didn't like the idea that someone could learn so much about her without her being aware of it. A defensive sarcasm laced her next words. "Didn't miss a thing, did you?"

"Actually, I felt that I missed a lot. I've wanted to know why you've worked so hard. Why you seem to be so driven."

She tried for a lighter tone. There were some things she wasn't ready to discuss with him. Maybe she'd never be. "So your investigation of me turned up nothing juicy?"

He watched her silently for a moment. "There hasn't been anything juicy in your life, Diann. You live in a modest one-bedroom apartment and sleep in the living room because your bedroom is the home for hundreds of laboratory mice. You pay your bills promptly. Periodically you date the professional men you call friends and have known awhile. You're not serious about any of them."

"How do you know that?"

"By the way you kissed me."

She watched the sudden decisive light in his eyes as he moved closer. His hands gently stroked through her hair and then circled around to her nape. Shimmers of excitement shifted down her spine.

His voice lowered to that deep, delicious sound that vibrated like an exciting hum in her ears. "I know having someone coldly gathering up the facts of your life seems intrusive, but understand we were after a murderer, and we sought to find out whatever we could in whatever way we could."

She looked into those eyes that could portray so damn much sincerity and fought against getting swept away. "All right. I suppose I can understand that."

He smiled that devastating smile of his and leaned over to brush her lips with his. Considering the quick chaste execution of that kiss, it left a hell of a heat ripple in its wake.

Diann felt the warmth right down to her toes.

Then he suddenly leaned back and dropped his hands to hers. "I could use your help."

His words surprised her. "My help? How?"

"I have some tapes I'd like you to listen to with me. They're in my room. Are you too tired?"

After that kiss? Was he kidding? "No, I'm fine. What are these tapes?"

"I'll explain when we get there."

ROBERT LIKED the idea of recruiting Diann from the moment it had popped into his head. For one, she knew the perfume business and could understand conversations in its technical jargon far better than either he or Cassel. And for two, by making her part of the investigation, he could keep her safely beside him.

Now that he was sure she wasn't a suspect, she had fallen into the other category—potential victim. And that thought sent a sliver of ice down his spine.

"You're frowning. Something wrong?" she asked from beside him.

He eased a smile onto his face. The thought would occur to her soon enough. No sense in hitting her with everything at once. "Everything's fine. As long as you're beside me."

She looked so lovely in the subdued hall light, her long, maple-sugar hair rustling past her shoulders, her skin flushing slightly at the meaning in his words.

For one mad moment back in her room, looking into that open lovely face, he'd had to fight an overwhelming desire to make love to her right there and then. But even if she had let him, and that was a big if, her room was still bugged, and he had no intention of letting Cassel listen in on some things.

But he would remove those bugs later. And then—

"You said you were the manager of the creative-arts division at Worldwide Insurance. Do you normally do your own hands-on investigation?"

"Sometimes I'm forced to when I can't find a particular expertise among my staff."

"Like when you became a major league pitcher last year?"

"Yes, although the manager, who was our informant on the team, hustled me in without putting me up against any real competition."

"Did you actually play in any games?"

"One. I legitimately struck out two batters before faking my shoulder injury."

"You faked an injury?"

"It was all part of the plan to catch an unscrupulous team doctor who was submitting false insurance claims on manufactured injuries."

"Oh, I see. Did the plan work?"

He hesitated. "Yes."

She looked at him closely. "But something went wrong, didn't it?"

Somehow she'd been able to sense his dissatisfaction. Had he let his guard down so much with her already?

"Diann, the doctor was a ruddy-cheeked, round little gal of sixty who spent her weekends giving free medical care to underprivileged youngsters who were being ignored by everyone else. She was scamming Worldwide with the false insurance claims on the baseball players so she could fund that clinic for the kids. And I was the one who masterminded the sting operation that caught her."

Diann's face clouded. "She went to jail?"

"No. We stopped her scam, of course. But when it was time to send the evidence to the police, my office... ah... misplaced it."

Robert suddenly felt her hand in his, the clasp of her fingers. He couldn't explain the feeling that swept through him then. He knew only that his heart beat stronger and lighter because she had not only understood what he had done, but approved.

As they approached his room, Robert and Diann halted as a door two rooms down opened. Out came the bushy-haired, mustached man whom Robert recognized as the hotel employee who had assisted at both Kohei's and Louis's presentations. He had a familiar-looking box cupped beneath his arm.

He turned his portly uniformed shape back toward the open door.

"I will see it is locked in the hotel safe immediately, Madame Strunk. You can count on me."

Helena's head emerged as she slipped the hotel employee his tip. Then she suddenly gripped the man's arm when she caught sight of Diann and Robert. A look of definite dismay crossed her face, before she wiped it off and sent a nod of acknowledgment in their direction. She retreated into her room and closed the door. Robert watched the rotund little man scoot off down the hall, whistling "April in Paris."

"Now, what do you suppose all that was about?" Diann asked.

Robert frowned. "I don't know. But I do know that that box looks just like one Louis Magnen was carrying the morning of his presentation. I wonder what Helena is doing with it? Come on in. Maybe we can find out."

Robert got out his key and began to worry about how he was going to tell Diann her room was bugged before she figured it out for herself. He had no doubt the thought would occur to her after listening to the taped conversations of the others.

She wouldn't be happy about it, of course. But he was going to have to take it just one step at a time with her. One very careful step at a time. He couldn't lose her now. Not now.

He wiped the growing frown off his forehead and sent her an easy smile as he opened the door and gestured her inside. Diann let out a small exclamation and halted almost immediately inside the door. Robert stiffened, then relaxed as he saw Cassel's copper-colored head slumped onto his chest as he lay sprawled across the couch. Robert stepped in and closed the door behind him.

He rested a hand on Diann's shoulder. "It's all right. I expected him to be here. He must have fallen asleep waiting for me."

Surprise skipped in her voice. "You have a roommate?"

"Not exactly."

Robert moved over to the couch and leaned down to give Cassel's shoulder a nudge. And then another.

"Come on, Cassel. Wake up."

Cassel didn't move. Alarm flashed through Robert.

Quickly he lifted Cassel's head and leaned it back against the sofa. Then he placed his fingers at the pulse point in Cassel's neck as he dropped his ear next to Cassel's mouth.

Diann moved alongside. "I recognize this man. He's one of the attendees to the symposium. What's wrong with him?"

After a long, silent moment, Robert straightened into a stiff, tight form beside her. His eyes took in the three tapes dotting the light beige cushions, the tape player sitting on the table. A full, open bottle of wine and a single clean glass sat next to the tape player. On the carpet lay a corkscrew, the cork still embedded in it.

"Robert, what's wrong?"

"He's dead."

"What?"

Robert grabbed for the phone and punched in the number for room service. "This is Robert Mize. Did you deliver a bottle of wine to my room this evening?"

"No, *monsieur*. Is there something we can get for you?"

"No, thank you."

Robert hung up the phone.

"Robert, how can this man be dead? What is going on?"

Robert turned to Diann, saw the shock on her face. His hands encircled her shoulders. "I'm sorry. I wish I could give you time to absorb this properly, but we haven't got time. This man was not just another attendee. His name was Cassel. He worked for me."

"Worked for you? You mean at Worldwide?"

"Yes. He was one of my top investigators. And now he's dead—without a mark on him."

She stiffened within his hold as her eyes saucered. "Robert. You mean, like the others?"

"Yes."

"But you said someone was killing off the top stars of the perfume industry. Why would this man be killed?"

"At the moment I haven't the faintest idea. I just know that this recorder and these tapes can't be found with him."

Robert looked into Diann's eyes, trying to judge if her outward calm went more than skin-deep. "Diann, you've got to trust me. Do you?"

She answered with a straight look from those clear eyes. "Yes. What do you want me to do?"

"I want you to hide this tape recorder and these tapes in your room."

"Why?"

"They'll search my room, since Cassel died in it. But they won't search yours."

"Who won't?"

"The police."

Robert watched her swallow uneasily. But she didn't flinch. "Will they find out he worked for you?"

"Eventually. But they mustn't find out about the tapes."

"What's on the tapes?"

"Conversations. Recorded illegally."

She licked her lips, but her look did not waver. "While I'm hiding the tapes, what will you be doing?"

"I'll be removing the rest of the equipment from Cassel's room. It's next door."

"When you say 'the rest of the equipment,' I assume you mean the equipment that was used to record these tapes?"

"Yes."

"After I hide the tapes, what do you want me to do?"

"I'll meet you back at your room. Then you'll accompany me here, where we will call the police and report finding him dead when we walked in. I'd leave you out of this entirely, but Helena saw us together in the hall outside my room and she's bound to tell the police. They'll know you must have come inside."

"I see. But neither of us will mention the tapes or equipment to the police. We'll say we came in, found the man and called them. Is that right?"

"That's it. But we'll have to move quickly so there's no obvious gap in time. Well, what do you say?"

She hesitated. Robert held his breath.

He was taking a hell of a chance with his freedom and hers. If she refused to help or talked, he'd be thrown into a French prison for an extended stay. If she went along with him on this, she'd become an accessory.

He was putting her in a hell of a position. But what choice did he have? If the police found out about these illegal tapes, he would go to jail. And if he went to jail, she'd be left alone with no protection against whoever it was who was preying on the perfume industry's top stars.

He could see a lot of figuring of her own going on behind those expressive eyes. When they finally refocused on his, a warm glow had formed in their liquid centers.

"We'd better hide the tapes and machine in a towel or something. We can't afford to have someone see me carrying them back to my room."

INSPECTOR PINCHOT seated Robert and Diann next to each other on the bed in Robert's room and stood over them. Diann decided his normally polite tone was definitely fraying around the edges.

"So you walked in to find this Monsieur Cassel lying dead in your room, is that right, Monsieur Mize?"

"Yes, Inspector. As I told you, I met Cassel at the symposium. I gave him my key and asked him to meet me here in my room for a drink."

"You meet this Monsieur Cassel and already you trust him with a key to your room?"

Robert smiled. "He was from Philadelphia, too. We call it the City of Brotherly Love."

Inspector Pinchot's brows pinched together. "And that is all of it?"

Diann could feel the tension in Robert. She circled her hand over his as it lay spuriously motionless on the spread.

Ever since Robert had come to her rescue that evening and taken her into his confidence, he'd won her trust completely. She found herself following his instructions without a qualm. As they faced the indomitable Inspector Pinchot together, she knew where her loyalties lay.

Robert leaned slightly forward. "If you're asking me how he died, I know no more than you do, Inspector."

"You know no more than I," the policeman repeated.

"That's right."

"You're just two innocent American tourists attending a symposium."

Diann bristled at the sarcasm in the man's words. "Inspector Pinchot, we have reported the death of a man. We have not caused it. You've no right to imply otherwise."

"And is that what you think I was implying, *mademoiselle?*"

"Well, wasn't it?"

"Withholding evidence is a serious offense, *mademoiselle*. Not as serious as murder, of course, but serious nonetheless."

Diann looked away from Pinchot's sharp eyes, knowing that the guilt was probably filling her own at that moment. Robert must have known it, too, because he hurried to intervene.

"Inspector, if you've asked all your questions, I'd like to escort Ms. Torrey to her room. This has been a very upsetting experience for her."

"And not for you, *monsieur?* You have no desire to shed a tear or two for Auguste Cassel?"

"What do you mean?"

Inspector Pinchot shook his head like an abused man. "Ah, Monsieur Mize, why do I think it would not surprise you to know that this symposium attendee, this Auguste Cassel, has identification in his pocket that says he works for Worldwide Insurance?"

Diann felt the tension increase in Robert, although his voice remained amazingly even and calm.

"Has he?"

"Monsieur Mize, please. No more we play these little games."

"What kind of game are you referring to, Inspector?"

"It does no good to pretend. You see, I know what you really do and who you really are."

Diann felt the air in the room suddenly get very heavy. It pressed in on her chest.

She watched an unreadable expression cross Robert's face. His eyes never left Pinchot's satisfied smile.

Inspector Pinchot folded his very neat and proper hands across his trim waist. "Robert Mize, there is no reason to deny your identity anymore."

"I've never denied my identity. I told you who I was when we first spoke."

"Ah, but you did not mention that your middle name was Duchamp."

"Duchamp?" Diann repeated.

"Nor did you mention who you really work for. It was not until I called Worldwide Insurance that I learned you managed their creative-arts branch. But then, even they do not know everything about your past, do they?"

Inspector Pinchot smiled as he tapped his temple. "I thought you looked familiar, but it has been more than twenty years and I was a young gendarme when it all occurred, and the boy has grown into a man, yes? But the memory, she sees a trace of the familiar and I do check the police records. And there I find you."

Diann didn't like the sound of this. Her stomach did a sick somersault. She turned to the man she had been assuring herself she absolutely trusted and studied his face.

"A police record? Robert, what is he talking about?"

Chapter Nine

Inspector Pinchot raised an eyebrow of inquiry in Robert's direction. "So you have not told *mademoiselle* all? Shall I do the honors or shall you, *monsieur?*"

Robert executed a beautiful French shrug, which did nothing to reassure Diann's unease.

Inspector Pinchot turned to her. "Monsieur Mize is known to the French police already, *mademoiselle*. He was a boy of twelve playing on the streets of Paris when he witnessed a local petty official murder his mistress. The gendarmes still speak of the local boy who gave witness before the magistrate like a man. They speak of him with respect."

Diann's eyes flew to Robert as relief washed through her. A police record had conjured up far-less-palatable possibilities.

Robert returned her gaze, looking decidedly uncomfortable, as well he should.

"Two years of high school French?" she said much too sweetly.

He grinned a bit ruefully as the shot hit its mark. "Did I happen to mention I got straight A's both years?"

She refused to let that sexy grin placate her. "I'll bet. So you're really French?"

"More accurately, half French. It's a long story."

"And one we presently do not have time for," Inspector Pinchot interrupted. "*Monsieur, mademoiselle,* perhaps we can return to the very important business at hand?"

"All right, Inspector," Robert said. "I do work for Worldwide. But I didn't lie to you when we first spoke. I also work for Man to Woman Perfumes and I am an official member of this symposium."

"That's true," Diann interjected.

"Please," Inspector Pinchot said, holding up his hands to halt further explanations or denials. "I know that is only your, how do you say, cloak?"

"Cover," Robert said, correcting him.

"Yes, thank you. Cover. And you need this cover because you know that Worldwide's investigators are not licensed to operate in France. Is this not so?"

"Cassel and I were just trying to find this murderer, Inspector. We weren't trying to step on anybody's toes."

"Well, my toes *have* been stepped on, *monsieur.* By omission you lied when I questioned you twice before. It is only because you were once that brave boy that this conversation is taking place in your room and not down at headquarters. But the surroundings can change at any time should I deem that any more less-than-truthful answers require it. I am making myself clear, yes?"

Robert nodded.

"Good. Now, I want to know how many more of your employees beside this Cassel are in Paris."

"None."

"You expect me to believe that a company the size of Worldwide sends only two investigators?"

"My company didn't want to send any, Inspector. Cassel and I came at my insistence."

"Your company did not want to investigate what it believes to be the possible loss of millions of dollars?"

"There were those who felt the way to handle the situation was to simply notify the various police forces of our suspicions and cancel the policies of those at risk, thereby removing our involvement and liability.''

Diann could see that Robert's explanation gave Inspector Pinchot pause. The sharp edge to his tone softened somewhat. "I see. But this was not the way you felt?"

"Someone's getting away with murder, Inspector. Stepping aside and letting him get on with it is not my idea of how best to handle the situation."

Inspector Pinchot rocked back on his heels and smiled. "So the boy can be found in the man. This does not displease me. What was Cassel doing in your room?"

"I had called him when Ms. Torrey and I returned from our evening out and asked him to stop by my room. When I later brought Ms. Torrey to my room, we found him as you saw him."

"So Mademoiselle Torrey was in your confidence? She knew about your real purpose here?"

"I only told her a few minutes before we found Cassel's body, Inspector. Prior to that she knew only that I worked for the same company she did."

"Mademoiselle Torrey's name was on the list of suspects Worldwide forwarded to my office. You no longer consider her suspect?"

Robert looked at Diann, interlaced his fingers with hers and smiled before turning back to Inspector Pinchot. "After getting to know her, I no longer consider her a suspect. On the contrary. I now feel her knowledge of the perfume industry might be able to help me trap this murderer."

Inspector Pinchot's brow clouded. "No, *monsieur*. You and *mademoiselle* will attempt to catch no one. You will leave this investigation to me."

"Inspector Pinchot, I have reason to have great respect for the French police. But as your medical examiner has not found a causative agent for these deaths and there is not a mark on the bodies, what can you do?"

"I can keep everyone involved in this perfume symposium in Paris until I do **find** a causative agent, *monsieur*. I plan to get to the bottom of these deaths. The very bottom."

"Did Gabrielle Rife talk to you about wanting to move the symposium from the hotel?"

"She did. And I have forbidden it. Everything has been thoroughly checked. The Hôtel de Crillon is perfectly safe. There is no Legionnaire bug here. Oh, yes. I have heard all about it. But then, you knew it wasn't such a bacteria we are battling. What will your company do now that Cassel is dead?"

"I don't know. His murder doesn't fit the pattern."

Inspector Pinchot pointed to the open bottle of wine. "Was that here when you left?"

"No."

"Did Monsieur Cassel bring it?"

"I don't know."

"Did you or Mademoiselle Torrey touch it?"

"No."

Inspector Pinchot eyed Robert silently for a moment. "And you have no idea how these people's hearts are being stopped?"

"I assure you, Inspector, if I did you'd be hearing about it."

Pinchot turned suddenly to Diann. "And you, *mademoiselle?* Can you not shed any light on these mysterious deaths?"

Diann was taken aback by the total lack of patience in the inspector's voice this time.

She straightened. "No, of course not. I didn't even know these deaths weren't natural ones until Robert told me this evening."

"And have you two been together all evening?"

"Yes, we have," Robert said quickly before Diann had a chance to put her foot in her mouth. She instantly understood that he lied to protect her secret visit to Dr. Béraud. She was very grateful for his quick thinking and his support.

Inspector Pinchot turned back to Diann. "Every moment?"

Diann knew it would be politically astute to throw him a bone. Besides, she was already sure her expression had displayed equivocation. "Well, not exactly every moment. When we got back to the hotel we did separate for about twenty minutes so that we could take our respective showers and get changed. We were quite wet."

"And how did you get this quite wet?"

Diann suddenly felt Robert's arm slipping around her waist and his pulling her to his side as his face smoothed into a smile. "We were walking in the rain, enjoying the evening in the City of Light."

The implication was clear. Two lovers out walking, oblivious to even the rain. Not a difficult image for a Frenchman to accept. Diann plastered a smile on her face and hoped to hell her guilty conscience wouldn't shine too visibly through it.

She needn't have worried. Inspector Pinchot completely wiped away that smile and her guilty conscience with his next sentence.

"You say Auguste Cassel's death does not fit the pattern. But have you considered, Monsieur Mize, that the fact that your man Cassel was murdered probably means that the killer is aware of your pursuit and now pursues you?"

"ROBERT, was Inspector Pinchot right? Does the murderer know who you really are?"

Robert pointed toward the liquor in Diann's bar, but she shook her head. He poured himself a straight whiskey and came to sit beside her on the couch.

"I don't see how. Cassel and I have been very careful. And if the killer murdered Cassel because he knew Cassel was working for me, why didn't he or she take the tapes? A murderer would have to be curious what was on them."

"Maybe the killer didn't know about the tapes."

Robert shook his head. "They were sitting right next to Cassel."

"Could the murderer have played them and decided they didn't implicate him or her?"

"You see someone killing Cassel and then calmly sitting down and playing the tapes they found with him? No, the killer would want to be away from the scene of his crime as quickly as possible. There's nothing about this whole business that makes any sense anymore."

Diann watched him take a slug of the whiskey and then rub his eyes as though trying to rub away some stubborn image. The calm demeanor he'd presented to Inspector Pinchot earlier was gone. Quite gone.

"What is it, Robert?"

He drew his hand away from his eyes. When he looked at her now, she saw the pain in them.

"Cassel wasn't just an employee. He was a friend. We were kids together on the streets of Paris. I owed him my life."

Her hand found his forearm, her fingers curling round the tightened muscles. "I'd like to hear about it."

Robert studied his whiskey glass as he exhaled a breath that seemed heavy with memories. Then he turned to look into her face. "Where to begin? I suppose the logical place would be to explain about my very hardheaded parents. My father was born in the States. My mother, in France."

"That's what you meant when you said you were half French?"

"Yes. They've had a tempestuous relationship throughout the years, always breaking up and getting back together again. They've separated at least a dozen times and have actually divorced each other twice. But each time they've remarried. At the moment, they're back together. But who knows what tomorrow will bring?''

"You must have had an interesting upbringing."

A subdued chuckle broke through. "Well, it was never dull, at least. Anyway, when I was five, my parents divorced for the first time and my mother took me to Paris to live with my grandparents. I was called Robert Duchamp then, my mother's maiden name. My parents reconciled when I was six, and my father came to live with us here. He left again when I was eleven. A year later I witnessed the murder Inspector Pinchot spoke of on the streets near our home in Paris."

"A man who killed his mistress?"

"Yes, a petty official. He shot her in a fit of rage when she walked away from his car. When he realized I'd seen him do it, he shot at me, too, but I ran. The day before I was to testify against him, he sent some thugs to quiet me for good."

Diann's hand tightened on Robert's arm. He paused to give it a reassuring pat.

"Cassel saw the men coming after me. He was only twelve, but he grabbed a knife, rounded up several of our buddies and came to my rescue. I was nearly beaten unconscious by the time he led his youthful gang yelling into that alley, waving kitchen knives. Amazingly, the thugs ran."

"And you testified despite the attempt on your life."

He smiled then and Diann thought she was seeing that very angry and very determined boy of twelve.

"On crutches, with one arm in a sling, both eyes nearly swollen shut and a face that not even my mother could recognize. You bet I testified."

"The man was convicted?"

Robert nodded. "Got a life sentence. He vowed he'd get me. That's when my mother decided to take no chances and moved us both back to the States. Soon afterward, she and my dad got back together again. For a while, anyway."

"Is the man you testified against still in jail?"

"No. He died several years later in prison."

"And you remained friends with Cassel?"

"Actually, we lost track of each other when I left France. We hooked up again when he came to the States looking for a job a few years back. I hired him as an investigator for Worldwide. He was a damn good one, too."

Robert took another gulp of his whiskey.

"What about his family? Will you have to call them?"

"His parents are both dead. There's an uncle. I phoned him when I got the equipment out of Cassel's room. He'll claim the body after the autopsy, let me know when the funeral will be."

"I'm so sorry."

He put down the half-empty glass, his handsome face drawn into an emotion so fierce it gave her a chill.

"We don't have time to feel sorry about Cassel, Diann. I want to, God knows I do, but I can't. We've got to go over these tapes. We've got to figure out who in the hell is killing these people and why. Or it's going to keep happening. You realize that? More people are going to die."

She knew then as he looked at her that his fear was for her. Ever since he'd explained about the deaths of the perfume stars, she had understood that she, too, was at risk. But this direct look sent an icy chill up her spine. She nodded silently as she reached for one of the tapes at random.

"The strip on this tape has some markings. It says HS to LM and has yesterday's date at seven p.m."

"HS stands for Helena Strunk. LM is Louis Magnen. The 'to' means that Louis called Helena on the phone. The rest is the date and time of the call. Put it into the machine and let's hear it."

Diann did so and pressed the Play button. A ringing of a telephone was the first sound. Louis answered almost immediately. Helena identified herself.

"Finally, Helena. What took you so long?"

"*I was with my man.*"

"*Well? He has looked it over, no? What do you say?*"

"*He is undecided, Louis. The style and color appear correct, but he wants to subject it to the full barrage of tests to ensure it's—*"

"*Helena, I do not have the time or patience for this. You have known from the first that these tests you speak of cannot be done. What do you think—I would cheat you? And where would I run after you found out? Tell me please, Helena, where do you think I would run?*"

"*All right, Louis. Enough. I will pay what you ask. But it will take time to get that much money.*"

"*How long?*"

"*A day. Could be more.*"

"*How much more? Two days? Three? I must know, Helena.*"

"*Well, I cannot tell you. Wilhelm is not at home when I call. The boys do not know where he has gone. I have left word. When he calls back it will be arranged. I can do no more.*"

"*Helena—*"

"*I will let you know,*" Helena said. Then she hung up.

Robert stopped the tape and turned to Diann. "What do you make of that?"

"I don't know. Who are the boys and Wilhelm?"

"The boys could be her teenage sons back at her home in Frankfurt. She's called them a couple of times from her room."

"Then maybe Wilhelm is her husband?"

"No. She's divorced. I'm interested in that merchandise Louis and Helena talked about on that tape. When they mentioned style and color, what does that mean in perfume terms?"

"Those don't sound like perfume terms to me, Robert. Oh, we talk about the style and color of different containers, of course, but—"

"Could Louis have been negotiating with Helena to sell her a new container idea he developed for La Belle perfumes?"

Diann's brow furrowed. "Louis always impressed me as an honest man. The idea of him selling his company's secrets just doesn't seem possible."

"Maybe not, but that box Helena asked that hotel employee to lock up for her was Louis's. And it has to be valuable. Otherwise Helena wouldn't have been trying to get it in the safe."

"But, Robert, putting something valuable in a cardboard box?"

"Could be a smart move, Diann. If the container is ordinary, then the contents might be considered ordinary, too."

"I can't think of what Louis could have possibly done to top those new scent-infused containers he presented."

"What about the secret of their manufacture? Could that have been what he was selling?"

"I suppose another company would pay handsomely for the process. Having the exact formula would certainly save a lot of time trying to dissect the containers and discover it on their own. Damn, Robert, I hate thinking this. Louis was at the zenith of his career, the undisputed top in his field. Why would he do anything so unethical as sell out a company secret?"

"Maybe he had to have the money."

"Why do you say that?"

"Cassel recorded an earlier conversation with his wife where Louis complained somewhat desperately about their finances."

Diann shook her head as she fingered the remaining two tapes. "I don't know, Robert. I still can't believe Louis would let financial need win over ethics. There's got to be another explanation."

"Like what?"

"If I had one I'd offer it. Maybe we'll find something else on the remaining tapes. This next one is labeled GR and PC. Gabrielle Rife and Peter Campbell?"

"Yes."

"It's dated this afternoon. Shall I play it next?"

"Might as well."

Diann slipped the old tape out of the recorder and replaced it with the new one. Then she hit the Play button.

The first thing she heard was laughter and the sound of a door opening. Then she heard Gabrielle's voice saying quite distinctly, *"Peter, close the door quickly. Someone might see us."*

"Don't worry, sweet. No one's in the hall."

The sound of the door closing came next and then a giggle from Gabrielle. *"Ooooh, that feels so good. I can't wait to get out of these clothes and get you out of yours."* Diann's eyes flashed to Robert. From his steady return gaze, she could see that nothing he was hearing was coming as a surprise.

The next few minutes of the tape were very uncomfortable for Diann. Not a whole lot of conversation could be distinguished. But the sounds were unmistakable. When the couple moved toward the bed and the tape kept recording, Diann finally stopped it, having had enough.

Diann turned to Robert, read the expression on his face. "You knew this about Gabrielle and Peter?"

"Let's just say I knew this about Gabrielle."

"Are you saying that she's done this with other men?"

"I don't know about other men. But she came on to me hot and heavy before Louis's presentation this morning."

Diann shook her head, let out a weary breath. "I suppose it shouldn't surprise me. I saw her with Peter in the bar this afternoon before I left for Dr. Béraud's."

"But it still surprises you. Why? Because of Peter or because of Gabrielle?"

"Because of Conrad, actually. He's quite in love with his wife. I can't understand a woman betraying that kind of love. I don't ever think I'll be able to look Gabrielle straight in the eyes again."

"Maybe you shouldn't. You don't have much of a poker face."

Diann took a deep breath and let it out slowly. "I know."

He rested a warm hand on her shoulder. "Don't look so unhappy about it, Diann. Being too genuine to pretend is one of your nicest qualities."

The way he said it and the glow in his eyes set Diann's heart to skipping. She returned her attention quickly to the tapes. "The mark on this last one says CR to GR, six p.m. and today's date. CR to GR means Conrad called Gabrielle on the phone this afternoon, right?"

"You got it."

Diann replaced the old tape with this last one and pressed the Play button. She instantly recognized Conrad's voice.

"Gabrielle, where have you been? I've been calling for hours."

Gabrielle hesitated, as well she might, Diann thought, considering who she was with and what she'd been doing.

"Conrad, I'm sorry. But I've had so many unexpected things to attend to. Things here have been so very...difficult without you."

"I know. I just heard about Kohei's and Louis's deaths on the radio. Dearest, why didn't you tell me about them when I phoned before?"

"I wanted to. But I was so afraid if I did you'd insist on coming back to Paris, and the doctor said—"

"To hell with the damn doctor, Gabrielle. I am coming to Paris. I'm leaving on tomorrow's train."

"No, Conrad. Please. This is exactly what I was afraid of. You can't—"

"Gabrielle, I know how much these very special people mean to you. Do you think I would let you face the horror

of their deaths alone? What kind of a husband would that make me?"

"But your heart—"

"Will mend much faster by your side. Now, don't bother about meeting the train. I'm not sure which one I'll be on. I'll see you in your room at the hotel. And, dearest..."

"Yes?"

"Don't worry. We'll get through this. You know I love you, don't you?"

"Yes, Conrad. And I love you, too. So very much."

The recording ended on Gabrielle's sigh.

Diann looked at Robert, her lips twisted in anger. "How can Gabrielle lie to him that way? How can she make a commitment to marriage and then turn her back on it and the man who loves her so much? I'll never understand people. Never."

Robert watched her quietly for a moment. "Gabrielle's a fool, I agree. But there are people who take their marriage commitments seriously."

She whirled on him. "Oh? You know any?"

"Diann, what's this all about?"

Diann felt a certain irritated bristling across the back of he neck. "I just hate to see Gabrielle acting this way. And Peter's no better. He's a single man. Why can't he direct his attentions to a single woman? Damn it, Conrad's in love with his wife. It would kill him if he found out how little she really cared."

"You don't think she really loves him?"

"You think she can really love him and still be with another man? That's not love. That's a joke. But then, I've often thought love is just a joke, and marriage merely one of its sicker punch lines."

"Is that what you've thought, Diann?"

Diann saw the serious light in his eyes. He hadn't asked a frivolous question. He wanted to know what she thought.

He might be sorry to learn. An unusual beep coming out of the recording equipment interrupted, making Diann give a little jump. "What's that?"

"A warning that someone is using a telephone in one of the rooms. I'll turn up the volume so we can listen to the conversation."

A man's voice answered, a bit sleepy and indistinct.

"Peter, I must see you."

"Gabrielle, it's nearly one in the morning. Is this really so urgent?"

"He's coming back tomorrow, Peter. He's heard about Kohei and Louis."

"Oh, I see. Tough luck, sweet. For us both."

"There's still tonight, Peter. I just took my bath, and what do you think I found in the bath salts but your wonderful Bouquet fragrance. It's all I'm wearing. How soon can you be here?"

"Gabrielle, in five minutes I shall be flying down the hallway and into your arms."

The phone went dead and the recording clicked off. Robert moved to adjust one of the knobs.

Diann moved beside him. "What are you doing?"

"Turning the volume up so we can hear what happens when Peter comes flying down that hallway."

She shook her head. "I don't understand this. Conrad called Gabrielle at six p.m., according to the markings on this other tape. Why did she wait until after one in the morning before calling Peter?"

"You forget, Diann. They spent a whole afternoon in similar activity. She probably needed some time to recharge her batteries."

Diann shifted in her seat at the images his words brought. She saw his hands moving over the controls, trying to fine-tune them. She felt absolutely miserable. "Robert, walking in on two people being indiscreet in a public bar is one thing. Having a microphone in someone's bedroom is another."

"My intent isn't to eavesdrop on anyone's sex life, Diann. But I want to know just how upset these two are that the husband is coming back."

"Why?"

"Someone already made an attempt on Conrad's life, remember? If it's his wife and/or her paramour, maybe we'll hear something."

"But what could Gabrielle's fooling around with Peter have to do with either Kohei's or Louis's death?"

"I don't know, and that's exactly the point. These killings are bizarre. Maybe their reason is equally bizarre."

Diann pushed the hair back from her face. "I don't care how necessary this is, it's awful. You bugged my suite, too, didn't you?"

He paused to look over at her. "The first night you let me into your room. One's under the lip of the liquor table. The other's in the phone."

Diann knew it, of course. On some level. But hearing him confirm it was another thing. Her stomach turned as the invasion of her privacy registered.

He read the distress in her face. "Shall I remove them now?"

She nodded silently.

He got up, walked over to the liquor table and, after running his fingers underneath an edge, slipped out a small cylindrical object barely a quarter of an inch long. Then he unscrewed the mouthpiece of the phone and removed another. He pocketed both, then walked back to the equipment.

"The tapes are sound activated. The equipment virtually runs itself. All we have to do is monitor the recordings while they're happening or by playback later if we're out of the room."

"Robert, I can't—"

"Diann, these bugs are where they are for one reason and one reason only. Cassel and I were after a murderer. I still am."

Robert's reference to Cassel in the past tense reminded Diann of the very dangerous situation they were dealing with. She lost a bit of her indignation.

"Isn't there any other way?"

"I'm open to suggestions. But you must see how important it is to know what's going on. I know you don't like the idea of snooping, but one of these people is a murderer. Something we hear could give us a clue as to which one it is. And that could save a life. And at the risk of repeating an old admonition, the life you save may be your own."

Robert saw his words were not bringing new information to Diann. She had obviously already faced the fact that she was on the list of potential victims. Her eyes were both resolute and accepting.

It struck him then how remarkably brave she was in her own quiet way. She had faced those two thugs on the street. She now calmly faced a possible attempt on her life. Her courage was yet another extremely attractive item in an altogether thoroughly irresistible package.

He leaned forward and his hands wrapped around her shoulders, then slid his hands down her arms. "I won't let anyone hurt you, Diann. I'm staying close to your side every moment from now on."

She had looked into that sincere blue of his eyes before. Each time it had washed away some form of resistance in her. Now it was threatening to wash away every defensive thought or impulse she possessed.

She had had a hard time resisting him when she thought him only a model and petty thief. But now that she knew who he really was, she recognized she was in real trouble.

She raised her hands to his chest. She felt the heat of him through their palms. Shooting it to every waiting and yearning cell in her body.

He studied her face, read the desire and the doubts. Suddenly he knew that the most important thing in the world to him was to rid her of those doubts. He pulled her close, pressed his lips against hers to seal his pledge.

A soft moan escaped her lips as she melted against him, and her vanilla-icing scent invaded his every pore. He had kissed her before, the first a mere taste, the second mad with hunger, the third when she had at first yielded and then pulled away.

She wasn't pulling away now. He took her lips to reassure, but that reassurance quickly changed into an exploration.

He wanted, needed, to know everything he could about her.

She was soft warmth and instant excitement—a thousand flavors from sweet to exotic, and he savored every one. But it wasn't enough. He was beginning to think he could never have enough of her.

He skimmed his hands across her shoulders and down her back, enjoying the incredible contrast of the yielding of her muscles and the yearning firmness of her body as she melted against him. He slipped his hands beneath her sweater and found the heated satin of her skin.

Diann felt herself drowning in sensations stronger than any she'd known. A sudden panic welled up inside her. "No. I can't—"

He felt the jolt in her voice and muscles. "I won't take advantage of you, Diann. I know what you've gone through this evening. I just want to touch you, to taste you."

She relaxed against him again. Hot, soft, smooth, her sighs helped him to map the sensitive nerves down her spine and up into her neck. He lowered his lips to the curve of her slim throat, skimming his tongue over its racing pulse.

Diann tried to fill her lungs again and again as the sensations he set off inside her robbed her of every breath. She moaned with pleasure and drew her arms across his shoulders, pressing against the ridges of his muscles, drawing him closer.

She totally forgot about Gabrielle and Peter until the tape recorder suddenly blared with the sound of voices.

Diann jolted up and right out of Robert's arms. He let her go instantly, although the heat in his eyes told her just how difficult it had been. She smiled and released her own reluctant sigh as they both turned their attention to the tape.

"Peter, you're here."

"In five minutes as promised. Gabrielle, you look divine and smell marvelous. Come. We have hours of pleasure ahead of us."

"Oh, yes, Peter. We will make this a night to remember. Who knows when the opportunity will ever present itself again?"

Suddenly a third voice answered, harsh and deep.

"I know. They're won't be any more opportunities."

Diann started at the unexpected anger of the voice being taped. Her eyes flew to Robert's, a question forming on her lips. She had no time to voice it.

Because in the next instant, the recording machine vibrated with the loud explosion of a rifle and a terrifying scream.

Chapter Ten

Robert took the stairs two at a time and then raced down the hall toward Gabrielle's room, knowing he was going to be too late but knowing that he must make the effort nonetheless. All he could think about was Conrad Rife's coming to Paris on an earlier train and finding his wife and Peter Campbell in a compromising embrace.

Had a husband's outrage pushed him to shoot Peter, Gabrielle or both?

With such images racing through his mind, it was with profound surprise that Robert ran through Gabrielle's open door to find not Conrad but a small-framed, white-faced woman with dishwater-blond hair, light eyes and bloodless lips, standing stiff as a statue, a smoking rifle still held in her hands.

Robert heard a shocked intake of breath as Helena came barreling into the room behind him.

"What has happened?"

Robert ignored Helena and her shouted question for the moment as he snatched the rifle away from the woman before him. Much to his surprise, she gave him no resistance. She didn't even move.

Helena circled behind Robert to the bed. "She shot Peter," she called in a surprised voice.

"Who are you?" Peter demanded of the assailant.

She didn't answer, just stared, not even appearing to see or hear him.

Helena stepped behind the woman, wrapping her sturdy arms around her captive's slight frame in a restraining vise.

"I will hold her. Do not worry."

Robert wasn't worrying. He had no doubt Helena could hold the slender woman. Hell, Helena could hold a tank if required. He turned away and went toward the bed, where he could see Gabrielle was bending over Peter.

As Robert got closer, he got a better look at Peter's gold dressing gown, seeping blood in the vicinity of his right leg.

"How badly is he hurt?"

Gabrielle wore one of the hotel's white bathrobes, as evidenced by an ornate *C* with a crown emblem monogram near the lapel. She pressed a thick white towel displaying the same monogram against the wound in what looked like a thoroughly competent effort to keep Peter from losing any more blood. She turned very briefly in Robert's direction.

Her voice was amazingly calm. "She shot him in the right thigh. Robert, you must ring for an ambulance. Quickly, please."

"One's already on its way, Gabrielle."

Gabrielle nodded, but did not turn away from administering to the wound on Peter's leg. Robert was reminded of how similarly calm and competent she had appeared when Conrad had been stricken. For all her faults and tears in the aftermath, the lady came through in a crisis.

He switched his attention to Peter's white complexion.

"Are you in much pain?"

Peter kept a perfectly straight face, but his normally precise diction was a bit fuzzy. "Not nearly as much as I'd be if her aim hadn't been off."

Gabrielle moved aside Peter's dressing gown to put more pressure on the wound. The torn flesh high on Peter's right inner thigh painted a clear-enough picture for Robert to catch Peter's meaning as to where his assailant had been aiming.

Robert gestured over to the woman who stood quietly in Helena's strong hold. "Who is she, Peter?"

"Jillian Bate-Land. My ex-ladyfriend."

"Ex?"

Robert watched Peter grit his teeth against the pain. "Well, old man, would you keep a woman like that around after she did this to you?"

DIANN FELT Robert ease into the chair beside her as she picked over her breakfast the following morning in the dining room. She didn't have to look to know it was him. His distinctive almond scent preceded him.

When she did look she saw his hair freshly washed and his sexy chin closely shaven. But lines of fatigue etched his forehead. He'd obviously been up all night.

"How's Peter? I called the hospital this morning, but no one would say."

Robert gave her a small smile before answering. "He'll mend. Bullet took out a chunk of his thigh, but it missed bone, arteries and other...ah...important parts. Pretty lucky, actually."

"Well, I can't say much for his morals, but I'm glad he's going to be okay. How did everything go with the police?"

"Tricky. I told Inspector Pinchot that we were returning to my room when I heard the shot. I said I sent you back to your room to call the police and an ambulance while I went to investigate."

"Good. That's the same story he got from me. Do you think he believed it?"

"I think he was too busy trying to sort out the shooting mess to give it much thought."

Diann shook her head. "Mess is right. Well, there's no way Gabrielle can hide her affair now. She's in for it."

"Maybe not."

"How can she not be, Robert? Conrad's not dumb. He'll be in Paris soon if he's not already. He's going to find out that Peter was shot in his wife's hotel room at one o'clock in the morning by Peter's jealous female friend."

"Ah, but that's not the story Gabrielle and Peter are telling."

Diann paused as the same dark-haired waiter who had served them on several occasions before came and took Robert's order. When he had gone, she leaned forward.

"But that's what happened."

"We know that because we were listening in. But according to Gabrielle and Peter, Jillian Bate-Land showed up in the middle of the night demanding Peter let her into his hotel room. When he opened the door, she pointed a rifle at him. He raced from his room, trying to get away. She followed and shot him as he passed the hallway in front of Gabrielle's room. Gabrielle heard the shot, opened her door, pulled Peter inside and immediately administered to his injuries."

Diann fell back into her chair. "I don't believe it. How can they tell such a story?"

"With perfectly straight faces. I watched them do it. Hell, if I hadn't known the truth, I probably would have been inclined to believe them."

"But how can they expect to get away with a story like that? Peter's friend is bound to say what really happened."

"Maybe. But for the moment Jillian Bate-Land is not saying anything. She didn't move an eyelash for a full twenty minutes while Helena held her for the police. When they took over and she finally came out of her shock at the hospital, she didn't even know her name."

"She has amnesia?"

"Who knows. It could be real, caused by the shock of having shot her lover. Or it could be faked, engineered to avoid prosecution. Take your pick."

Diann just shook her head as the waiter delivered Robert's steaming coffee and warm croissants.

"Well, at least we're sure that Jillian Bate-Land wasn't responsible for Kohei's, Louis's, and your friend Cassel's deaths."

Robert took a gulp of his coffee as though he needed it. "About now, Diann, I'm not sure of anything. The pattern began changing with Conrad's collapse. Prior to then, everyone who'd been stricken had been a prominent star in the perfume world."

"You mean, Conrad was an exception, since he doesn't contribute to the perfume industry in anything more than a supporting role?"

"He was the first exception. And then Cassel was killed and that shot the pattern all to hell. I feel like I'm pitching to the other team's top batter only to find that instead of hitting the ball, he's running it to the goal line of a football field. The games and the rules are all mixed up."

"What would happen to the pattern if you took the exceptions out?"

Robert saw the sudden speculation in her eyes. "What are you thinking?"

"Well, when I put a perfume together, what I leave out is sometimes as important as what I put in."

"Meaning?"

"What if you were to leave out Conrad's collapse? What if his illness was legitimate and had nothing to do with the fatal attacks on the others?"

Robert nodded. "That's always been a possibility. Actually, I think it's not only possible but logical to assume his collapse to be unrelated. After all, he didn't die like the others."

"Okay, so then Kohei and Louis die. Now their deaths fit the pattern, right?"

"Only until Cassel's death, Diann. His death scatters the pattern back into a hundred pieces."

"Only because Cassel was not a star in the perfume world."

"That's a big 'only,' Diann. That's the basis of the pattern, remember?"

"I haven't forgotten. But ask yourself this. If someone wanted to kill Cassel, why didn't they kill him in his own room? Why did they wait until he came to your room to do it?"

"What are you trying to say?"

She looked directly at him, the intelligence in her eyes pole-vaulting with speculation. "Robert, your advertisement for HEAT perfume is revolutionary. Remember the conversation at the banquet on the first night? Remember what Gabrielle said about adding a new PERFUME Award for the most effective advertisement?"

"Well, yes, but—"

"If there were such an award this year, there is no doubt in anyone's mind that you would be responsible for MW receiving it. Don't you see? Robert, you're a star in the perfume industry now. The murderer wasn't trying to kill Cassel. The murderer was trying to kill you!"

Robert nodded as the import of her words made themselves felt. "I think you're right. I've never for once imagined that my *undercover* position might have set me up as a victim, too. But if it has, then that explains so much. And most important it tells us the pattern is running true. The game hasn't changed."

Diann took a sip of her coffee. "We've got to figure out how these people are being killed. Could there have been something in that wine Cassel ordered? It was uncorked."

"That was my first thought, too. But the wine bottle was full and the glass was clean. Looked like he had just opened it."

"You called room service. They hadn't sent it to your room?"

"No."

"Was it likely Cassel would bring a bottle of wine?"

"It wasn't unlikely. But I would like to be sure of where he got it."

"Wouldn't it have had to come from the kitchen in the hotel?"

"Absolutely, since it was the les Ambassadeurs house wine. I suppose now is as good a time as any to check with the staff," Robert said as he rose.

"Shall I come along?" Diann asked.

"No. Since Cassel didn't drink any of the wine, I rather doubt there is any mystery to this. He probably just purchased a bottle and whatever the murderer used to kill him took effect before he had a chance to have any. Still, it's a loose end that needs tying. This will just take a minute. Be right back."

Diann nodded and shifted her attention back to her coffee. She felt as if she'd been living on caffeine the past few days. She tried to remember the last good night's sleep she'd had. It certainly hadn't been since she'd arrived in Paris.

"Diann. I am glad to see you. I will join you."

Diann's thoughts were so far away she was startled by the voice coming from directly behind her. She turned to see Helena pulling up the chair just vacated by Robert.

Helena looked rested and wrinkle-free in her plain buff-colored pantsuit—not at all like a woman who had probably spent a good part of the night with the police. She sported a red and runny nose.

"Please, Diann, do you have a tissue?"

Diann dug into her purse and came out with an entire packet, which she handed to Helena.

Helena took one gratefully and dabbed at her much-abused nose. At Diann's insistence she pocketed the rest of the tissues. "Such a nuisance, but I can't find my last container of scented tissues this morning. Perhaps it is hiding under the bedclothes I threw onto the floor when the sound of the shot awoke me. Perhaps the maid will find it when she makes up the room."

"You have these tissues scented specially, don't you?"

"*Ja*. And sealed in a custom aluminum scent box. I have learned this from the Grasse fragrance containers. They say the scent can last in one of the aluminum containers for ten years. But now that I have seen Louis's special polymer containers, I will probably change to them."

Helena signaled with a small jerking motion of her hand and the waiter was immediately beside her to pour a cup of coffee. She declined any other breakfast and took a large gulp of the coffee before turning back to Diann.

"You were the one who contacted the hotel management last night and had them call the police?"

"Yes."

Helena's ginger head shook as she took another gulp of coffee. Competent fingers with short, unpainted nails circled the cup. "Such foolishness. He is not the kind of man worth shooting."

"Come again?"

"This Jillian Bate-Land. She cares too much for Peter. So few men are worth such care."

Diann was reminded once more of how little she knew about the personal lives of her fellow perfume stars. Looking at Helena's set mouth, she saw her chance to learn more. She leaned forward.

"You're saying she shot him because she cares for him?"

"Of course, Diann. If she did not care, she could just walk away when he takes up with another woman."

"Peter says she came after him without provocation."

Helena's ginger eyes looked straight into Diann's while she passed the tissue beneath the red tip of her nose. "You believe this?"

Diann sat back and smiled. "No."

"I did not think you were that dumb. It does not pay to care too much for these worthless men, but there are so few of the others around."

Helena sighed as though weary. Diann didn't know if the sigh had been generated by the conversation topic or the woman's battle with her ever-drippy nose. She decided it was probably both.

"I don't ever think I've seen you without this sinus problem. Isn't there anything you can do?"

"No. Oh, the doctors have shots that dry up the fluid. But the only time I took them I could not concentrate or smell well. They had to be stopped."

"But doesn't the dripping interfere with your sense of smell?"

"Only if it gets very bad. And when that happens, I use my tissues doused with one of Mit Luv's perfumes to help to clear my passages temporarily. It is the one that includes menthol."

"Yes, I've smelled it. Actually, it's quite pleasant and invigorating. Is this sinus thing a year-round problem?"

"*Ja,* but spring is the worst. And being outside. But somehow I manage. Without my sense of smell I cannot function, and it is for our work that we live, is it not?"

"Yes, work has always been very important to me."

Helena's eyes glowed at Diann. "*Ja.* Work, children, these are the things that fulfill women's lives and make us strong."

"You have children?"

"Two boys."

"And their father?"

Helena stared into her coffee cup. "Rudolph left us when my eldest was three and my youngest nine months."

"That must have been difficult for you."

"My brother, Wilhelm, and his wife, Anna, help. I signed on at Mit Luv. The boys are now fifteen and seventeen, and I make more than their father ever would have. It was a good thing that he left. If he came back, I do not need to shoot him. When he saw how well we live, he would probably shoot himself.''

She smiled, possibly conjuring pleasurable mental images as she raised her coffee cup in a mock toast.

Diann found herself smiling back and raising her own cup. She liked the strength she saw behind that look on Helena's face and the confident glow in her ginger eyes.

"So there you are," Gabrielle called out as she crossed the dining room toward them.

Diann put down her coffee cup and turned to see the Fragrance Foundation's codirector.

Gabrielle was beautifully and expensively dressed, as always, but her late night definitely showed in the prominent bags underneath her eyes, despite her attempt to cover them with makeup. She swept into the chair on the other side of Diann with a dramatic flourish.

"Such a night! How thankful I am that it is over and poor Peter will be well. Where is the waiter? I am simply dying for a cup of coffee. Oh, there he is. *Garçon!*"

After the waiter had taken her order, Diann caught Gabrielle's eye. "Did you get any sleep at all?"

"No. But it does not matter. Conrad is coming to Paris, and I must be awake to greet him."

"He is well?" Helena asked.

"So he insists," Gabrielle answered. "And his courage has emboldened me. I mean to continue with our symposium despite all our trials. Helena, Diann, you must both be prepared to give your presentations."

Helena positively scowled. "Gabrielle, you cannot be serious? Even if I felt like it, which I do not, who do you think would attend?"

"Everyone, Helena. Inspector Pinchot has refused to allow any of the symposium's attendees to leave Paris. He is not even allowing them to seek accommodations outside of this hotel. What else have they to do but attend? Come, Helena, what harm is there in going on as planned?"

"We have not gone on as planned since the first day. None of the afternoon workshops have taken place because of all the disasters occurring at the morning presentations. Nor have the evening activities been pursued." Helena dabbed at her nose. "If someone had meant to intentionally sabotage your symposium, Gabrielle, they could not have done a better job."

Helena's comments shot a quick thought into Diann's head. Had the woman inadvertently stumbled on the reason for these deaths? "Gabrielle, is there anyone you know who would like to see this symposium fail? Or *Redolence* magazine?"

Gabrielle's nose scrunched at Diann as though she had dabbed kerosene behind her ears.

"What a strange question, Diann. Why ever do you ask it?"

"Is there, Gabrielle?"

"I suppose the other industry magazines might benefit if *Redolence* were to fail, but my magazine is not at the mercy of the success or failure of any one symposium we might sponsor. These dreadful deaths of Kohei and Louis—although so tragically similar—are related only in that they both occurred at this symposium. They cannot have any bearing on the magazine."

Diann could barely believe her ears. "Gabrielle, you can't have convinced yourself that the only thing Kohei's and Louis's deaths share is that they happened at this symposium."

"And why not? That is all they do share. Inspector Pinchot assures me his men have checked the air-circulation system in the hotel and the kitchen and wine cellars. All is in perfect working order."

"Then why did two men die here?"

"I do not know. But it has to be a coincidence. A dreadful coincidence, but a coincidence nonetheless. There simply is no other explanation."

"Isn't there?" Robert said as he strode up and pulled out the fourth chair.

Diann came immediately alert when she saw the grim tightening of his jaw.

"What do you mean?" Helena immediately demanded.

ROBERT SAT DOWN and looked at Helena steadily. "Kohei and Louis did not die from natural causes."

"But they did," Gabrielle protested. "From heart attacks. The inspector, he told us."

Robert switched his steady look to her. "Oh, they died from heart attacks, all right. But those heart attacks were not the result of natural causes."

Gabrielle nearly choked. "What are you saying?"

"Someone is murdering the stars in the perfume industry."

He watched for a reaction. Gabrielle turned several shades whiter beneath her makeup.

Helena's spine straightened into a stiff board. He refocused his eyes on her face.

She was visibly agitated as she punched her tissue at her nose. "You have made a very serious statement, Robert."

"I realize that, Helena. But four of the perfume industry's top stars have met mysterious deaths from unexplainable heart attacks. It is simply impossible for these heart attacks to have been the result of natural causes. Which means someone has deliberately caused them with malice aforethought. And unless the killer is stopped, more will die."

"Four?" Gabrielle squeaked. "But there have only been Kohei and Louis who—"

"And Terry Wonnacott and Annette Prince," Robert interjected very matter-of-factly.

Gabrielle blinked several times.

Helena frowned. "Terry Wonnacott and Annette Prince are dead? When?"

Robert decided that if Helena was an actress, she was a good one. "Right after the conventions they attended in Toronto and Las Vegas this past year," he answered, trying to watch the reaction of both women.

Gabrielle's face went stiff with its pallor. Helena's, on the other hand, flushed. She looked angry enough to chew nails as her eyes traveled from Robert to Diann and finally rested on Gabrielle accusingly.

"Why have I not been told of this before?" she demanded.

The waiter took that moment to set Gabrielle's coffee, orange juice and croissants in front of her.

Gabrielle ignored him and her breakfast. Her expressive hands flew into the air. "Helena, do not look at me that way. What was I supposed to have told you? That people have died? I write a perfume column, not the obituaries!"

"You knew!"

"Of course I knew Terry and Annette died. I also knew they died of natural causes."

"What natural causes?" Helena asked, but Gabrielle's white face shuttered as she reached for her coffee.

Helena's eyes sought Robert's. "What natural causes?" she repeated.

"Both Terry and Annette also died of sudden heart attacks."

Helena's eyes flew back to Gabrielle. "So you also knew that there has never been a convention bug. How cleverly you tried to confuse us!"

Robert heard Gabrielle's sharp intake of breath. In place of her previous pallor, a roaring flush raced up her neck and into her cheeks. She dropped the delicate china cup she held in her hand onto its saucer, spilling the coffee.

Then she rose regally and looked down at Helena as a queen might at a particularly displeasing subject—a queen with the power to cut off the head of that particularly displeasing subject. "Helena, I am going to assume you are not yourself and that is why you say these things and behave in this manner to me."

A tense moment passed between the two women. Anger flushed both faces. Robert wondered which one of the women would end this confrontation and how. He would never find out, because Conrad Rife took that moment to make his appearance at the edge of the dining room. When he saw his wife, he came running.

"Gabrielle!"

She turned, and Robert watched the anger drain from her face to be replaced by great relief. She threw her arms around Conrad's shoulders as though he was her stalwart Romeo and she his chaste Juliet. Several murmured French endearments escaped her lips before she finally pulled back, seeming to remember where they were.

Conrad's face and voice wore all the vulnerability of his love for his wife. Robert shook an internal head. Was it better for the man to know or not to know the truth? "Gabrielle, the concierge said there was some new trouble. Tell me, dear, what has happened?"

"Peter was shot."

Robert watched total bewilderment strike the concern from Conrad's face. "Peter...shot?"

"Yes, dearest. By his deranged ladyfriend. But do not worry. He will be all right. Come, we will order room service and I'll tell you all about it."

And with that Gabrielle whisked Conrad out of the dining room, her elegant high heels clicking confidently on the gleaming floors.

When the couple had left, Helena leaned across the table toward Robert, her eyes still too bright. "Did someone really murder Terry, Annette, Kohei and Louis?"

Robert looked Helena directly in the eye. "Yes. I caution you to be on your guard."

"Me? You think I am a target?"

"You are a perfume star. It's perfume stars who are being killed."

"But how? Why?"

"Those are good questions, Helena. Answer one for me. What secret business did you have going with Louis?"

That brought her up straight and stiff as a rod. A mixture of surprise and dismay fought in her eyes. "Any business I did with Louis was personal. You have no right to ask me such a question."

Robert smiled, one of those empty charming smiles he saved for moments just like this. "If you don't want to give me an answer, I can arrange it so that Inspector Pinchot is the next one to ask the question."

Helena shot to her feet. Robert definitely didn't like being at the receiving end of this woman's angry look. That look alone convinced him that Helena Strunk could commit murder. "Be careful who you hurl your threats at, Herr Mize."

With anger sizzling in her eyes and her every step, Helena Strunk plowed out of the dining room.

Beside Robert, Diann let out an audible breath. "Well, I'll say this for you. You sure know how to bring up the subjects that empty a table."

"You finished your breakfast?"

"Yes. Why?"

"Let's go back to the tapes. We're going to listen to every one—front to back."

"Robert, what is it?"

He rested his hand on her arm, trying to convey his urgency in its pressure. "Cassel didn't bring that bottle of wine to my room last night. One of the room-service waiters distinctly remembers seeing the bottle, with a wineglass, on a tray in front of my door at least ten minutes before Cassel was supposed to arrive."

"Are you saying someone other than room service delivered a bottle of wine to your room?"

"Yes."

"But who? Why? And how can that undrunk bottle of wine have anything to do with Cassel's death?"

"When we learn the answers to those questions, Diann, maybe we'll know the answer to who's been killing the perfume industry's top stars."

Diann was out of her chair in a second.

Too impatient to wait for the elevator, they took the grand staircase up to her suite. Robert quickly followed her inside, but he stopped in alarm when he didn't see the equipment.

"What happened?"

"I shoved it into the closet. I didn't want the maid wondering what it was."

Robert flashed her an appreciative smile. "Good thinking." He brought the equipment back into the room and started to check the counters on the tape. "According to these meters, there have been several conversations in a couple of the rooms. Let me remove the recorded tapes and put in new ones. Then I'll rewind these and add them to all the others so we can listen."

Robert was just about ready to do that, when the now-familiar *beep, beep* of a call being placed sounded into the room.

Diann and Robert exchanged glances and then stared back at the recording equipment as Robert increased the volume so they could hear the forthcoming conversation.

A woman's voice answered the phone in French.

"Madame, *this is Helena Strunk. We must meet immediately and settle this business between us.*"

"*Immediately? But I thought you said I had a day to think this matter over.*"

"I am sorry, madame. *But I have found that I have no more time. I will come to your house now."*

"No, not here. I have company."

"Then somewhere else, madame. *Somewhere we can be private."*

"This is so inopportune. Can you not wait—"

"No, madame. *I have sent a hotel employee to get it for me from out of the safe. I do not intend it to be found in my possession."*

"All right. I will be at the Champ-de-Mars in forty minutes, near the children's puppet show. You will bring the check?"

"Yes."

"And you will let me see it one last time as promised?"

"Yes. But I must have the agreed-upon letter."

"Of course."

"Then in forty minutes, madame. *At the Champ-de-Mars."*

And with that Helena Strunk hung up.

Diann turned to Robert. "What was all that about?"

"I think that I succeeded in nudging Helena into some action. Whoever she's going to be meeting in forty minutes, she's going to be paying her for something she doesn't want the police to know she has. And I have a feeling that something was what Louis was selling to Helena. This could be it."

He paused as he looked at her face. "What's wrong?"

"Damn it, Robert. I've just been getting to know Helena personally and I really like her. She's strong, independent, reliable."

"She may also be a killer, Diann. One of these people is."

His hand encircled her arm in a reassuring clasp. "We don't have the luxury of liking any of them until we've found out which."

"How do you do this, Robert? If I had to constantly be spying on and suspecting the people I'm with, all the joy of life would be lost."

His hand traveled to her cheek, where it traced a path to a lock of her hair. "When you know what you're doing is right, you can put up with a lot of unpleasantness. Are you ready to go?"

"We're going to follow Helena to the Champ-de-Mars?"

"No. We're going to get there first and be in position. I know where the children's puppet theater is performed."

Diann grabbed her purse as she threw her next comment over her shoulder sweetly. "Some information you found in a guidebook, no doubt?"

Robert had the grace to laugh. "Am I ever going to live this down?"

"I'll let you know. By the way, what is the Champ-de-Mars?"

He wrapped an arm around her shoulder and gave her forehead a quick kiss. "It's a formal garden at the base of the Eiffel Tower. Used to be used as a military parade ground. Rather pretty. You'll like it."

DIANN FOUND Robert's prediction accurate. The Champ-de-Mars was enormous and engaging, with arches and grottoes, lakes and cascades. Robert led them to the area where the puppet shows were performed, but none was taking place that day. They waited opposite the pebbled walkway in a beautiful green blind of blooming daffodils and regal red tulips.

Sun rays periodically squeezed through a restraining net of clouds. Diann felt an expectant spring breeze on her cheeks and in her hair, full of the blooming scents of the surrounding plants and flowers. She looked up at the majestic Eiffel Tower, soaring above them. The straining sunlight swept across its seven thousand tons of steel, making it a startling sight of beauty and strength.

And then she looked at the man beside her, sunlight glinting in his eyes, too. A tense, focused expression fixed the muscles of his face. It reminded her of a hunting dog that had caught the scent of his quarry and would follow it to the end.

And suddenly Diann knew that was exactly what this man would do. He would find this murderer. He wouldn't give up until he did. He was not a man who did anything half-way.

Exactly forty minutes from the moment she had agreed to the rendezvous, Helena arrived. She wore a purse over her shoulder and had a large box cupped underneath her sturdy arm and an anxious look on her face.

Helena quickly scanned a couple strolling by. She twisted again to see a lone woman walking her full-size poodle. All passed her by without a returning glance.

Diann watched as the spring breeze puffed at the hems of Helena's buff pants. The woman alternated between dabbing at her nose and checking her watch.

Finally, after fifteen minutes and a good chunk of Helena's patience, another woman skirted the edge of the garden surrounding the arch. She was petite and pretty, with dark hair and eyes. She walked with a furtive step. She didn't approach Helena straightaway, but looked nervously in every direction first.

Diann felt the tension increasing in Robert as he stood beside her. Like her, he must feel certain that this was the woman on the phone.

Although still cautious, the petite woman finally walked up to Helena.

Diann and Robert were too far away to hear the women's conversation. But they could see Helena reach into her purse, pull out a white envelope and hand it to the woman. The woman in turn handed Helena an envelope.

Then the newcomer sat down on a bench and Helena gently set the box on her lap. Unfortunately when Helena did so, she also stepped between the box and Diann's and Robert's line of sight.

Robert whispered in Diann's ear. "Let's go see what it is."

Robert took Diann's elbow as they advanced on the two women. The seated woman saw them approaching first and gave a startled little jump. Helena whirled around to face them. Her cheeks colored angrily.

"What are you doing here?"

Robert turned to the still-seated woman and took her hand, blowing a small kiss over its knuckles. "We're here to see what you're buying from this lady, Helena. Madame Magnen, I presume?"

The woman blinked. "How do you know who I am?"

"An educated guess. I knew Helena had a business deal going with Louis. With his death, it just seemed logical that she would continue to conduct that business deal with Louis's widow. My name is Robert Mize. Please accept my condolences, *madame,* on the death of your husband."

"Thank you, *monsieur.* I—"

"Stop this," Helena interrupted. "Do not speak to them, Madame Magnen. They do not belong here. This is not their business."

Robert turned to face her once again. "You're wrong, Helena. There's a killer loose, remember? As far as I'm concerned that makes anything and everything that has to do with Louis's death our business. Now, if *madame* will be so kind, I will take a look in that box."

Robert didn't wait for permission, despite his words. He just leaned down, grasped the large box and lifted it off Madame Magnen's lap. Diann's curiosity had her stepping to his side and watching over his shoulder.

Diann didn't know what she had expected, but the translucent container, which she recognized as one of Louis's magnificent new plastic polymers, and its contents came as an absolute surprise. Although she had never seen the item before, she had seen pictures of it—no, more correctly, she had seen Egyptian stone carvings of it.

She stepped around Robert and lifted the container and its precious contents carefully out of the box.

Robert was completely perplexed. "What is it?"

Diann's tone was as reverent as her expression. "It's an Egyptian scent cone."

Robert looked blank. "A what?"

She twirled it in her hands, letting it catch the light. "Liquid perfumes had not been invented back in the days of Egyptian pharaohs. Women wore their fragrances by setting decorated cones of scented wax on top of their heads. As the heat from their body melted the wax, the fragrance was released around their faces."

"And this is one of those Egyptian scent cones?"

Diann shook her head. "No. It can't be real. Nothing so delicate could have lasted since such ancient times."

Madame Magnen flew to her feet. "But of course it is real! Is there not the letter from Louis's grandfather authenticating its find?"

Robert turned to Madame Magnen. "You have a paper that proves this is real?"

The widow turned to Helena. "Madame Strunk. Give it to him."

Helena didn't appear happy about turning it over, but with thin, disapproving lips, she finally did.

Robert started a quick perusal of the document, while Diann gave all her attention to the beautifully shaped wax cone. Set on its broad end, its diameter looked to be about six inches wide. It rose to a point about eight inches high, with the bands of red concentric circles spinning ever wider from its top. And embedded in these circles were the graceful figures of women, drawn with a bluish ink in the stylized precision of Egyptian art.

She brought the container to her nose and had the fleeting impression of an ancient frankincense. Had Louis infused his special polymer with a semblance of the original fragrance of the scented cone? What an absolute genius he had been! The idea that this scent cone could be authentic absolutely thrilled her.

Her attention refocused on Robert as he interpreted the document he had read. "This paper says that a Pierre Magnen smuggled this scent cone out of the tomb of an Egyptian queen while he was a member of an international archaeological team nearly seventy years ago."

Diann turned to Robert. "Smuggled?"

"Yes. Possession of this cone by anyone but the proper authorities in Egypt is technically illegal. All objects found in unearthed tombs are supposed to be cataloged and sent to the Cairo Museum."

Robert turned to Madame Magnen. "Has this scent cone remained in your husband's family all these years?"

"Oui, monsieur."

"The authorities don't know of its existence?"

The petite woman's dark eyes watered as her voice wavered. "Louis's grandfather was a good man. He only took this scent cone because he wanted to preserve it. The only other scent cone removed from a tomb melted in the Egyptian heat because the authorities would not spend the money and act quickly enough to protect it. He wanted this second one to survive."

"So he didn't report finding it?"

"Oui."

"But how did he get it out of Egypt without it melting?"

"He kept it in ice, at much inconvenience and great cost. Ever since then his family has stored it in a refrigerated vault. Then Louis invented his special polymer. Louis carefully wound the translucent fibers around the cone until they were an inch thick, insulating it from heat and air. Now that he has encased it, the wax and scent are preserved without refrigeration."

Robert turned to Helena. "And you're buying it. For how much?"

"Twenty thousand dollars."

"That seems like a lot."

Helena looked insulted. "It's the only one of its kind in the world—an incomparable piece of both Egyptian and fragrance history. It does not seem like a lot to me."

Robert turned back to Madame Magnen. "Why did your husband decide to sell this treasure after it has been kept in your family so long?"

"We need the money, *monsieur.*"

"But your husband held an important position at La Belle Perfumes. Hasn't his compensation been sufficient?"

"It was, *monsieur.* Until our daughter became very ill this past year and in need of many specialists."

Robert paused, remembering Cassel's having told him of the money problems of the Magnens. A lot of things were beginning to make sense. "*Madame,* did Louis offer to sell this scent cone to anyone else?"

"*Oui.* When Madame Strunk told Louis she did not know when she could get the money, Louis contacted Peter Campbell. Louis heard Monsieur Campbell is also interested in Egyptian artifacts."

"But Campbell declined to buy it?"

"On the contrary. Monsieur Campbell was very eager to buy. He even offered twenty-five thousand dollars."

"Then why didn't Louis take him up on his offer?"

"Perhaps Louis would have, but Louis...died." Mrs. Magnen's eyes filled with quick tears. She was holding herself together, but only just. "Afterward, Madame Strunk called. She told me she had the scent cone in her possession because Louis had let her have it examined by the expert in Egyptian antiquities. Madame Strunk could have simply kept the cone. You see this? But *madame* is honorable. She offered to buy the cone at the agreed-upon price. I agreed to sell it.''

''I see.''

''Do you, *monsieur?* My Louis, he is gone. The insurance, she is little. My daughter must be cared for. If the authorities learn of this fragrance cone, it will go back to Egypt.''

Robert gave Madame Magnen a little bow. ''They will not learn of it from me, *madame.* I thank you for your explanation.''

Helena sneezed loudly as she leaned down to repossess the box. ''So now Robert, Diann, if you are satisfied, I will conclude my business with Madame Magnen before this wind blows all the pollen of Paris into my sinuses.''

Diann stepped toward Helena, gently placing the polymer-protected fragrance cone back into the box. ''I feel privileged to have seen your treasure.''

Helena closed the lid and circled her hefty arm around the box as a small smile claimed her full lips. ''*Ja.* It is special. I am not angry anymore that you followed me here, Diann. You are one who can understand what this scent cone means.''

The breeze whipped past them, and Helena dug into her shoulder bag. Diann caught the flash of aluminum.

''I see you found your special tissue container.''

''*Ja.* Next to the bedside. A night without rest. It will fool the eyes.'' She punctured the seal of the special container and reached in for a fresh tissue. She brought it to her nose to wipe away its perpetual drip and to inhale a whiff of menthol.

For just an instant Diann watched a curious look come over Helena's face.

She wondered what had caused it, until she smelled it, too. Very faint, but very distinctive. And then Diann knew much of what had previously eluded her.

But it was too late.
Helena had already fallen to the pebbled walkway.
And Diann was right behind her.

Chapter Eleven

Diann awoke to a buzzing in her ears and a feeling of total disorientation. She opened her eyes, only to find herself lying on a cot in what appeared to be the emergency room of a hospital. A nurse looked at her, said something in French and then disappeared.

Diann closed her eyes again. Like a turtle slowly sticking its head out of a very dark and heavy shell, her mind began to poke out of its fog to locate its lost memories.

A windy day. She and Robert standing among the lovely daffodils and tulips in the Champ de Mars. Helena and Madame Magnen standing in the sun by the bench near the puppet stand. The beautiful Egyptian scent cone. Then, in slow motion, Helena reached for her fresh tissue, sniffing it, and the last look on her face before she fell. And the memory of that faint odor.

Diann opened her eyes and sat straight up. By the time she had swung her feet over the edge of the cot, Robert had reached her, with Inspector Pinchot not far behind.

Diann fought back a wave of dizziness as the blood rushed from her head. "Careful, *mademoiselle,*" Inspector Pinchot's voice said, but it was Robert's arm that had encircled her shoulders to steady her.

"I've got you," his warm voice said in her ear. "I've been worried. It's taken nearly three hours for you to come around."

She raised her head and looked into his eyes, fighting the dizziness and the awful buzzing in her ears. "Helena's dead, isn't she?"

His eyes held a gentleness that cushioned the awful bite of his response. "Yes."

Inspector Pinchot gave a little cough. "We can postpone our conversation if you do not feel well enough, *mademoiselle*."

Diann tried to silence the buzzing that only she could hear. "No, I must talk to you now, Inspector. I know how Helena died. And the others."

Robert's arm tightened. "Diann, you do?"

Inspector Pinchot took a step forward. "Mademoiselle Torrey, please explain."

Diann took a deep breath, fought through the slowly dissipating dizziness, thankful for the steady support and warmth seeping into her from Robert's arm. "Helena had special sealed containers of tissues she kept in her purse. They had been saturated with a perfume her company produces. Helena used the high menthol concentration of that perfume to assist her in keeping her sinuses clear."

Inspector Pinchot nodded thoughtfully. "Yes, I saw Madame Strunk use these tissues. What is their significance?"

"The first—and last—tissue she got out of the new container did not contain that perfume, Inspector. It contained another chemical."

"What chemical?"

"I do not know. But I do know that when she inhaled the scent, it killed her."

"And how do you know this?"

"Because I smelled it, too, being so close to her at the time. It was the same odor that I smelled just before passing out during Kohei's presentation."

"An odor? You did not mention you smelled an odor before passing out at that presentation."

"Inspector, please understand it was so faint and so unlike anything I'd smelled before that I knew I couldn't describe it. Frankly, I thought I might have imagined it."

"But now you do not think you imagined it?"

"No, now I'm sure it's real."

"But then, why did not anyone else mention this smell?"

"That's not unusual. As human beings our knowledge of smells is based on experience. Unless we've experienced a smell before, its odor often doesn't even register in our minds. But I've trained myself to pay particular attention to odor. That's my profession. And I'm sure I've smelled this chemical twice now. The first time just before I passed out at Kohei's presentation. The second time when Helen brought out her tissue today."

Inspector Pinchot's brow furrowed. "So you are saying these people have been killed when they inhaled this chemical with this particular odor?"

"Yes, Inspector. I'm sure of it. And if you test out Helena's tissue carefully, I'm sure you'll find it."

"Hmm. We shall see. But even so I am still confused. I can understand how you might have been affected today. As Monsieur Mize explained, you were standing right next to Madame Strunk. But, *mademoiselle*, how could a whole roomful of people be affected by the chemical odor you claimed killed Monsieur Kanemoto?"

Robert spoke up. "I think I can answer that. Remember the scent tubing underneath the tables, Inspector? The residue of the full dose that killed Kohei must have been blown around the room, incapacitating everyone else."

Diann was thankful for Robert's quick grasp and deduction. As soon as she heard his words, she was sure he was right. "And Louis must have inhaled it when he opened the seal on the large replica of his Genie perfume," she offered. "That's how he died."

Inspector Pinchot pursed his lips as he frowned. "But what chemical is this? We have autopsied the victims. No mystery chemical has been found."

Diann ignored a new wave of buzzing. "Somehow when this new chemical is inhaled, it stops the heart and leaves no obvious traces. I would imagine that unless your forensic medical examiners knew exactly what they were looking for, they would not have known the right toxicological screen to run in order to identify it. There may not even be a current toxicological screen that can find it."

Robert sent Diann a small, quick smile. "As a chemist reminded me recently, new chemicals are being discovered all the time. That must be what's happened here."

Diann found a small smile to send back. "The killer knew what the top stars would touch or come in contact with and went about planting this chemical where a victim would be bound to inhale it."

"And has just waited for the traps to be sprung," Robert said.

Inspector Pinchot nodded thoughtfully. "Yes, this fits in with what we now know. You have been very helpful, *mademoiselle*. So, we find this chemical and we will have solved this most troubling case."

Diann leaned forward, feeling the warmth in Robert's arm come with her. "Solved? But, Inspector, just identifying the chemical won't solve the case. You have to also identify who discovered it and is using it to kill."

"You are correct, *mademoiselle*. Fortunately we already know who is to blame."

Diann blinked at Inspector Pinchot, sure she must have heard wrong through the persistent buzzing in her ears. "You know who it is?"

Robert gave her shoulders a reassuring squeeze. "Inspector Pinchot got a call from Armand Vuillard's head assistant earlier this afternoon. The man was worried because Vuillard hadn't been seen or heard from in a week. When Inspector Pinchot's men broke into this apartment, they found an angry letter Vuillard had written to his sister in Provence. In it Vuillard talks about the murders of two perfume stars and his intent to kill the remaining ones."

The buzzing increased in Diann's brain. "Wait a minute. Armand Vuillard is responsible for these murders?"

Inspector Pinchot rested his sharp black eyes on her face. "It is all in the letter, *mademoiselle*. Monsieur Vuillard's company, once the foremost and most exclusive perfumerie in Paris, has been suffering some major financial reversals recently. In his mental derangement, Monsieur Vuillard blamed the Fragrance Fraternity and the perfume stars who were selected from without his company. He planned to kill all of you, and Conrad and Gabrielle Rife for selecting you."

Diann shook her head. "Armand. It's so hard to believe! What is the deadly chemical he's using?"

"He does not say, does not even mention it is inhaled. All he says is that he discovered it quite by accident when it knocked him out for several hours. When he came to he realized a more concentrated dose would kill and he decided to use it."

"But Armand isn't even at the symposium. How could he have—"

"He's here, Diann," Robert interrupted. "We may not recognize him, but you can bet he's here in some disguise. Now that you've identified this unusual odor, we finally have the clue that can focus the search."

Robert turned from Diann then. "Inspector, you will have your men carefully search the rooms and any of the equipment that the presenters have or were going to use for something that can be inhaled?"

"*Oui, monsieur.* This has been my thought, also."

Inspector Pinchot gave Diann a little bow and left the hospital room.

Diann immediately turned to Robert. "But what if he searches my room, Robert? The record and the tapes—"

He smiled and kissed her forehead. "It's okay, Diann. They're gone."

"What about Madame Magnen?"

"She disappeared, too, when I called the ambulance for you and Helena. I didn't mention her presence on the Champs-de-Mars to the inspector. There's no way she could be involved in these deaths. I didn't see any point in causing her any more grief."

"And the fragrance cone?"

"I hid it in my rented Peugeot, along with the letter alluding to its authenticity. I'll get it to Helena's next of kin somehow when all of this is over."

"Helena's next of kin," Diann repeated, a wave of sadness engulfing her. "Her sons. Her brother and his wife. Damn it, Robert. Why couldn't I have understood the significance of that odor before Helena became the next victim?"

"Diann, don't take the burden of her death onto your shoulders. You're probably one of the few people in this world who could even smell the stuff and be able to figure out its significance. Now, how are you feeling?"

"The dizziness is gone, but the buzzing remains. It's so hard for me to accept that Armand is responsible for this insanity. From the first moment I went to work at MW, he has been my idol. The fragrances he has created are legendary. He's a genius—an absolute genius."

Robert ran his fingers from her temple to her chin, his smile gentle. "Wouldn't be the first time genius and madness existed in the same mind. And it won't be the last."

INSPECTOR PINCHOT stood before Diann, Robert, Gabrielle, Conrad and Peter after he had gathered them together in his office mere hours later. Robert noted the pleased expression on his face as he treated Robert to a conspiratorial nod.

"We have found them," Inspector Pinchot announced. "Monsieur Vuillard has been a very busy, clever man."

"What did you find?" Peter asked.

"In your room, Monsieur Campbell, we found the chemical embedded in an unopened bottle of shaving cream.

In Madame Rife's room there was a special bottle of Armand Vuillard's floral chypre perfume that had the chemical in the seal of the cap. In Mademoiselle Torrey's presentation kit, a scent strip had been doctored with the chemical. And in Monsieur Rife's new heart medicine bottle, its seal also contained this deadly substance.''

Diann sat forward. "What is the chemical?"

"We are not quite sure yet. But we have seen it on our registering equipment. It appears that two harmless chemicals combine into a harmful one when they come into contact with oxygen.''

Conrad's domed forehead puckered into an uncharacteristic frown. "Please explain, Inspector."

"We had all these items opened in the laboratory in sealed containers, you understand. Thanks to Mademoiselle Torrey, we knew we were looking for something in a sealed vessel that when unsealed, released a gas. So when we opened all these seals in contained environments in the laboratory, we checked our instruments for any indication of a forming gas.''

"And you found . . . ?" Peter prompted.

"A gas was released when each of these items came into contact with air. A very deadly but fragile gas. It dissipates very quickly.''

"Were you able to capture any residue of the gas?" Diann asked.

"Yes, and we have sent it to be studied under electron microscopes, along with the seals. We will soon know what this mysterious gas is and what substances produce it. The chemists will be the ones to officially close this inquiry.''

Peter sat forward. "Close the inquiry? You have found Armand Vuillard?"

"Armand Vuillard's name was on a passenger list of a flight to Quebec yesterday afternoon. He must have seen my men at his apartment and fled. We have notified the Canadian authorities. It is now up to them.''

Gabrielle sighed loudly and sank into her chair. "So. It is finally over."

Conrad wrapped an arm around her shoulders. "I assume we are free to go now, Inspector?"

"You may leave, Monsieur Rife. I am also releasing my hold on the attendees to the symposium. But *madame* and the others in this room must remain in Paris while the matter of Mademoiselle Jillian Bate-Land and her attack on Monsieur Campbell is resolved. *Madame, mademoiselle, messieurs,* I will be in touch."

"IF WE HAVE to stay here, we might as well try to salvage the symposium. No use wasting the time," Robert said as they walked down the hall toward the exit of the police station.

Gabrielle turned to him. "What do you mean, Robert?"

"The danger is past, Gabrielle. Armand has fled. The chemical time bombs have been discovered and defused. We are safe. If the symposium attendees, many of whom are major perfume buyers, break up now and go home with the vivid memories of these deaths the last thing on their minds, how many do you think will return for the next symposium?"

Gabrielle frowned as she turned to her husband. "Conrad, Robert makes a good point. As we are forced to stay, why not go on with the symposium?"

Conrad's perpetually happy-looking face studied his wife's. He let out a tired sigh. "But, dear, do you really think the attendees will stay to participate after being witnesses to so much tragedy?"

Peter's jaw set in determination as he limped along, supporting his right leg with the use of a cane. "It's up to us to see they do. My major contacts come from these symposiums. Robert is right. If this one ends on this unsatisfactory note, I doubt there'll be another symposium."

"But, Robert, how can we possibly talk these people into continuing?" Diann asked.

He smiled at her. "Humor is a wonderful healer, Diann. I suggest we have a 'survivors' party tomorrow night on one of those dinner cruises along the Seine. Get cups and T-shirts printed up for everyone that say, We Survived The Symposium From Hell. Give everyone a good feeling for having been here."

Gabrielle's hands flew into the air. "A wonderful idea, Robert! You think so too, Diann, no?"

"It's probably brilliant," Diann conceded. "But even if everyone can be contacted in time, will they come?"

Peter paused to lean on his cane. "If we get back to the hotel and make the effort to get them to come, I don't see why not. Even when Inspector Pinchot gives them the okay to leave, few will be able to get last-minute flights out tonight or tomorrow. And even if they can, we can entice them not to by promising to do small samples of our original presentations on board the boat."

Gabrielle's hands, which had been moving excitedly with the prospect, suddenly stilled. "But Inspector Pinchot took all your presentation materials from me with his *autorisation*."

Peter waved away the problem as insignificant. "I can have my company express new materials, and I'm sure Diann can do the same. What do you say, Diann? Could they be here by tomorrow night?"

"If I call them now, I suppose so."

Gabrielle turned back excitedly to Conrad, her hands once again flying about her face. "Conrad, this would be so wonderful. Do you think we can?"

Conrad gave a small resigned sigh in response to the energy and enthusiasm in his wife's voice and gestures. "Of course we can. If that is your desire. Peter, Diann, you concentrate on getting the new materials. Robert, I would be grateful if you could see to those 'survivor' souvenirs you spoke of. Gabrielle, I will help you notify the attendees and set up the cruise for tomorrow night."

"Conrad, no. I forget. You are not well enough."

He gave her cheek a quick kiss. He looked tired and gray to Diann, but his tone was cheery enough. "Of course I am, my sweet. We will conclude this symposium in the proper manner."

"I DON'T KNOW about this dinner cruise tomorrow night. You really think it's a good idea?"

Robert looked across the small, exquisite table in the world-renowed Tour d'Argent restaurant to see Diann's clear questioning eyes and tried to choose his words carefully. "What's bothering you?"

Diann took a deep breath. "I still think I'm going to see Kohei, Louis and Helena every time I turn around, as though each has just momentarily stepped out of my vision and will be back. I know on some level their deaths are still not real to me. I still can't believe Armand... I so looked up to him, Robert. I..."

Her voice just faded away. She looked so sad. Robert wanted to put his arms around her and tell many things then. But the time was not right for them.

He leaned across the table and took hold of her hand. "I know. This afternoon I went to help arrange the services for Cassel. He's still on my mind. The past few days have had their tragedies. But they've also been filled with good things, Diann. That's why tomorrow night is a good idea. It will help us focus on the good. We need to try to forget the rest."

Diann felt the heat of his stare and the intent of his words. She knew she could forget many things by gazing into those eyes. And after the emotional turmoil of the past few days, she wanted to.

She smiled and nodded. Then she gave her attention to the Tour d'Argent's fabulous night view of the serenely flowing Seine beneath the window and the Gothic architecture of the Notre-Dame cathedral, lit beautifully in the distance. For the next hour she just concentrated on the beautiful sights, her sublime meal and the man by her side.

After dinner they walked hand in hand across a beautifully lit bridge lined with stone ladies who held up the lamps to light their way. The night was brilliantly clear. The air, sweet and warm.

They didn't speak for a long time, but Diann felt the communication between them nonetheless. She had never paid much attention to body language before, but feeling the warm sensuality of this man was as simple as the brush of his palm against hers and the briefest of smoky glances.

When they returned to the Hôtel de Crillon, Robert wrapped a claiming arm around her waist as they walked up the grand staircase to her suite. She opened the door, and he followed her inside and closed it behind them.

Diann knew she could say good-night and he'd leave. But she didn't say good-night. He reached for her hands, took them into his, caressing her fingers lightly. Chills raced up her arms.

He gently ran his fingers over her shoulders to her neck in incredibly sensual strokes that set her nerves to singing. He touched her jaw and chin and cheeks, then circled his hands back to cup her head as he slowly brought his mouth to hers.

His kiss was a mere brush that gradually deepened, urging sigh after sigh from caverns so deep inside her they'd never been charted.

She moaned as his touch became more urgent and insistent.

Something strong and unstoppable seemed to be rapidly building within him. Within her. She knew now that it had begun the moment they'd first met. Each time they'd been together it had grown. Now it seemed larger and stronger than even her heartbeat.

Robert's hands ached to touch the satin heat of her skin, his lips to taste her hot, sweet vanilla-icing flavor. He slipped the strap of her dress off her shoulder and traced her collarbone with his tongue. She sighed exquisitely.

With every taste and touch of her, he felt a small tease of his appetite. His hunger became greater and greater until he was ravenous. And it was this woman he was meant to devour. It was only this woman who could satisfy that hunger.

Robert felt his control slipping precariously fast in the face of her all-consuming sweet heat and heady scent. He'd given himself up to passion before, but never like this. No, never like this.

Diann felt his hands and mouth drawing such pure pleasure from deep inside her that she shuddered. When his hand cupped her breast, his thumb feathering her nipple, it was taut beneath his touch and she was quivering beneath him. His voice was a ragged whisper as he said what he had to say and hoped to hell he wasn't lying.

"Diann, if you tell me to stop now I will."

She answered him with just one word. The way she said it stripped him of any lingering thought he had in his head.

"Robert."

The passion in her voice shook him. He swept her into his arms and carried her into the bedroom.

He tore at their clothes. Then suddenly, gloriously, she was naked beside him and his hands and mouth were exploring her silky thighs and belly and breasts.

She called out his name again and again.

He was in pain, torture, he wanted her so badly. But he knew that if he let himself go, it would be over much too fast.

He wanted it to last forever. She was a woman to be savored. He concentrated on pleasuring her with just his hands and mouth. She moaned in delight with every flick of his tongue and writhed frantically beneath his fingers. On and on he built her sensations until they spilled over into a cry of joy and he marveled at how this woman's pleasure could sharpen his own pain and make him relish it at the same time.

But then he got too close to her hands, and they found him. And he knew all his good intentions to take this slow were about to be sorely tested.

She brought him to her, joining their bodies, and he could offer no resistance. She folded him inside her and wrapped herself around him with a smile bright enough to give a Paris night competition.

He looked at her lovely face as she lay beneath him on the bed—her eyes flashing, cheeks flushed, lips swollen from his kisses. He knew he'd never seen a more beautiful sight than the light of desire for him in her eyes.

He closed his eyes and dragged in a breath of air, trying to remain motionless, to regain even a semblance of physical control.

But then she was arching up against him, bringing his head down to nuzzle her nose against his skin and hair. "Robert, I love your smell. It's heated almonds and deep, rich forest woods and peppery sage."

Robert couldn't explain the incredible intimacy he felt while she drew every scent from his body into her. Her hands greedily grasped his shoulders as she rocked against him, squeezing him, inside and outside. Every effort he was making to take this slowly just shattered to hell.

"Diann, please."

He was met by the determined set to her flushed jaw as she inhaled and exhaled with uninhibited ecstasy.

"Robert, if you tell me to stop now I will."

He recognized the echo of his earlier promise and laughed, gave up and gripped her waist. He matched her enticing movements with a powerful stroke that brought a new cry of delight from her.

She rose with him on every thrust, joining their rhythms of body and mind in perfect pitch. He was part of her. She had thought she understood passion before, but she realized she had only had a whiff. This was the full fragrance. She inhaled greedily, knowing she was spoiled now for anything less.

She was part of him. Her scent, her feel. This was a woman as he had never known a woman. This was *his* woman. And when he finally could hold the fire in no longer, he released it into her and felt her ricocheting heat scorch his very soul.

DIANN WATCHED the Paris night stream through the bedroom window to light his magnificent naked body. Even after several hours of being introduced to its most intimate delights, she still couldn't take her eyes off him. He lay on his stomach, the muscles of his back in bold relief as he spread his arms under the sheet, reaching for her yet again.

"I can't get enough of you." His voice was husky. "You're going to have to tie me up if you want any sleep."

She sighed with pure pleasure as his strong, competent hands continued to work their magic over her skin. "I'll sleep when I'm back in New Jersey and you're back in Philadelphia."

She closed her eyes as he nuzzled the sensitive nerve endings in her neck, bringing back to life desire she could have sworn only seconds before had been thoroughly sated.

"Don't count on any sleep there, either. I'm coming back to New Jersey with you."

His words had her eyes opening in surprise. "You're going to pursue your career with MW's advertising department?"

His lips moved to munch on her earlobe. "No, thank you. I'm quite content with insurance investigation. What I had in mind was a more personal pursuit. Of one luscious chemist."

Diann stiffened at the meaning in his words as she slipped out from under his hands. "Robert, this has been . . . well, wonderful, but my work has to come first. I thought you understood that."

He raised his hand to her cheek and traced a line to her lips. "I told you I'm not into casual affairs. I thought you understood that."

Diann swung her legs over the bed, suddenly needing distance between them. "Robert, you mean a lot to me. I don't take what's happened between us lightly. But I simply do not have time to pursue a relationship with you. I have an enormous amount of work to do. Nothing can interfere."

He swung his body next to her and put his arm around her. "Why would you think I'd interfere? I would never expect you to give up what you love to do. It's part of what makes you the person you are—the very exciting person you are."

He punctuated his last words with a strategic string of kisses over her right shoulder. Diann felt her spine liquefying as resistance melted from her muscles.

"I told you once I've been looking for you a long time, Diann. It's true. And now that I've found you, I'm not going to let you go."

His lips traveled toward her breast. She closed her eyes and fought for all her normal superb control. "No. I can't."

Robert raised his head. "Can't? Or do you mean won't?"

His eyes were searching into her very soul. She had to look away. "I must focus my complete attention on these upcoming experiments. They have to be my sole focus. I can't let any other thoughts interfere."

He sat back for a moment, but his hands remained on her shoulders. "I don't think the idea of my interfering with your work is what you're really afraid of here."

"You don't understand."

"Then help me to. Tell me what this is really all about."

If he had demanded or gotten angry, she could have refused. But his gentle insistence undid her remaining restraint. She took a deep breath and let it out slowly. It was time for him to know. Time for him to understand. "You remember when you did a background check on me and found out that my parents were divorced when I was fifteen and my father got custody of my sister and me?"

"Yes. I thought it unusual that you went to live with your father rather than your mother after your parents' breakup. But since you and your sister were both old enough to make a decision as to which parent—"

"We made no such decision, Robert. It was made for us."

Her voice had grown very soft and calm, but the caramel in her eyes had dried to become hard and brittle.

Robert scanned her face carefully, reading every tightened muscle, every stretched nerve. "What happened?"

Again her voice reflected that soft calmness. "My father contracted Legionnaires' disease when I was twelve. He was one of the lucky ones. He survived the infection. But it knocked him out, and it took four bedridden months before he began to return to normal—four months of my mother feeding, bathing, dressing, doing everything for him. She took a leave of absence from her position as an executive at an advertising company to do it, too. It cost her a promotion."

"You say this as though you don't think she should have."

Diann's voice went ever softer, deadlier. "I know she shouldn't have."

Robert was getting uncomfortable with the look in Diann's eyes and the conflicting calmness of her voice. "Diann, he was her husband. She obviously loved him and didn't want to trust his care to a stranger. What's the problem here?"

"The problem is two years later my mother developed Alzheimer's. It came on like a devastating tornado. Within months she was having difficulty functioning, even remembering who we were. My father hired a nurse. He didn't miss a day of work. When she could no longer function, he had her committed to a state sanitarium and filed divorce papers. He said he couldn't handle the financial burden her private care would cost. On my eighteenth birthday, two days before I was graduated from high school, my mother died in that sanitarium."

Robert wrapped his arms around Diann and brought her head to rest against him. She spoke against his chest in that soft calm voice that now chilled him to the very bone.

"I promised her on her grave that I would work to find a cure for Alzheimer's. She's why I enrolled in Dr. Béraud's class at Cornell when I found out he was going to pursue getting a research grant to study Alzheimer's. She's why I can't let anything or anyone sidetrack me."

Robert didn't know what to say. Her father's response to her mother's devastating illness might be understandable to an outsider, who could reason that with her mind gone, Diann's mother was no longer alive to her father. Reason might even be found for the divorce if he did it to save the family's money for his daughters' education. Diann might understand these things someday and forgive him. But that dead, soft calm in her voice told Robert that day would not come soon.

He held her face in his hands, seeing the stone-cold tears she held in her heart, tears she had not permitted to warm so they could be shed.

"Diann," was all he said as he tenderly kissed her forehead, her eyes, her cheeks and cradled her in his arms.

Diann accepted the comfort he offered, indulging herself only for a moment. Then she took a deep breath and sighed and gradually leaned out of his arms.

"So you see, Robert, I don't have time for anything but my work."

"No. It's not your work. What I see is that you're really afraid you'll learn to care for me too much and I'll let you down someday. The way you believe your father let your mother down."

Diann sat back out of his arms. "You don't think he did?"

Robert took a deep breath, let it out very carefully. "Whatever happened between your parents does not have to happen to us. I know that our first and sometimes most insistent impressions of love and marriage come from our parents' example, whether we admit that to ourselves consciously or not. Watching my parents' seesawing relationship put me off the idea of both love and marriage for a long while, I can tell you."

He ran his palms up and down her arms gently as his blue eyes caressed her face. "Meeting the right woman helped to put things in perspective for me. I've fallen in love with you, Diann. I'm not interested in just having an affair with you. I want commitment. For a lifetime. I'm not going to accept anything less. I'm not going to give anything less. I'll be there for you. You can believe in that."

Diann felt herself tumbling into the bottomless blue sincerity of his eyes as she searched inside herself for that belief. But as much as she wanted to find it, it eluded her. Her next words were blurted out in a strangled voice. "I can't put my belief in love. It isn't I don't want to, but I just can't."

His eyes and voice were gentle. "Can't you, Diann?"

She gazed down at the rumpled bed, where only moments before she had been so happy beneath his touch, and sighed.

She rubbed her eyes, suddenly feeling very weary. "It's late. I'm tired. I think we should say good-night now."

She felt him stiffen beside her. "You want me to leave?"

She didn't look at him. She couldn't look at him. "Yes."

A long moment passed where neither of them moved. Then he got up off the bed and dressed in absolute silence. When she raised her head less than a minute later, he was gone.

And with him seemed to go every bit of warmth she'd ever known.

Chapter Twelve

Riding on the Bateau Mouche floating restaurant on the Seine at night was absolutely glorious. So many beautiful landmarks graced the shores in illuminated splendor. Spotlights attached to the side of the boat lit up the remaining buildings.

Looking out at the spectacular sights, Diann decided that if this had to be her last night in Paris, at least it would be a beautiful one. From the standpoint of scenery, anyway.

A boat guide was speaking through a loudspeaker to a handful of attendees gathered at the bow. "We travel atop the powerful River Seine, which has worn away the limestone and sand of Paris's foundation for centuries. Facing toward the sea, we observe that the Seine divides Paris into the rich Right Bank and the intellectual Left Bank."

Diann thought it was nice that the banks were described that way. One either lives in a rich environment or an intellectual one. Couldn't lose that way.

She walked back toward the interior of the boat. The guide's voice faded into the background. An entire section of the dining room had been cordoned off for the Fragrance Fraternity's attendees.

And they were there in force and in formal dress, happy to claim their "survival" T-shirts and commemorative cups. Minutes before when Diann had stepped aboard and into the smiling throng, she could see that Robert's idea had been a rousing success.

They all knew now about Armand Vuillard and his victims. Yet here they were. A lesson in human nature. When given a chance, people wanted to make the best of things.

Just as she should be making the best of things.

She hadn't seen Robert since he'd left her room early that morning. She had walked the length of the boat twice, but had not spotted him in the milling throng.

He might not even show up here at this dinner cruise. Now that Armand had been unmasked, his work was done. He might have already left Paris. She might never see him again.

She told herself it was better this way. A clean break. Robert and she had had a night to remember. It should be enough. Her work should be enough.

But nothing seemed enough, and she felt the terrible pressure of tears that could not be shed.

Gabrielle swept next to her, bringing a whiff of HEAT with her. "What's wrong, Diann?"

She tried to perk up. "Last-night-in-Paris syndrome."

Gabrielle nodded. "*Oui*, I understand. Still, I was happy to receive the call from Inspector Pinchot this afternoon to say we could all leave. I was not looking forward to this Jillian Bate-Land prosecution, you understand."

"No, I can't imagine you were," Diann replied noncommittally.

Diann's attention was distracted as a man with dark hair passed. But it only proved to be the dark-haired waiter she recognized as being from the hotel. He was carrying a box of commemorative flags with "I Survived The Symposium From Hell" printed on them. Her eyes automatically flicked up to his face and then away again in disappointment.

"You look for Robert, no?" Gabrielle asked.

Diann sighed. She didn't realize she was so obvious. "Have you seen him?"

"Not yet. But he will come. He is not a man who gives up easily. He wants a more serious relationship than you offer, yes?"

Diann blinked back her surprise. "How did you know?"

Gabrielle waved her expressive hands. "Robert only has eyes for you. I see this from the first day. Every woman in Paris envies you. Diann, you are silly to say no to such a man. A man with such devotion toward a woman brings her much happiness. Ask me, I know."

"You're talking about Conrad's devotion to you?"

"*Oui.* Oh, do not mistake me. I look at the other men. And you and the other stars are so clever that I confess I cannot resist the way you give your perfumes such sexual power. So sometimes I am driven to do more than look. After all, life is to be lived. But always I come back to my Conrad. He is the kind of a man a woman wants to come back to. Like your Robert."

Diann decided that Gabrielle's idea of devotion to her husband had both a touch of sincerity and lunacy. "Actually, Gabrielle, he's not my Robert. I don't even think I'll be seeing him again."

Gabrielle arched a finely penciled eyebrow. "Oh, you will be seeing him again. He is walking up to us right now."

Diann whirled around, trying to keep her silly heart from battering against her breast.

He looked so absolutely wonderful in his tuxedo that she actually felt her breath getting caught in her lungs. He smiled charmingly and executed a formal bow between them before holding out his arms. "Ladies, dinner is about to be served. I am here to conduct you to the head table."

Diann took his right arm as Gabrielle took his left. Gabielle chatted on gaily as Robert led them to a table adorned in white lace and red ribbons. Diann didn't hear a word she said. All that was real to her was the solid feel of Robert beside her.

He sat down next to her, and his wonderful almond fragrance came with him. Only now she knew it was him and not a concoction prepared in some lab. He and his scent were one of a kind. He turned his blue eyes directly on her in a grazing heat and leaned close to whisper in her ear.

"You look wonderful in that rose-satin gown, Diann. Almost as wonderful as you'd look out of it."

The breath ran from her lungs and she couldn't seem to coax more in. She didn't know what she had expected from Robert after she had asked him to leave her hotel suite that morning. Anger. Hurt. Aloofness.

Any other man probably would have responded in one or more of those ways. But this man treated her as he always had, with a heartbreaking charm and focused regard.

She had no idea what to say or do. She only knew she wanted this man for all she was worth, and she couldn't afford to have him.

"Robert, I have a question to ask," Gabrielle said from the other side of him. Robert turned toward his hostess.

Diann drew in some needed air into her lungs. Peter slipped into the chair on the other side of her with somewhat less than his usual grace because of his injury.

"Diann, you look smashing."

She tried to concentrate on his compliment as she sent him a small smile. "Thank you. How's the leg?"

Peter managed to wrap a brave smile about his lips. "Healing nicely, thank you. What a relief it is to see things beginning to return to normal."

Normal? Diann didn't think she knew what normal was anymore. "Peter, Inspector Pinchot called me today to say they won't be prosecuting Jillian Bate-Land so I was free to leave Paris. He didn't mention why they had chosen not to prosecute. Do you know what's behind that decision?"

"They decided Jillian is ill and have opted to have her committed to a sanitarium."

Diann couldn't be sure—Peter was very good at projecting an emotional distance—but she thought she heard a note of concern in his voice.

"This must be very hard on you, Peter. Emotionally as well as physically, I mean."

He flashed Diann a very stalwart smile. "I'm holding up."

"Do you agree with the decision of the police?"

"Yes, I'm rather pleased actually."

"Do you think Jillian is . . . ill?"

He reached for the glass of wine the waiter had just poured. Took a small sip. Put down the glass. Adjusted the sleeve of his pristine white shirt beneath the cuff of his tuxedo. "Quite. For four years we have enjoyed a relationship. No tiresome demands or expectations. She has to be off the mark. What other explanation is there for her shooting me?"

"What, indeed?" Diann echoed after a stunned moment, but Peter didn't hear the edge of sarcasm that lay beneath her words. Four years and Peter didn't think he had a commitment to Jillian? Diann thought about Helena's comment that Jillian had shot Peter because she cared too much and that Peter wasn't worth it. Diann decided that Helena had been right on both counts.

Diann swiveled toward Robert. Now, here was a man who made tiresome demands and insisted on unrealistic expectations. Here was a man who believed in commitment and would settle for nothing else.

He must have felt her scrutiny, because his eyes skipped to hers. The sincere blue of their concern was as gentle as a spring rain. "What is it?"

"I was just thinking that you are a man worth shooting if there ever was one."

A look of growing perplexity grew on his face. Diann felt a smile forming inside her heart.

"So, Robert," Gabrielle called from the other side of him. "We will do the spread as agreed. You will talk to your company then and recommend they approve the inclusion of your magazine ad in the next issue of *Redolence*?"

Robert returned his attention to the director of the Fragrance Fraternity. "Of course, Gabrielle. Although I'm sure they won't need my urgings. They'll no doubt view an article and a running of the picture as free advertising. What company wouldn't welcome that?"

"Good. It is settled. I will have my staff contact you at MW. You return tomorrow, yes?"

"Yes."

Diann felt confused. Robert was acting as though he were still just a male model for MW. And then she realized that he had yet to say anything to the members of the Fragrance Fraternity about his real position.

Was he concerned that they might resent his representing himself as something he wasn't?

Diann had just decided to ask him, when Gabrielle suddenly rose from her seat and rang a little bell to bring those assembled to order.

"*Mesdames* and *messieurs*. Thank you all for coming. On this the last evening of our symposium, we have our two final stars of the perfume world ready to regale you with their presentations. Now, originally, Peter Campbell, our unsurpassed winner of the DISTRIBUTOR Award was to go first. But as the equipment he needs is more extensive than that of Diann Torrey, our incomparable winner of the NOSE Award, they have agreed to switch and Diann will go first. So without further delay, *mesdames* and *messieurs,* I urge you to welcome Diann Torrey, the number one nose in the entire perfume industry."

A rapid applause followed Diann as she strode over to a magnificently lit display table, where more than two-dozen bottles of the world's most fabulous perfumes graced an impeccable yard of deep-red velvet.

Of course, her presentation here couldn't compete with what she had planned for the more formal setting of the Salon Marie-Antoinette at the Hôtel de Crillon, but she had to give Conrad and Gabrielle credit. A microphone had been provided and all her presentation materials had been arranged just as requested.

She moved up to the portable podium and battled a few butterflies that always gathered in her stomach before making a speech. "Thank you, ladies and gentlemen. This evening I want to teach you how to enrich your lives by enriching your sense of smell."

She paused to look around at the audience, giving them time to settle. Then she went on.

"As human societies moved away from a close relationship with nature, they moved away from their sense of smell. This is understandable when you consider that when we were outside, we had the wonderful, invigorating scents of fresh earth and pine and grass and ocean to inhale.

"Now we are surrounded by chlorine and car exhaust and spray starch. Is it any wonder that we've switched off our noses?"

A small chuckle made its way around the dining room. Diann smiled and continued.

"Unfortunately we are also missing many pleasant smells. Reeducating our noses takes motivation and practice, but the rewards are well worth it.

"And to prove that, tonight I'm going to teach everyone in this room to differentiate from among the five basic types of perfume themes. And I'm also going to tell you what it says about your personality when you have a distinct preference for one basic type of perfume over another."

Diann stopped to pick up the packaged strips of perfume samples that she'd developed years before to help newcomers to the MW lab catch on quicker to the differences in the fragrance notes. Both Conrad and Gabrielle rose and helped to distribute them. When she was sure everyone had a strip, she continued.

"There are five fragrance strips in each one of your packets, representing the extremes of the five main perfume themes. You can see their surfaces as small pink squares. You can test out their scents by scratching at the pink squares with a fingernail or the edge of your spoon. We'll all start with the strip on the top labeled number one. Ready? Scratch. Then sniff.''

Diann waited until scratched strips around the room were passed beneath noses. Then she continued. "This first fragrance is a mixture of exotic blossoms and spices and is known to noses as the 'Oriental' blend. If you're one of those people who have a preference for the intense Oriental blends, you probably prefer life in the exit lane, are a real homebody and consider even the slightest rain shower a perfect excuse to cancel your evening out in exchange for a quiet candlelit dinner around the fireplace and hours of making love under the covers.''

At that very moment a patter of rain sounded on the glass ceiling of the boat. One of the male attendees got to his feet and looked meaningfully at his female companion. "I'm ready.''

She batted his arm away as the entire group responded with an appreciative chuckle.

Diann smiled at her audience's antics. They certainly were in good spirits tonight. "Let's go on to strip number two. All set? Scratch and then sniff.''

Diann gave everyone around the room a chance to try out the second strip before resuming. "This is called chypre and is reminiscent of grass and leaves, with hints of light woods and moss. If you like the chypre fragrance, you also probably like life in the slow lane, have never worked a minute of overtime in your life and think the ultimate in making love is in the middle of a sunny meadow after a long nature hike.''

"This one is for me. Anybody else for a hike?'' one woman called out. Diann gave the resultant chortles time to dissipate before picking up the third strip.

"Your next strip is a rose floral. Florals can have a single theme like this rose one or be a mixed bouquet of many different flowers. In contrast to the Oriental and chypre fragrances, if you prefer floral fragrances, you generally like the center lane of life, giving noisy parties that go on for days and making love in a bathtub filled with petals and champagne."

"That's me!" several people called out simultaneously, to the laughter of all.

Diann smiled. "Well, if these first three haven't struck a responsive chord, perhaps this fourth strip will. It's mostly fruity, redolent of the fragrances of lemon and orange and other citrus. If you find you like this scent, you're definitely traveling through life in the fast lane, rush to lunches and board meetings with equal glee and enjoy making love best in the back seat of long black limousines."

An appreciative murmur followed this description, accompanied by more laughter.

Diann picked up the last strip. "Finally, this last fragrance theme is called woodsy/spicy and is often a blend of aromatic woods like sandalwood and rich spices like cinnamon. This theme makes some of the most powerful of feminine perfume blends. If you find you like this theme, you crave the oncoming lane of life as a test to your razor-sharp reflexes and instinct, you don't leave the house ever without your passport and the man you want most to make love to is the one who refuses to take off his gun first."

An appreciative *ooooh* went around the room at this description.

"If you haven't found yourself in any of these five fragrances, it's probably because your preference, like your personality, is a mixture of more than one. But like your personality, every perfume has a dominant theme. And now that you're familiar with the five dominant themes, I'd like to introduce to you a sensational new scent from Man to Woman Perfumes."

Diann turned to the display table and picked up an exquisite white bottle shaped like a sparkling ice crystal.

"As you can see on the label, this new fragrance is called ICE. Unlike other perfumes, this fragrance is not liquid but comes out of its bottle in small crystal shapes like tiny chunks of ice, each chunk a perfectly measured dose that warms to life when it comes in contact with a woman's skin.

"In a moment I'll be handing out samples of ICE for each of you to try. But I have promised that the first woman to experience this new perfume, outside of my lab at MW, will be Gabrielle Rife, our gracious hostess. Gabrielle, would you like to step forward?"

Gabrielle rose amid encouraging applause and made her way excitedly to the podium. She had just reached Diann's side, when suddenly a loud shout made both women jump.

"No!"

Diann spun around in the direction of the protest to see Conrad had sprung to his feet, his face as white as the tablecloth.

Gabrielle immediately called out anxiously to him from the podium. "Conrad, what is wrong?"

The jovial crowd had gone absolutely quiet. Conrad Rife's perpetually smiling elf face just stared at his wife's. He did not say another word.

"Do you not feel well, Conrad?"

"No, dear. I don't feel well. Please, can we go?"

Gabrielle hesitated. Diann could see she was obviously torn. On the one hand, her husband was saying he did not feel well and wished to leave. But on the other hand, how urgent could it be? He was standing talking to her.

Gabrielle reached her decision. She quickly tore at the seal on the bottle of perfume. "Yes, darling. We'll go. It will take but a second to anoint myself with this new perfume."

"No!" Conrad screamed again. He leaped across the table separating him from his wife, desperately trying to get to her before she could open the bottle. But it was too late. Gabrielle had already twisted off the cap and removed a glowing ice crystal of fragrance from inside.

Conrad crashed into the podium and landed in a heap at her feet, sobbing in a gut-wrenching bellow. "No! No! No!"

Gabrielle dropped the perfume bottle and the small crystal of ICE perfume. Both fell to the carpet. She stared down at her husband in total and complete shock.

Diann felt Robert's warm, firm hands on her arms then, slowly, gently pulling her back, away from the couple. She was so stunned herself that she gave not a thought to protest.

Seemingly from out of nowhere, Inspector Pinchot appeared and dropped next to Conrad, firmly drawing his arms behind his back and handcuffing his wrists. "It is all over, Monsieur Rife."

Conrad's shoulders shook as he sobbed into the carpet.

Gabrielle's lost voice returned with a roar. "What are you doing, Inspector? Have you gone mad? Release my husband. Release him immediately!"

Conrad raised stunned eyes to his wife, the tears still flowing down his round cheeks. "Darling, you're all right? I can't believe it. You're all right!"

"Yes, *monsieur,*" Inspector Pinchot answered. "Madame Rife is quite safe. We found the doctored bottle with the deadly chemical you planted in Mademoiselle Torrey's presentation materials earlier and replaced it."

Gabrielle's cry roared through the room as her hands flew to her mouth. "No, no!"

Conrad's elfin face stared lovingly at his wife, the tears drying on his cheeks. He smiled. "It's all right, dear. You're safe." Then his eyes turned to the inspector. "I'm so glad you changed the bottles. How can I ever thank you? You saved my wife's life, you know."

Inspector Pinchot's voice was very soft and polite as he helped Conrad Rife to his feet. "Yes, *monsieur.* I know."

Gabrielle stepped forward and grasped her husband's arm. "Conrad, what is this? You were trying to hurt Diann? No, I cannot believe it. Why would you do such an insane thing?"

Conrad Rife looked at his wife with a face full of worship. "Gabrielle, you were not at fault. It was the perfumes they bombarded you with and the sensuous ways in which they presented them that drove you to be unfaithful. You could not help yourself."

Gabrielle's hazel eyes widened. "Conrad, are you saying that—"

"I had to remove their temptations, dear. These perfume stars shamelessly seduced you with their fragrances and their packaging and presentations."

Gabrielle's face drained deathly white as she released her husband's arm and stepped back. "It was not Armand! It was you! Conrad. Oh, no, Conrad!"

Conrad Rife shrugged his portly shoulders, his expression that of a man who knew he had committed a regrettable but necessary faux pas. "I did not want to cause you distress, of course, but I had to kill them. Then their temptations would be gone and no one would ever come between us again. You see that, don't you, dear?"

Something passed through Gabrielle Rife's eyes then that made her go rigid. Diann had the strangest feeling that Gabrielle had been looking at an internal mirror and had seen herself in it. And the image shocked her to her core.

Then amazingly, Gabrielle shook off her shock, stepped forward and curled her arm around her husband's bound one. She smiled as a mother might at her young child. "Yes, dear. I see that," she said calmly. She raised her head regally, resolutely, toward Pinchot. "We are ready to go, Inspector."

"Yes, *madame*," Inspector Pinchot answered with a small bow.

DIANN WAS exhausted when she and Robert finally returned to her hotel suite, closing the door behind them. She threw her evening wrap and purse onto a table and immediately sank into the couch with a tired sigh.

What an incredible end to an incredible symposium. And still so much of what had happened eluded her. But one thing was clear. Somehow, nothing that had happened that evening had come as a surprise to Robert. As Robert came to sit beside her, she determined to find out how.

"How did you know that it wasn't Armand Vuillard?"

He sent her a tired smile as he rested his arm on the back of the couch. "Actually, you were the one who told me it couldn't be Armand."

"Well, I'm glad I was so helpful. Now maybe you'll tell me how I managed this feat."

He chuckled. "Remember when you convinced me that because of my appearance in MW's advertising campaign and Gabrielle's insistence that advertising become a PER-FUME Award category, I had become a perfume star and therefore a target?"

"Yes."

"Well, Gabrielle spoke of making advertising a category for the PERFUME awards and me a perfume star at that banquet table on the opening night. And Armand Vuillard was not there."

It took a moment before her tired mind absorbed his meaning. Once it had, she swiveled toward him. "And yet later someone tried to kill you with the doctored seal on the bottle of wine!"

Robert flashed her a smile. "Exactly. So since it couldn't have been Vuillard, that meant someone else had to be involved. Someone at the banquet table. That's how I finally convinced Pinchot."

Diann still shook her head. "Still, if Armand is innocent, why did he flee to Quebec?"

"He didn't. That was an employee of Conrad's, acting under Conrad's directions. The employee didn't know why he was using Armand's name on that flight. He was just following Conrad's orders. Conrad was also the one who planted that false evidence in Armand's apartment."

"But then, where is Armand?"

Robert bent his head to rub at his tired eyes. "Inspector Pinchot found him in his lab yesterday. He'd been dead about a week."

Diann slumped under the weight of the news. "Oh, no."

Robert slid closer to her, wove his hand through her hair. Gently he massaged the back of her neck with his fingers, as though knowing she needed his soothing touch. "Conrad had doctored some of Armand's new absolutes from Grasse with the chemical so that Armand would be killed when he opened them."

Despite his welcome touch, Diann frowned at Robert's words. "Yesterday you found out Armand was dead and knew he couldn't be behind these murders, but you said nothing?"

"I'm sorry, Diann. I wanted to tell you. But with those damn honest eyes of yours, I just didn't think you'd be able to playact through what you had to do tonight if you knew the killer was still out there. And if we were going to catch Conrad, he had to think he had gotten away with framing Armand."

She smiled at the sincerity in his eyes, a warm, forgiving smile. "But how did you know Conrad would expose himself tonight?"

"He was paying the taxi that first day when you told Gabrielle you'd let her be the first to experience your newest perfume, so he didn't hear. When the inspector and I found the deadly chemical in your ICE perfume, we knew all we need do was step back and wait for Conrad to give himself away when he tried to prevent Gabrielle from being his unintended victim."

"But Inspector Pinchot said the deadly chemical had been found in Conrad's and Gabrielle's things, too."

"Yes. Clever move on Conrad's part. He made it seem as though they were targets, as well."

"But he had a heart attack, Robert. We saw him. I don't understand how he could fake his own heart problems well enough to fool the doctors."

"He just stopped taking his medication for a while, and his chronic condition reappeared. He wanted a bed-rest prescription so he could move about surreptitiously, planting that deadly chemical while everyone thought he was in Macon. He wore a bushy hairpiece, a thick mustache and glasses and pretended to be a hotel employee helping out at the symposium.''

Diann straightened as earlier images flashed into her mind. ''Of course! I remember seeing that man! How clever he is. How ever did you get wise to him, Robert?''

Robert's warm arm encircled her shoulders. ''Actually, I got my first clue when he came out of Helena Strunk's room carrying the box. He had offered to assist her so he could get into her room to doctor her tissues. He was supposed to be a Frenchman, but he was whistling an American tune. Then, when Inspector Pinchot found Vuillard's body, I suggested he send a man to the Rifes' home in Macon to see if Conrad was really there. He wasn't.''

''But Gabrielle said she took Conrad home to Macon. Did she lie?''

''No. She took him there all right. Conrad just didn't stay in Macon.''

''Isn't Macon quite a distance from Paris?''

''About four hundred kilometers or two hundred and forty miles away. That's just a little over an hour's trip for France's *train à grande vitesse,* or TGV, the fastest in the world.''

''But if Conrad took the train right back to Paris, what happened when Gabrielle called him in Macon?''

''She never got a chance to call, because he called her constantly to prevent it. That might have been what Cassel finally stumbled on when he wanted me to listen to one of those tapes. Remember the conversation between Conrad and Gabrielle and how he admitted he kept calling her?''

Diann exhaled and gave a heavy nod. ''Conrad planned it all so thoroughly. Where did he get the deadly gas?''

''Conrad told Inspector Pinchot that it was discovered accidentally by a scientist working at one of his waste-recycling plants. The chemicals actually produce a gas that packs a wallop of an electrical charge that stuns both the brain and heart. If enough of the gas is inhaled, the charge is deadly enough to cause the heart to stop completely. Which is what happened to Conrad's victims.''

''And if a smaller amount is inhaled, it induces a blackout with a residual buzzing inside the brain.''

He kissed the top of her head. ''Exactly, my lovely chemist.''

Diann shook her head. ''It's so sad. Conrad loves Gabrielle so much. But that love got twisted somehow. I never would have thought him capable of such terrible crimes. He must be mad.''

''Yes, I believe he is.''

She looked into Robert's serious face, framed by those brown curls, the sincere blue eyes so clearly focused just on her. ''I was standing so close to Gabrielle. If you hadn't found that chemical inside my ICE perfume, I might have died along with her.''

Robert smiled at her as he raised a finger to caress her cheek. ''I promised you I'd stay close, Diann. That I wouldn't let anyone harm you. I'm a man of my word. I'll convince you of that yet. Even if it takes a hundred years.''

Diann's throat swelled with the emotion she was trying to contain. ''Robert, I—''

''No, hear me first. Yes, I know that commitments between two people can be broken. We've both seen enough of that in our lives, not to mention the past few days. But if we don't make commitments and act like they will last and believe in the power of love, then what can we look forward to but emptiness and solitude? Diann, do you understand?''

''Yes, Robert, I understand because I believe in you.''

Robert's arms came instantly around her and he held her to his chest as he gently stroked her hair and whispered her name over and over again. ''Diann, *je t'aime. Je t'aime.*'' And the sound of the love in his voice echoed in her heart.

She was surprised to feel the wetness on her cheeks. Her mind told her she cried because she was exhausted, emotionally spent after all those grueling days and nights. But her heart knew she cried because suddenly, in the arms of this special man, she could. Her love for him had made her strong enough for tears.

Her heart felt both full and light, and she knew at that moment she was happier than she'd ever been.

She sighed as she buried herself against all that wonderful warmth and strength of him. "Robert, I love you so much. With all there is in me, I love you. And I believe in our future together."

His arms tightened around her—strong, solid, sure. His natural scent filled her with all its exotic, enticing warmth. His deep voice dipped into her heart to stir its beat. "Diann, my love. I've needed you for such a long time. Remember when I told you that Paris is like a shiny unexpected promise?"

"Yes," she murmured. "You said that it seems to say that here you'll find the brightest of your dreams."

"And I did find that dream. I found you."

Diann sighed from a deep contentment in her soul. Yes, this enchanting city had indeed sent this marvelous magician to weave its spell around her for all time. She looked up at that mysterious glow in his eyes, at that sexy smile.

"Do something for me, Robert."

He nibbled at the soft lobe of her ear, sending thrills through her. "Anything, *cherie.*"

"Don't let MW talk you into doing the advertising for ICE. The planet is already in danger of global warming. Another one of your nude appearances, and the combined panting breath of the world's women might cause a complete meltdown."

He laughed in his honest, robust way. Then he tightened his grip on her as though he never meant to let go. "You're the only woman I'll ever take my clothes off for again, Diann. And I mean to do that every day for the rest of our lives. Marry me. Today. I don't want a moment of our futures to be wasted apart."

She blinked and drew back to look up at his face. "Today?"

He smiled into her surprise and his warm spring-sky blue eyes bathed her in their light. "We'll honeymoon right here in Paris. There are so many wonderful things I know about the heart of Paris that I'd like to show you."

He was serious. Absolutely serious. Her handsome half Frenchman wanted to marry her today and show her his Paris. Diann's heart felt as though it could sing.

She plastered as innocent a look on her face as she could manage and let a sweet sarcasm drift into her voice. "Wonderful things you read about in a Paris guidebook?"

A warning glint entered his eyes as that sexy smile lifted the side of his lip. Then suddenly he grabbed her, hoisted her over his shoulder and carried her into the bedroom. Diann tried to protest, but she couldn't enunciate through her bubbling squeals of laughter.

When he finally plopped her onto the bed, he bent over her with blue eyes wet enough to quench the hottest feminine thirst. "What I'm about to show you, *cherie,* you'll never find in any guidebook."

Diann exhaled a breath of pure pleasure as she wove her fingers through his hair and brought his lips to hers. Leave it to a Frenchman to know that to have found love is to have found the real heart of Paris.

HARLEQUIN®

Don't miss these Harlequin favorites by some of our most distinguished authors!
And now, you can receive a discount by ordering two or more titles!

HT #25551	THE OTHER WOMAN by Candace Schuler	$2.99	☐
HT #25539	FOOLS RUSH IN by Vicki Lewis Thompson	$2.99	☐
HP #11550	THE GOLDEN GREEK by Sally Wentworth	$2.89	☐
HP #11603	PAST ALL REASON by Kay Thorpe	$2.99	☐
HR #03228	MEANT FOR EACH OTHER by Rebecca Winters	$2.89	☐
HR #03268	THE BAD PENNY by Susan Fox	$2.99	☐
HS #70532	TOUCH THE DAWN by Karen Young	$3.39	☐
HS #70540	FOR THE LOVE OF IVY by Barbara Kaye	$3.39	☐
HI #22177	MINDGAME by Laura Pender	$2.79	☐
HI #22214	TO DIE FOR by M.J. Rodgers	$2.89	☐
HAR #16421	HAPPY NEW YEAR, DARLING by Margaret St. George	$3.29	☐
HAR #16507	THE UNEXPECTED GROOM by Muriel Jensen	$3.50	☐
HH #28774	SPINDRIFT by Miranda Jarrett	$3.99	☐
HH #28782	SWEET SENSATIONS by Julie Tetel	$3.99	☐

Harlequin Promotional Titles

#83259	UNTAMED MAVERICK HEARTS	$4.99	☐
	(Short-story collection featuring Heather Graham Pozzessere, Patricia Potter, Joan Johnston)		

(limited quantities available on certain titles)

	AMOUNT	$
DEDUCT:	10% DISCOUNT FOR 2+ BOOKS	$
	POSTAGE & HANDLING	$
	($1.00 for one book, 50¢ for each additional)	
	APPLICABLE TAXES*	$ _____
	TOTAL PAYABLE	$ _____
	(check or money order—please do not send cash)	

To order, complete this form and send it, along with a check or money order for the total above, payable to Harlequin Books, to: **In the U.S.:** 3010 Walden Avenue, P.O. Box 9047, Buffalo, NY 14269-9047; **In Canada:** P.O. Box 613, Fort Erie, Ontario, L2A 5X3.

Name: _____

Address: _____ City: _____

State/Prov.: _____ Zip/Postal Code: _____

*New York residents remit applicable sales taxes.
Canadian residents remit applicable GST and provincial taxes.

HBACK-AJ

HARLEQUIN®

I N T R I G U E®

*When lovers are fated, not even
time can separate them....When
a mystery is pending, only time
can solve it....*

Timeless Love

Harlequin Intrigue is proud to
bring you this exciting new program
of time-travel romantic mysteries!

Be on time in May for the next book
in this series:

**#275 TIMEWALKER
by Aimée Thurlo**

It was a lot to ask of a tough FBI
agent—to believe that a Navajo
medicine man was held suspended
in time in a turquoise amulet...but
the man before her needed to right
a hundred-year-old wrong—done
him by the one and only Kit Carson.

Watch for
TIMEWALKER...
and all the upcoming books in
TIMELESS LOVE.